"Someone is co[...]
relaxed, but her [...]
mane and a restless whining growl sounded from somewhere in her larynx.

"Impossible, Lady," said the thief just as a rising blast sheared a hole through the main door. The smoke cleared to reveal the black uniforms of the fanatical secret police answerable only to Timur Khan Bey. "Black Tumans!" the thief bleated.

With inhuman speed Rama was at the back door, slapping it back with her palm. It snapped open, and more BT troopers burst into the room. Rama's claws raked two of them, but their protective uniforms saved them from gutting. She got at one through the opening in his helmet, and he staggered back clutching at a ruined face. . . .

THE CINGULUM

Look for this other TOR book by John Maddox Roberts

CESTUS DEI

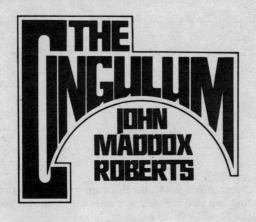

THE CINGULUM

JOHN MADDOX ROBERTS

TOR

A TOM DOHERTY ASSOCIATES BOOK

THE CINGULUM

Copyright © 1985 by John Maddox Roberts

First printing: February 1985

A TOR Book

Published by Tom Doherty Associates
8-10 West 36 Street
New York, N.Y. 10018

Cover art by Norma Segrelles

ISBN: 0-812-55200-8
CAN. ED.: 0-812-55201-6

Printed in the United States of America

For my daughter, Day Alayne:

With love and gratitude
for all those years of music,
optimism and encouragement.

PART I

ONE

Corrections Officer Tsinsit lounged in his office overlooking the quarry. The office was a transparent bubble perched on the edge of a granite cliff. Below it stretched a depression many acres in extent, where naked men reduced solid stone to rubble with primitive hand tools. The Bahadur System had no real need of gravel produced by such inefficient means. What went on at Corrections Facility Five was pointless, man-killing toil for the purpose of reducing rebellious, antisocial men to a state of conformity with the rules of the Bahadur System. Most often it killed them before this end was accomplished.

"Aircraft approaching," said Tsinsit's assistant.

A sleek, government-model hovercraft unfolded its spindly legs and settled next to the quarry office. It extruded a gangway and from its portal emerged two men in the tight-fitting black uniform of the Black Tuman.

"What do the BTs want here?" muttered Tsinsit apprehensively. The Black Tuman was the super-elite military arm of the Bahadur System. Their powers were almost unlimited and they upheld the rule of the Syndicate through terror and brute force.

"Honored warriors," said Tsinsit as the two entered the office, "how may I be of assistance?" Hands pressed together, he bowed deeply. The soldiers made no acknowledgment of his bow.

"We have come to pick up a prisoner," said the one who wore the insignia of a Subadar. He handed Tsinsit a paper ordering the release of prisoner 2694445 to Black Tuman custody.

"A moment, sirs," Tsinsit said. He punched the number into his console and examined the readout a moment later. Then he depressed the button of his communication system and spoke into its grille. "Commander of Gang Ninety-five, bring the prisoner 2694445 to the office at once." He turned to the BTs. "Will there be anything else, sirs?" They did not bother to reply.

Their arrogance surpasses belief, Tsinsit thought. Both were tall and lean, and they wore knives and pistols on their belts. Their close-fitting black helmets exposed little of their faces, but they had the straight, spare features of the Turkic-Mongol ruling caste. Tsinsit wondered what they wanted with the prisoner. He was willing to bet that the man would soon wish he were back in the living hell of the quarry.

Timur Khan Bey stood on the balcony of his office suite in the tower called the Black Obelisk. The building was the embodied symbol of fear for a whole system. Fifty yards from the balcony a small target hovered, held in place by a small anti-g device. Timur Khan slipped on his thumb ring and selected an arrow, fitting it to the string.

The bow was a compound, recurved type of traditional design.

He drew and released in a single fluid motion. The arrow sailed across the intervening distance and skewered the center of the target. Had it missed, it might have impaled some citizen on the streets below . . . but Timur Khan Bey never missed. He continued until one hundred arrows bristled from the target. The ancient art of the bow was almost the only recreation he allowed himself, and he shot one hundred arrows every day at this time unless more pressing activities prevailed.

He walked from the balcony into his stark, spare office and hung the bow from its peg on the wall. He was a tall man and deceptively thin, but only a man of exceptional strength could have drawn his powerful bow. He crossed to his desk and spoke into the console. "Is the prisoner here yet?"

"Yes, Noyon," replied his secretary.

"Send him in."

Two uniformed guardsmen entered, the prisoner between them. They forced the man to lie face-down on the polished stone floor; then they knelt and bowed until their helmets touched the stone.

"This is the prisoner you wished to see, Noyon," said the Subadar.

"Rise," Timur Khan ordered. He was the commander of the Black Tuman, and the most feared man in the system. Even the Lords of the Syndicate feared him. "You two wait outside." The guardsmen bowed their way out of the room and the prisoner rose to his feet, awkwardly since his hands were bound behind him.

Timur Khan studied the portfolio opened on his desk, containing the prisoner's official history. The likeness supplied showed a young man with long, wavy blond hair, wearing the uniform of a cadet of the Space Naval Academy of Delius. He was elegant in dress cape and sword and had the refined features common to the higher classes of that republic. The face was sensitive, with bright blue eyes. At least the eyes were still the same.

The man before him wore only cheap gray trousers. He was completely hairless, like all convicts. The years of brutal labor under a merciless sun had turned him deep brown. He was tall but so muscular that he appeared to be shorter than he actually was. The body carried not a trace of surplus flesh but more than its share of scars, and his nose had been broken more than once. The face was deeply lined.

"Your name is Haakon," Timur Khan said without preamble. "You were commander of a light cruiser of the Three System Alliance during its war with the Serene Powers. Taken prisoner off Gallus and spent two years in the quarries. You were released at the cessation of hostilities and drifted into smuggling activities. You were apprehended by the authorities and are now in the fifth year of a life sentence. Is all that correct?"

"In essence, although I dispute the criminality of breaking your laws." The voice was mild for such a fierce-looking man, and Timur Khan was pleased with its evidence of deep self-control.

"Your interpretation of our laws is of no importance. You must live by them because we will make you suffer if you don't."

Haakon listened attentively, with every evidence of polite interest. Timur Khan was impressed; he knew the man had to be terrified. Anyone summoned to this office expected the worst. Timur Khan was known to have done truly awesome things to those who displeased him.

"Still," he went on, "there is yet hope for you. I take it that you would like to leave the quarries?"

Haakon almost smiled. "Of course. Unless it is possible that the alternative could be even worse."

"Just so. It's an incautious man who trades even the most miserable of existences for another sight unseen. I think you'll like my proposition though. How would you like your freedom, and command of a ship and crew?"

The dark face registered something akin to shock. "Is this some form of torture?" Haakon asked.

"No," Timur Khan answered coldly. "I leave that to my subordinates. My time is valuable, convict, don't waste it. Are you interested? There are other prisoners on my list for interview; yours was the first name to come up."

"Yes!" Haakon said hastily; then, under better control: "It's just that you are not a man famed for charity, Noyon."

"Nor should I be. Of course I have a purpose in releasing you. I am a man of affairs, Haakon. I have a great many things to accomplish. Among them is the restoration of the Bahadur System to its former preeminence. To this end I plan to undertake a series of missions outside the system. In order to accomplish these missions, I must have at my disposal a force of agents who are not of Bahadur.

"I chose you for a special reason. I need an experienced ship's captain. You are one such. I need a man of uncommon strength and endurance. Only two kinds of men come out of the quarries after five years: shambling wrecks, and hard, bitter men with an uncommon will to survive. You seem to have thrived on the existence. However, you are not unique in these qualities. Do you accept enrollment in my service?"

"I accept!" Haakon replied.

"A man of prompt decision," Timur Khan said. "That, too, is a quality I require."

He turned toward the wall and took down the bow. Idly he thrummed the string a few times as though to check its tension. "This is the ancestral weapon of my people," he began, almost as though to himself. "Once we dominated a world with it, and with our matchless steppe ponies. The world changed, and we became an obscure people. Then came the leap into space, and it was time for a people like us again: a strong and savage race, with no tolerance for weakness, not in ourselves or in others. But as always, with conquest came softening, corruption and the onset of decadence."

Haakon listened to this peculiar monologue without comment. He knew he was in the presence of a madman. Only a madman could be capable of the things Timur Khan had done in his climb to power. But he was that strange kind of madman who, when the currents of the times are just right, can achieve a great, worshipful following and seize the reins of power, changing the course of history forever. Haakon knew too that he had no choice but to play the man's game.

"Once," Timur Khan went on, "every high-born male of my race had to become expert with the bow. It was our link with the past, our way of acknowledging the virtue of our ancestors. Now the art is almost dead. I intend to reverse this trend. I've made a start with my Black Tuman. They are all men who will make any sacrifice to restore the glory of my people. As members of the steppe people, however, they would be under suspicion anywhere outside the Bahadur System. I am forced to make use of those who are not of pure blood."

"And my crew?" Haakon asked.

"Likewise, they shall be persons of the lower races."

Haakon searched Timur's face, looking for a glimmer of humor, some indication that the man didn't seriously believe what he was saying. There was none.

Timur took another printout from his desk. "Here are four persons now listed for arrest and execution by the Black Tuman." He held the paper before Haakon's eyes.

"No trial?" Haakon asked.

"Are you serious?"

"Silly of me," Haakon said. "Go on."

"These persons have the requisite skills to perform the tasks I shall require. All are human, within limits. They are at present being rounded up. You may be wondering how I intend to secure your obedience."

"I don't suppose an oath of loyalty would be sufficient?" Haakon hazarded.

"Don't insult my intelligence. I trust totally the loyalty of my own men; lesser races obey only through fear. You and each member of your crew shall have implanted in your brains a device that shall ensure your obedience—a poisonous explosive that will bring about instant death at my command. You and your crew will continue to live solely at my pleasure." There was no arrogance, no gloating. Timur Khan did not consider the matter worthy of more than passing interest.

Haakon was appalled, but not surprised. He had spent too many years in the quarries. When he had been sentenced the Black Tuman had been a mere bodyguard, commanded by the new Minister of National Security, Timur Khan Bey. In those days Timur Khan and his minions had had nothing like the powers they obviously now enjoyed. Summary execution had not been among their privileges when Haakon was condemned to the hammer and pick. Times had changed, obviously. Haakon was ready to accept that. It had happened often enough before.

*   *   *

The jewels sparkled more brightly than stars in an unpolluted sky. They were not beyond praise though, and the man who had stolen them was willing to supply all that was needed.

"From the crown of a queen, lady," he pleaded earnestly. "Each a fabled gem, with its own tale behind it." He pointed to a yellow diamond. "The Star of Betelgeuse, lady," he urged, "once in the crown of the queen of. . . ."

The lady who sat across from the thief purred, and he relaxed a little. She also smelled content, and that was a good sign. She reached out daintily and unsheathed an inch-long claw from the tip of her forefinger. With the claw, she drew the gem closer and studied it with slit-pupiled eyes. The thief was still uneasy. Rama was a Felid, and Felids were bioengineered humans. The thief was more comfortable with aliens than with creatures like Rama. They seemed so human—up to a point. Beyond that they were controlled by whatever strange genes had been grafted onto their human inheritance.

Rama was a human female, but she was also a cat—from her clawed toes to the tips of the long, sensitive whiskers that flanked her nose. Her sleek, well-groomed hair was striped gray and black. When she purred, it was no figure of speech but a genuine cat's sound of pleasure and contentment. Her lithe, rangy body was enormously powerful, and he would have expected her ears to be long and pointed, but instead they were small and perfectly human, although inhumanly acute. Just now they were twitching and Rama was giving off a new, bitter scent.

"Were you followed?" she hissed.

"Of course not," the thief said, alarmed. "What's wrong?" The chamber they were in was supposed to be secure from raids and snoops, and Rama paid handsomely for its use. It was deep in the offworlder's quarter of Baikal, the capital city of Bahadur. The doors were double-blocked, and piercing them would be a task far beyond the capabilities of the Baikal police.

"Someone is coming," Rama warned. She seemed relaxed but her hair began to fan out into a leonine mane and a restless, whining growl began to sound from somewhere within her larynx.

"Impossible, lady," said the thief, sweat beginning to bead his brow. "The police have been paid to leave this place alone."

"Not the police then," Rama said.

"It makes no sense," the thief protested. What rival gang would dare to stage a raid against Rama? He swept the gems into a bag and stuffed the bag beneath his shirt just as a ringing blast sheared a hole through the main door. The smoke cleared to reveal black uniforms.

"BTs!" the thief bleated. With inhuman speed Rama was at the back door, slapping its lock with her palm. It snapped open and more BT troopers burst into the room. Rama's claws raked two of them but their protective uniforms saved them from gutting. She managed to get one through the opening in his helmet, but as the man fell back, clasping his hands to his face, the others bound her hands and feet. It took three of the powerful men to hold her still. Another sprayed knockout gas into her face and her hissing and squalling subsided.

The thief was standing with hands high, petrified with fear. No attention was paid to him. Unbelievingly, he watched as Rama was trussed up and carried out. The man she had clawed had taken his helmet off; he stood cursing quietly as a companion applied disinfectant to his slashes. Then they filed out, leaving the thief alone with his trembling knees. Not a word had been spoken to him.

* * *

Haakon left the city transport at the edge of the clean, orderly New Town section of the city and began his descent into Lower Baikal. The old section of town near the spaceport was a warren of narrow streets and alleys and dilapidated buildings. It was crowded with humans and aliens of many types, and there was a notable absence of government enforcement personnel. From time to time, police observation 'bots floated by overhead, but little attention was paid to them. In all probability their sensors weren't even turned on. The Bahadur police didn't care much what offworlders did to one another, so long as they stayed out of the New Town.

Haakon was wearing spacer pants and boots and a lorix-hide vest. Everything seemed a little unreal to him. He had spent the last five years in the quarries and adjusting to the outside wasn't going to be easy. Not that he felt exactly free. The little device implanted in his head saw to that.

He stepped into a nearby bar-restaurant for his first unsupervised meal in five years. He ate slowly, relishing the sensation. The air was full of narcotic smokes and incense, and soothing music came from the little speaker set into the table top. He heard a low babble of conversation in several human tongues. It seemed that this place didn't serve XT food. He punched an order for pseudo tequila and lime, and it was brought to his table by a Ganthan, who set the thermoflask before him. The Ganthan was squat and covered with long, rough fur. It had no visible features, and its head was little more than a bump atop its torso; it looked rather like a small, ambulatory haystack. The Ganthi were native to Delius, and Haakon addressed it in the High Speech.

"Could Younger Sister's Eldest Son inform me where fighting dens are?"

After a moment's hesitation, the Ganthan said, "One trusts that my lord is not associated with the authorities?"

Haakon dialed his favored temperature on the flask. "Has my nephew ever met a person of the Bright World who would deal with the authorities of Bahadur?"

"One must be careful," the Ganthan replied. "In the warehouse district, near the abandoned Centauran docks, is an establishment called Spacer's Delight. It is a rough place. I urge my lord not to go there alone or unarmed."

"I thank my nephew," Haakon said. He rubbed salt around the rim of his glass and poured the chilled liquid from the flask into it.

Before going into the warehouse district, he went to a shop that sold, among other things, arms and protective equipment. Guns of all types were forbidden to offworlders, but he bought an eight-inch powerblade. Unsheathed, the blade was transparent. Haakon thumbed the button on the handle and the blade turned shimmering silver, its edges sparkling with static discharge. A useful tool as well as a weapon, the powerblade was carried by nearly every spacer. He added a pair of wide steel bracelets to protect his wrists and forearms. He paid for his purchases with the credit chip supplied by Timur Khan. The chip was also a good way of keeping track of his movements, but just now Haakon wasn't worrying about that.

The warehouse district was in the seediest section of the old city. Lighting was supposed to be provided by the glowing sidewalks, but many panels flickered or were entirely dark. Occasionally Haakon was approached by small bands of street toughs; invariably they steered clear when they got a good look at him. His powerful frame, grim face and ex-con's depilation were enough to send them in search of easier prey.

Whores and pervs were more persistent, but he shrugged

them loose. Once he was stopped by a stunning hermaphrodite who wore nothing but sandals and glowing gems. A ring of scarlet comet-rubies outlined the two sets of genitals, male above female.

"New from the pits, spacer?" the herm asked, blue stars twinkling from the corners of its eyes. "Come to my place and I'll get the taste of rock dust out of your mouth." It pressed a large, bejeweled breast against his arm.

"Where's the Spacer's Delight?" Haakon asked. The herm seemed to be as good a source as any.

"Why, are you a sado? I go there myself, sometimes. I don't go for the blood so much, but some of the customers come away really horny. It's this way."

Haakon followed the herm. From the cleft of its buttocks a line of green gems ran all the way up its spine. The body was as voluptuous as bioengineering and surgery could make it, and the herm exuded an aphrodisiac pheromone from glands in its armpits.

The herm turned down a darkened alleyway and Haakon followed, ready for trouble. The glowing gems stopped before an unmarked door. "This is it." The herm leaned close and laid a hand on the front of his trousers. "Are you sure you wouldn't rather go to my place?" Its breath was sweetly scented and also charged with pheromones.

"Sorry," Haakon said. "My taste runs strictly to women."

"You silly chauvinist, when you could have the best of both worlds. 'Bye now." Haakon watched as the twinkling lights went back up the alley. Then he went inside.

Immediately his way was blocked by a giant, scaly Pirian. "You not p'lice?" it hissed. He held his arms out as it ran a snoop over him.

"I want to talk to Jemal," Haakon said. "I hear he fights here. Is he here tonight?"

"Jemal fight tonight. He in warmup pit." The Pirian had a long, fanged snout and no visible eyes. Its visual organs were located behind a band of red scales encircling its head. It made an intimidating bouncer. With a taloned hand, it waved Haakon inside.

A bar came floating by and Haakon ordered another tequila and lime. The big room was filled with beings of many species, but the majority were humans of one sort or another. A surprising number were Bahadurans. The amtosphere was not one of conviviality, and most of the conversation was in low, muttered tones. What little Haakon could catch seemed to be devoted to betting.

He saw a railing encircling a pit at one end of the room. A number of beings were leaning on the railing, intent on the action taking place below. Haakon sauntered over. Down in the pit the men and aliens who were to fight that evening were sparring with dummy blades. He saw Jemal immediately.

Unlike himself, Jemal had not changed much. He was an old friend, and when Haakon had seen his name on the arrest list, he had asked to make this contact, instead of their putting Jemal through a BT arrest. Jemal still looked much as he had when they were young, idealistic students at the academy. He was small, lithe and swift, with olive skin and black hair.

They'd graduated together early in the war. Haakon had been commissioned into the fleet and Jemal had gone into intelligence. A few years before, he'd run into Jemal again. All former members of the Delian armed forces had been exiled from their home system; Jemal had drifted into forging, counterfeiting, burglary and a number of other equally nefarious pursuits for which his training suited him. He had ended up in the same quarry with Haakon.

Still barred from most legitimate employment and unable to get off Bahadur, he was now a prize fighter.

Jemal broke off sparring and wiped the sweat from his face with a towel. Haakon managed to catch his eye and beckoned. Jemal, looking amazed, left the pit through a side door. Haakon found a vacant table and sat down, sipping his drink. A few minutes later, Jemal appeared and joined him.

"What're you doing here, Hack? I thought you were doing life in the pits."

"I was. I got released."

"It's good to see you. How long have you been out?"

"About a day. Have a drink, Jem. I have a proposition for you."

"Uh-uh. I'm fighting tonight."

"No you aren't. You're coming with me. I've got a ship."

Jemal stared at him in disbelief. "A ship? How could you get a ship?"

Haakon told his story. In the center of the room a stage rose from the floor and the first pair began to fight. There was noise and shouting and betting, then quiet as the badly wounded loser was carried to the infirmary. Another pair took their place.

"Timur Khan!" Jemal said. "You'd work for that butcher? No, thanks. At least as a thief I could live with myself."

"You think I like it?" Haakon demanded. "I had no choice, and neither have you. You think you can escape the BT on their own world? Maybe someplace we can find a way out of this, but in the meantime we'll be spacing and off Bahadur."

"Who else?" Jemal asked.

"A Felid named Rama."

Jemal whistled. "Rama! So they got her at last. I've never met her but they say she's the most dangerous creature in the lower city, and that's saying something. Anybody else?"

"A man named Soong and a woman named Mirabelle."

"Never heard of her, but Soong is a gambler. I didn't know that he'd done anything to attract BT attention. Any idea of what kind of jobs the bastard has in mind for us?"

"Do you think he'd tell me? Look, I know how it goes against the grain to work for Timur Khan, but we're dead if we don't, and who profits from that?" He stared at his glass, idly flicking specks of salt from its rim. "We didn't think it would ever come to this, did we? Back at the academy, I mean. We were going to fight for the cause, defeat the Powers, make the spaceways a free environment for all sentients." He brooded into his glass, lines etching bitterness into his face.

"Have you stopped believing it?" Jemal demanded. He waved a hand, taking in the room full of excited, sweating gamblers. "This is paltry, but it keeps me alive. I stay alive just so that someday, somehow, I can hit back at the Powers. I've operated as a crook but the only laws I've broken have been Bahadur laws." He took a sip of the drink he had finally ordered. "Look, I'll go along on one condition: whatever job Timur Khan gives us to do, we sabotage it as best we can without getting killed for it."

Haakon grinned. "Did you think I intended anything else?"

Jemal clapped him on the shoulder. "That's the Hack I used to know!" He relaxed now and took a long pull at his glass. "Hey, why don't you get repilated? I know a good clinic not far from here. I got my hair back in a few days."

Haakon ran a palm over his bare scalp. "I'm used to it

now. Hair would feel funny. Maybe I'll get some eyebrow implants.''

"What kind of ship is the bastard giving us?" Jemal mused. "I'll bet it's some war-surplus cargo bucket."

"Who cares? A ship's a ship—if it'll just get us out of this system. Come on, let's go to the port. There's a shuttle waiting to take us up to her. She's in parking orbit right now.''

TWO

There were thousands of craft in orbit next to the big maintenance station. Most had been mothballed after the war, inert but ready for new battles, new conquests, needing only their crews and their orders. The shuttle headed toward one of them.

"I don't believe this!" Jemal said, examining the ship that was their destination. Compared to the squat, utilitarian cargo craft that surrounded it, their ship was lean and sleek, its sides unscarred, its lines those of a vessel designed for atmosphere flying as well as spacefaring.

"Did you think I would assign an inferior craft for my purposes?" Timur Khan asked. The warlord appeared to be standing next to Haakon and Jemal, but it was an illusion. He was actually in his office in the Black Obelisk. What stood next to the two men was a holographic projection. He was no less fearsome for that.

"This is the *Eurynome*," Timur Khan said. "She was built on a light cruiser frame, to be the Prince Admiral's personal yacht in the last year of the war. The war ended before she could be commissioned. She is unmatched in every aspect of spacefaring. Her armament is formidable, although she is better suited as an explorer than as a warship.''

The shuttle drifted toward the boarding hatch. The sides of the ship had a black finish, applied by some process that was new to Haakon. The hull was entirely devoid of markings. Shuttle and ship made contact and the connecting hatches opened. Haakon and Jemal stepped through. They were met by a wave of scent so powerful that both men were stopped in their tracks.

Standing in the center of the lockroom was a female Felid, fingers and toes splayed, claws out and mane ruffled. Two other humans were in the lockroom but the Felid easily dominated. She was radiating a scent of hostility strong enough to be felt through the skin.

''Damn it, stop smelling up my ship!'' Haakon shouted.

''Your ship, is it?'' said the enraged Felid. ''You don't look much like a Bahaduran.''

''The name is Haakon. Captain Haakon to you, late of the Delian Fleet of the Three System Alliance, now commanding *Eurynome*. I take it you're Rama.''

The Felid relaxed a little and sheathed her claws. ''Delian? What're you doing here?''

''Same as you, trying to avoid death. Who are these two?''

A man came forward. In build he was slighter than Jemal. He had the slant-eyed, small-nosed features of the Bahadurans, but his face was round and his frame too small to belong to that race. ''I am Soong,'' he said. ''Once an intelligence officer of Han, now a gambler, or, rather, a prisoner. The lady with me is Mirabelle.''

At Soong's gesture the other human came forward. She

was small, with brown skin, hair and eyes. Her body was as voluptuous as the hermaphrodite's had been, but on her it looked natural.

"And what might your offense be?" Haakon asked.

"I'm a technothief," Mirabelle answered.

Haakon was impressed. It was an exacting trade, that of stealing technological secrets and selling them on the underground market. All the more exacting in that the detection devices installed in computer facilities rendered it almost impossible to smuggle out chips, film or other recording devices. Technothieves had not only to get into the facilities and retrieve the information, they had to be able to get out, carrying the encoded data in their heads.

"Each of you suits my purpose," Timur Khan said. "You are all criminals with backgrounds in military operations and intelligence. Should your histories be investigated, there is nothing to connect you with Bahadur save a record of hostility toward the Serene Powers. You may now acquaint yourselves with your ship. Assemble in the briefing room at twenty-one hundred hours to receive your first assignment." The holo winked out.

The new companions looked at each other, taking measure. It was not a new experience for any of them. The dislocations of war, the ephemeral arrangements of military life, the vicissitudes of life in the underground and in prison—all had accustomed them to being thrown together in close proximity with total strangers, expected to live and work with them in relative harmony.

"I suggest we follow the Noyon's instructions and examine our new vessel," Soong said.

They left the lockroom, Soong in the lead. Haakon followed him. Soong had a quiet voice, and all of his movements were delicate and precise. Haakon could picture him working at some intricate and infinitely painstaking task such as biosurgery or carving netsuke.

The interior of the ship was lavish, as befitted a royal yacht. The fittings were of carved and polished woods or of mellowed bronze. Even the control panels were finished with exquisite lacquer. Even so, nothing was garish or ostentatious. No surface had been altered for the sake of decoration, but all had been made of carefully chosen materials, finished in the highest taste.

"I've seen herm brothels that weren't as luxurious as this," Jemal said.

"I like it," said Rama, running a hand caressingly over a panel of fretted bronze given the greenish finish of *shakudo*.

"You would," Mirabelle said.

Haakon usurped for himself the captain's quarters, which opened directly off the bridge. A much larger suite of rooms on a lower deck had obviously been intended for the Prince Admiral, and the rest of the crew drew lots for it. Rama won, purring and exuding a cinnamon scent of delight.

Soong, it transpired, was the only one besides Haakon who had bridge-officer experience. Together the two checked out the instruments and controls.

"Soong," Haakon said, "I've known Jemal for a long time. The rest of you I need to learn more about if we're to accomplish anything. You've said you were an intelligence man for Han. What were your duties?"

"Oh," Soong began with a self-deprecating wave of the hand, "I was not an important man. A mere functionary, in fact. My task was one of reducing the expense in Han lives by neutralizing enemy forces. I removed our most capable adversaries through the most expedient means on the most cost-effective basis possible." He continued to check the readouts on the crystal screen before him. Haakon ran that through his mind for a while.

"You're saying that you were an assassin?"

"Crudely but accurately put."

"Did you ever try for Timur Khan?"

"He was not that important in those days. Still, it is an intriguing thought and one to which I have devoted much consideration."

"And your conclusion?"

"That he would be a very difficult man to get to. Also, I suspect that he has rigged some sort of deadman switch to these clever devices implanted in our skulls. The moment he dies, so do we."

"I fear you may be right. Not a comforting prospect, considering that he's spent years in making deadly enemies."

In spite of their situation, Haakon could not suppress a surge of joy at getting his hands once more on a ship's controls. And what a ship! *Eurynome* was a spacer's fantasy come true. Not only was she the most modern craft imaginable, she was adept at fighting, trade and exploration. She was agile enough to go anywhere and fast enough to get away from anything. Her lines were superbly functional and, at the same time, aesthetically pleasing. The young, starry-eyed Haakon of a dozen years earlier would have called her the embodiment of man's aspiration to inhabit all of space.

"How did those Bahaduran savages ever build a ship like this?" he wondered aloud.

"They didn't," Soong said. "This vessel is the product of the shipyards on Amaterasu. Only their ships utilize lacquer, and no others have the secret of giving bronze the *shakudo* finish."

"I should've thought Timur Khan wouldn't give us a Bahadur-built ship."

Haakon went through the remainder of the pre-voyage checkout automatically, without really thinking. Mentally he was still back in the quarry, breaking rock. The change was too sudden, and the shock was just setting in.

In the briefing room, the others gave their reports.

"Fully supplied," Mirabelle said. "Bulk foods and liquids for months, and enough concentrates to keep us alive for years. All the medical supplies we're likely to need too."

"Communications gear is all in order," Jemal said. "So are the engines as far as I can tell, but I'm no engineer."

Haakon looked at Rama. "Anything to report?"

"My suite is marvelous. Especially the bath." She purred.

"Bath?" Mirabelle said. "I assumed you Felids just licked yourselves." The Felid only purred louder, but she shed an acrid scent of annoyance.

Without warning, Timur Khan's image appeared among them. Even Haakon jumped slightly. "All is in order?"

"We need an engineer," Haakon said. "I can handle the mills for a short hop. So can Jemal. But we're not specialists. If anything went wrong, we'd be in trouble."

"I have a man for you. A suitable engineer was more difficult to find than the rest of you were." For good reason. Engineer was the most hazardous of spacing jobs. The highly temperamental Tesla Drive generators could be deadly, and attrition among engineers was high. Since the wars the ports were choked with spacers looking for berths, but a skilled engineer could always find work.

"Now," Timur Khan continued, "your first assignment."

Abruptly the lights extinguished and a holographic projection sprang to life at one end of the small room, turning the wall into a three-dimensional starscape. The picture magnified, showing a yellow star banded by a brilliant ring of myriad particles.

"This is the Cingulum," Timur Khan said. "Millions of years ago it was a standard system of perhaps ten planets. Its inhabitants somehow dismantled those planets and rearranged them into a band of worldlets equidistant from the primary star. Except for some rather enigmatic but impressive ruins, nothing remains of its former inhabitants, vanished more than a million years ago. The worldlets are now a warren for exiles and refugees fleeing the wrath of the Serene Powers."

The picture flickered again, this time displaying a small spaceport located within a narrow canyon. Large numbers of ships were unloading passengers onto the crowded field. All wore life-support suits and the place obviously had little gravity.

"The inhabitants of the Cingulum fondly think that the Serene Powers do not possess the coordinates to their hideaway. This was true until recently. Now, as you can see, we have a visual record of both its location and its main immigration facility. This is where you will go to do my bidding. You will thoroughly infiltrate the power structure of the resistance command and bring me the heads of its leaders. You will destroy this port facility. You will bring back a full readout of the defenses of the Cingulum." His holographic glare settled on Mirabelle and she nodded slightly.

"If you know where it is," Haakon said, "why not just send in a fleet and wipe it out?"

"Their Majesties do not wish a major military action at this time. In any case, it is not your place to analyze my instructions, only to carry them out."

"We're the knives and you're the butcher," Jemal said. Suddenly he jerked back, his eyes starting almost from their sockets as his spine bent into an agonized bow and he fell writhing to the floor.

"Small insolence will bring pain," Timur Khan said, "and major infractions, death. You will now carry out your orders, as soon as your engineer arrives. Fear me and obey."

The holographic image disappeared. Haakon, Soong and Mirabelle helped Jemal to his feet, while Rama ignored them, licking the back of her hand.

"That man," Jemal said, "has no sense of humor."

"Keep it in mind," Haakon cautioned.

A faint bell note sounded throughout the ship. "Someone at the airlock," Soong said. "Our new engineer, I would presume."

They met the final crew member as he, she or it came aboard from the shuttle. Sex and even species were not immediately apparent. What they saw appeared to be a human in gray battle armor, but there were none of the usual weapons systems visible, and they could see liquids bubbling through transparent tubes exposed at the joints. Instead of eyes or lenses, it had a pair of large visual receptors bulging above a voice-grille, giving the face an insectoid look.

"I take it you're our engineer," Haakon said.

The figure dropped its spacebag to the deck. "I'm Rand." The voice, muffled and made metallic by the voice-grille, seemed to be male and human.

"Why are you dressed like that?" Rama asked.

"Five years ago I was standing too close to a Tesla generator when it blew."

"How close?" Haakon interrupted.

"Two meters."

Jemal snorted. "Nobody ever survived anything like that."

"I almost didn't. We were on Galen at the time. The meds there gave the victims free treatment if they'd try out a new tissue-regeneration system they were working on. I was burned down to the bone over most of my body. No skin left at all. I'm regenerating in here.''

They looked him over sceptically. He looked more like a robot than a man. "How do you move?" Mirabelle asked.

"Partially with regenerated muscle tissue, mostly by servomotors. In about ten years I can take all this off and look human again. I expect I'll be pale though."

Rama rapped the plating with her knuckles. "Stop that!" Rand ordered. "I'm not an exhibit."

"How did Timur Khan get you?" Haakon asked.

"The Powers have Galen now. No more treatment for me if I fail him."

"No crimes on your record?" Jemal asked.

"Nothing official. Why? Do you have to be a crook to sign on here?"

"Timur Khan seems to like it that way. He's made an exception for you. I'm Haakon, captain of *Eurynome*."

It was the first time he'd said it and he hadn't anticipated the rush of pleasure, almost of exaltation, that the simple assertion brought. A ship! A crew! All of space to wander in! Then he remembered Timur Khan and returned to reality, still as much a slave as he had been in the pits.

"There are some vacant crew quarters left. Find yourself a cabin and stow your gear, then check out the engines. We head out as soon as your report's in. You can get acquainted with your new crewmates on the way."

"I'll show you where you may lodge," Soong said. Rand threw Haakon a sketchy, metallic salute and followed Soong down a passageway, his therapeutic suit clicking slightly.

Gesturing to Jemal to follow him, Haakon made his way to the captain's quarters adjoining the bridge. There he punched a combination below the refreshment niche in the wall and two frosted glasses appeared. He handed one to Jemal and then sat down in the big, padded float-chair.

"All right, Jem, tell me what you think."

"This is suicide."

"It's suicide if we fail Timur Khan."

"Fail him? What can we accomplish with this crew?" He began ticking off points on the spread fingers of a fine-boned hand. "First we have two alumni of the Academy of Delius, splendid specimens both but aging and with spacer skills untested in several years. Next we have a half-human, half-cat Felid, mean and dangerous, criminally inclined and with no discernible talent except as a generator of smells. Third, a lovely walking memory-bank too young to have taken part in any war. Fourth, a delicate little gambler who probably paints landscape scrolls in his spare time—"

"He was an assassin for Han," Haakon interrupted.

"Lovely. Just wonderful. An assassin. How can I contain my joy? Now fifth, we have something that looks like a cross between a spacesuit and a garbage processor and claims there's a man growing inside it. All we know about him, if it is a him, is that he was standing next to a Tesla when it blew. He probably caused the explosion."

"You've grown pessimistic in your old age, Jem," Haakon pointed out. "Time was when you'd take on a fleet with a training ship and a slingshot."

"Well, you know how it is. Lose a war, spend a few years busting rocks, get explosive devices implanted in your brain, first thing you know your sense of invincibility loses its edge."

"But that's not it, is it?" Quizzically Haakon raised the bare skin where he had once had eyebrows.

Jemal stared intently into his drink. "No. It's what

we're going to do. We're going to go to the Cingulum and betray all those people.''

''You can't betray people unless they trust you.''

''Don't play with words. If it weren't for these little bombs in our heads, we'd be off to the Cingulum so quick we'd leave our ship behind. Those are our kind of people out there, Hack.''

''Do you have any constructive suggestions to make, or are you just bitching? Of course they're our kind of people. That's why Timur Khan's sending us there. We may run into people we know. There's not a damn thing we can do about it either. We do as he says or we die. We talked about this before. We'll do what we have to to stay alive. Beyond that, we'll do what we can to minimize Timur Khan's accomplishments. What other choice do we have?''

Jemal stared into his drink again. ''None,'' he said at last.

''Their *heads*?'' Even through the voice-grille, Rand sounded incredulous. ''He really wants their heads?''

''Barbarous, certainly,'' Soong said, ''but not unexpected.'' He looked at the others, gathered about the mess table. They were under Tesla Drive, on their way to the Cingulum. ''The Bahadurans are great followers of traditional forms. In the last years of the war, Their Majesties had victorious commanders send back the heads, suitably preserved, of enemy generals. A return to the pristine customs of their ancestors.''

''It figures,'' Mirabelle said. ''If there's any nasty historical atavism lying around unused, count on the Bahadurans to revive it.'' She glanced distastefully at Rama, who had a large hunk of something raw and bloody lying on a plate before her. With two swift slashes of her talons, the Felid reduced it to bite-sized chunks.

"You worry about the defense readouts, dear one," Rama said. "Let me worry about taking heads. That's more my line." She speared a chunk of meat on the talon of a forefinger and delicately nibbled at it with small, sharp teeth.

"Nobody takes any heads until I decide," Haakon said. "We'll have a lot of exploring and sizing up to do before we take any irreversible action. Clear?" He looked around.

All nodded assent except Rama. He glared at her until she gave a slight, almost imperceptible nod. She was going to be trouble.

They were still far from the Cingulum when the picket ships stopped them.

THREE

Petty Officer Scanlon took in the readout on the strange ship, but the figures weren't helpful. It was time to pass the problem on to higher authority.

"Hey, Chief," he called, "you know that ship the point satellites picked up a while ago?"

"What about it?" Captain Chang asked. He was bored stiff. Security picket was the dullest duty imaginable. He wore oddments of several military and civilian uniforms, as did the rest of the crew. The Cingulum had never settled on a uniform and probably never would.

"It doesn't match up with anything in the banks," Scanlon said.

"Nothing new about that," Chang commented, refusing to get excited. All kinds of obsolete tubs were wandering around space, too old to be on current record, or cobbled together from junked ships and fitting no category, or built by some obscure shipyard on some backwater that wasn't even on the charts. The computer now had enough data to construct a holographic image and it was beginning to appear, in tiny cubical increments, in the tank.

"Chief," Scanlon said, "I think you better have a look at this."

Chang sighed and got up from his deep chair. He was cut off in mid-sigh when he caught sight of the image in the tank. "Big gods and little devils! What's a beauty like that doing here?" He'd seen nothing but scruffy smugglers and tattered refugee ships since he'd fled to the Cingulum, and now *Eurynome* glittered in his tank like a jewel.

"That's our job, isn't it?" Scanlon asked. "Finding out what it's doing, I mean."

Chang looked at him bleakly. "Thanks, Scanlon. I really needed that reminder." The petty officer just looked back blankly.

Chang returned his attention to the image in the tank. "Communication?" he asked.

"I've sent the regulation stand-and-identify order," said Hori, his commo officer.

The image of the ship blanked and was replaced by that of a female Felid, head and shoulders. The crew was gathered in a circle around the tank, but all saw the same full-face view. Chang studied her with interest. He had never met a Felid before. She was, in her way, as beautiful as the ship.

Chang stood before a blank panel and heel-kicked a pressure plate at its base. The panel turned into a starscape and in its foreground was a circle of multicolored spheres; the sigil of the Cingulum. When he appeared in the other ship's holo tank, he would be framed by the symbol, to suitably dazzling effect.

"Give the 'open communication' signal, Hori."

The slight widening of the Felid's eyes told him that

visual and audio contact had been established. "Yes, dear?" she said.

This was not a contact formula Chang was familiar with. "Unidentified ship, give your name, registration number and port of origin."

"Why don't you tell me who *you* are, you handsome devil?" Chang turned red, while his crew snickered.

"Of course. Captain Chang, of the light cruiser *Sakura*, Cingulum security forces."

"Well, then, I'm Captain Rama of *Eurynome*."

"And your business?"

Her eyes went wide in mock amazement. "Why, I'm on the run of course, silly man. Why else would I be heading for the Cingulum?"

"Why indeed? Any contraband aboard?"

"Hmm, let's see," Rama said. "I'm not sure. What's illegal here?"

"Good question," Chang said. "They've never told me. No Bahaduran personnel or snoop devices aboard, I trust?"

"I should hope not! Who do you think I'm running from?"

"Almost anybody. I'm going to have to notify my superiors. In the meantime you will bring your ship to boarding approach. Take care not to make any hostile action."

"Why, Captain," Rama said with a slight purr, "would I endanger so lovely a man as you? The very thought wilts my whiskers."

Several of Chang's crewmen left the bridge so they could enjoy their convulsions without being overheard. Chang was made of sterner stuff and kept a straight face. He did, however, make certain disciplinary plans for later.

"I shall have to board you as soon as you arrive," he said.

"I hunger for the moment, Captain Chang."

Chang fumed nervously at the lock. Three crewmen accompanied him on the shuttle, along with Leila, the shuttle pilot. They had docked with the strange ship thirty seconds ago and still the lock was not open.

"What's taking so long?" Chang wondered aloud.

"Maybe she's still putting on her makeup for you," Scanlon said.

"Perhaps her hand trembles with lust on the control," Leila suggested. Chang groaned silently. It was getting out of hand.

Abruptly the lock snapped open and the men were hit in the nostrils by a wave of pheromone so powerful that their scalps tingled, their mouths dried, their knees trembled and their eyeballs grew bloodshot. Pulse rates soared and hormones shot through their systems like a horde of ravening rats. Leila just wrinkled her nose. To her it was merely a disagreeable stink.

Rama appeared in the lock, her hair fanned out and her whiskers aquiver. Chang hadn't expected her to be so big. He was not a large man, and her intimidating aspect helped to calm his biochemically induced lust. "Captain Rama?" he managed to choke out.

"The same, beloved," she said, gathering him into her arms and lifting him from the deck in a spine-cracking hug. She licked his ear and he winced. Her tongue was like a file. She set him down and drew him inside with an arm around his shoulders. "Let me show you the wonders of my ship. Is it not beautiful?" With a wave of her hand she indicated the rest of her personnel. "Oh, and these are my crew. The hairless one is Haakon, my second. The one who looks mechanical is Rand, the engineer. These two are Jemal and Soong. They do something or other, I'm not sure what. That plain little one with the uninteresting smell is Mirabelle. She provides a pleasing contrast to me." She led the slightly benumbed officer into the ship.

Scanlon looked at Haakon. "She like that all the time?"

"When it suits her," Haakon said.

Scanlon shook his head, clearing the last of the phero-mone from his senses. "Well, she's got Chang under control, but that stuff won't work with Lopal Singh."

"Who's that?" Jemal asked.

"He's our boss, the head of security for the Cingulum. He's on his way over now." The petty officer looked about him with interest. "How'd you get your hands on a ship like this?"

"We stole it, of course," Haakon said. "Where else would working spacers get hold of a royal yacht? Come on, let's go to the lounge and have a drink." He began to lead the way.

"I don't know," Scanlon said. "We're on duty. Ah, what the hell. Lopal Singh's going to give us a tube-reaming anyway. Might as well have a drink while we're waiting."

Haakon drew drinks while Scanlon and the others gazed in wonderment at the fittings of the lounge. Jemal took up the story they had agreed on. "We were in a BT holding tank for various indiscretions," he said. "We knew what we faced, so we pulled a break. There were a couple hundred of us. I don't know if any of the others made it. The six of us grabbed a shuttle and headed for the moth-ball fleet. We keyed the shuttle to find us an explorer-scout or light cruiser. We never expected to luck into anything like this. They were keeping her in orbit around Bahadur. Pretty nice berth, don't you think?"

"Not bad, not bad," Scanlon said, turning the cut-crystal goblet he had been given. He wondered what planet produced purple crystal streaked with yellow. "I hope Lopal Singh lets you keep it."

"Keep it?" Haakon said sharply. "You mean they confiscate ships from refugees? I thought this was the one place where we could be safe from Bahadur. We heard that the Cingulum welcomed people on the run from the Powers."

"Sure," Scanlon said. "But you're going to have to convince our boss that you're real refugees, not just a bunch of escaped crooks. We've had a lot of those come here, and they're not an element we want to have around. Several ships have been confiscated and the convicts sent to Coventry. If I were you, I'd think real hard about what I was going to say to Lopal Singh."

"And what is this Coventry?" Soong asked. "I recall an ancient Earth city of that name."

"It's where the authorities quarter people they aren't sure about until it's decided whether or not they're safe. I don't know why they named it that. It's not a bad place, not like a real prison, but you don't go anywhere else until your case is decided. I was there for a few days when I first got here."

"Just our luck!" Jemal fumed. "Get out of one slammer and jump right into another! I thought arbitrary tyranny was what we were getting away from."

Actually this was exactly what they had been expecting, but a little show of indignation had been deemed to be in order. Complacency is the most unimpressive of attitudes.

"It can speed things up if you can find someone here to vouch for you," Scanlon advised. "Do you know anybody who's already made his way here?"

"Not for sure," Haakon told him. "Jemal and I fought

for Delius. Soong was with Han. But you know how they split us up. Besides that, we've spent a lot of time in the slams. I haven't been in contact with my old associates in years. They could all be dead by now. Not many of us survived the wars anyway.''

"We've got some Delians here. Some from Han too." Scanlon looked at Mirabelle. "What about you?"

"I'll do all right for myself no matter what they decide," she said.

"I expect you will. Now, when you meet—" The ship's proximity alarm proclaimed the approach of another vessel. "That's the boss," Scanlon said. He turned to his crewmates. "Ditch the drinks. Mister," he said to Haakon, "you better go tell your captain that the real trouble is about to arrive."

Lopal Singh had to stoop to get through the door of the lounge. Nearly two and one half meters of NeoSikh from the heavy-grav world of New Rann of Kutch, he dwarfed everyone else present. He wore a tan uniform based on a nineteenth-century British design, complete with Sam Browne belt from which hung a holstered pistol and a curved tulwar. His never-cut black beard was parted in the middle, its ends tucked up beneath his violet turban.

Rama immediately transferred her attentions from Chang to his superior. "How may I supply your lordship with the utmost gratification?" she asked.

"You may begin by explaining the circumstances leading to your arrival here." His rumbling voice was slightly distorted by the nostril filters he wore. He had encountered Felids before.

Rama gave him much the same story Jemal had given Scanlon. Lopal Singh listened impassively, his black eyes revealing nothing. "This prison satellite," he said at last, "tell me more about it."

Rama beckoned to Mirabelle. "You, memory person, come here and give this incredibly gorgeous gentleman all he wants to know."

The security chief unclipped a computer terminal from his belt and handed it to Mirabelle. The technothief took it and began to recite in the special symbolic language of her profession, speaking with mind-boggling speed and flawless diction. The performance went on for perhaps thirty seconds; then she handed the terminal back to Lopal Singh.

"Only two types of people can master that language and skill," he said. "Computer intelligence officers of special education, and technothieves. Which are you?"

"Come now, sir," she said, "need you really inquire?"

"Freelance or organizational?" he asked.

"I'm a licensed technothief for the House of Akagi. I was working on assignment in Baikal when I was picked up." This part was true. The prison satellite was one she had been held on. Just to keep in practice, she had passed the time by raiding its computers and memorizing anything that looked useful.

"Did your assignment in Baikal involve military, political or commercial information?"

"I'm alive. Commercial, naturally. Anything you'd like to know about the Bahadur-Valerian secret trade agreements I can tell you, right down to the bribes and kickbacks at bottom management level."

"You could be useful." He looked at Haakon, Jemal, Soong and Rand, who stood behind Rama. "You four, if you are being truthful about your situation, will probably be given freedom of the Cingulum, after a stay in Coventry while we check you out. But you—" he turned his stony gaze to Rama. "I've heard of you, none of it good. You're a thief, a fence and probably much worse. You've run gangs noted for ruthlessness.''

She gave him a needle-toothed smile. ''Mere propaganda put forth by my enemies, sir. Surely you don't believe what the Bahadurans say, you ravishing creature?''

''I am not among those who believe that an enemy of Bahadur is necessarily a friend of ours. In any case, the decision is not mine. My assignment is merely to take charge of you and gather the facts. The Council will decide. For the present, your ship and its contents are confiscated and you will all accompany me to Coventry. If the Council so decides, all will be returned to you exactly as it is now. Come with me, please.''

Rama's expression remained unchanged, but her hair began to shift and her whiskers flattened to her face. A faint squalling sound came from her larynx and she shed a metallic scent. She gripped the arms of her chair, her claws indenting its covering.

''I could kill you where you stand, you insolent fool,'' she said. ''You could be dead before you touch your pistol or sword.''

''I very much doubt it,'' Lopal Singh said. He did not change his position in the slightest, but that meant nothing. Men from New Rann of Kutch were fast and powerful and known to fear nothing.

Haakon laid a gentle hand on Rama's shoulder. She turned her head and hissed at him, the movement so fast it was a blur. ''Easy, Captain,'' he said. ''They have us surrounded and outgunned. Let's go along with them. After all, they should let us go as soon as they know we're no threat to them.'' His words were quiet and soothing, but his glare was savage, as though by sheer willpower he could stop her from destroying their slender chance of gaining refuge here. The bit of byplay wasn't lost on Lopal Singh.

"Of course," she said at last. "By all means, take us to your Coventry, sir. May I pack a few things to take with me for this durance?"

"Certainly." He turned to his subordinates, still in the process of relaxing after the threatening moment. "Da Souza, accompany this lady and make a list of everything she takes from the ship." He faced Haakon. "Your ship will be inventoried and sealed until the Council's decision. Go get your things but take no weapons of beam or missile capacity."

"What about a powerblade?" Jemal asked.

"Powerblades, knives and swords are permitted. I would even recommend them. Your new neighbors in Coventry are sometimes unsociable."

Five of them gathered in the holding cell aboard Lopal Singh's ship. Rama was still selecting from among her possessions those she would take with her.

"What impression did you form of our esteemed host?" Haakon asked Jemal.

"Hard as any I've seen. Bad man to fall afoul of. I think he could have taken Rama if she'd attacked."

Haakon looked at Mirabelle.

"He has police instincts," she said. "He can spot a real crook with his eyes shut. We'd just better hope he finds us useful. Rama's going to ruin us all if you can't keep her leashed."

"Leave Rama to me." He looked at Rand inquiringly.

"It's all the same to me," he said. "They'll find a use for a good Tesla man. I didn't ask to come on this little expedition, you know."

"Are you forgetting that interesting device planted in your head?" Haakon asked. "For all we know, they'll blow it if the team splits up. We stick together and we back one another or we die. Remember it.'' He turned to Soong.

''Lopal Singh is most devoted to his duty,'' the little gambler-assassin said. ''He will keep us under watch until he is sure that we represent no harm to his nation.'' He considered further for a moment, then: ''I think he is an honorable man.''

FOUR

Coventry was a roughly spherical chunk of rock with no distinguishing features. A massive lock set into a cliff side admitted the shuttle into the interior. The shuttle dock was an immense cavern in which tiers of balconies towered out of sight, seemingly carved or molded from the native rock by some unknown process.

"How did you build all this?" Haakon asked, staring with the others from the shuttle's transparent nose. Weird-looking passageways twisted at odd angles from the docking area.

"We didn't," the shuttle captain answered. "It was here when it was first explored. We simply added the locks and baffles. There are some parts you shouldn't go into, but you'll find out about that soon enough."

There was a humming as the landing stair extruded. "All right, all ashore and good luck," the captain said. "Keep an eye on your goods, and don't let anyone get too close behind you until you know the place better. I hope

I'll be back to pick you up before long.'' It sounded as though it were a spiel he had performed often.

They descended to the dock surface, carrying their spacebags. Rama, who enjoyed her creature comforts, was the exception. She had brought along an anti-grav sled piled high with what she deemed necessary, and she towed it along behind her like a pet. The gravity had to be artificial, but it felt just below Earth-standard.

A small group of men and women greeted them as they trudged from the shuttle toward the nearest cave entrance. The dominant figure was a fat man with a jolly, florid face and hard blue eyes. Clothing among the group ran the gamut from rags to finery, from body armor to near-nudity. The *Eurynome* crew lowered their spacebags to the ground, not wishing to have encumbered hands when meeting strangers of unclear intent. The greeting committee was armed with simple hand weapons: knives, hatchets and powerblades.

"Welcome to our little world, pilgrims,'' the fat man said. "We'd like to help you get yourselves established. Start off on the right foot, so to speak. You'll be needing quarters, a place to eat, some kind of work, things like that. We'll be of assistance to you. We take care of all the newcomers.''

"Are you official or self-appointed?'' Haakon asked. The fat man shot him a sudden, appraising glance.

"Nobody's really official here, friend,'' he said. "But things work for the best when people cooperate.'' He went on, addressing himself to Rama. "You'll find it a place where some live better than others. It's largely a matter of being on good terms with the right people. I can see you aren't just some bunch of small-timers, like about half the population here. You wouldn't want to associate with the wrong element, and if you'll allow me to be your guide and advisor, so to speak, you could save yourselves a lot of grief.''

"What if we don't figure we need any help?'' Haakon asked.

The fat man's gaze returned to Haakon, harder than ever although the friendly grin remained fixed. "Excuse me, friend, but we were told that the Felid owned the ship you came in on. Also, the name of Rama the Felid is not exactly unknown to some hereabouts. Not to pry, but I like to keep these relationships clear. Ignorance can lead to misunderstanding.''

"The ship's hers,'' Haakon said. "Groundside, I'm in charge.'' He glanced up. From some of the lower balconies people were watching the byplay below, and more onlookers were arriving.

"I can see you've spent some time in the pits,'' the fat man said. Haakon nodded. "Then you know how these things work.'' Haakon nodded again. "And you're going to cooperate?''

"No,'' Haakon replied.

"Then you could be in big trouble,'' the fat man said.

Behind him the others were subtly shifting stance and position. Nothing was overt, but only the hopelessly unperceptive could have missed the transition from neutral to combat status.

"I'm McTeague,'' the fat man continued, "the boss of this place, I'm good to people who want to get along with me. Troublemakers get all the trouble they can handle.''

"For the sake of my shipmates,'' Haakon said, "allow me to explain. Some of them have never been in the pits or the slams.''

Without taking his eyes from McTeague, Haakon addressed his crew. "Fat man here is offering us a chance to join his mob. That means we'd be under his protection. None of the other cons here could threaten us without incurring his displeasure. But his protection doesn't come free. Anything we have is his. Anyone he tells us to kill or maim, we kill or maim. Any sexual service he requires, we deliver upon request. That about covers it, fat man?''

"You got it," McTeague said. "I don't like your tone though." He turned slightly, toward his myrmidons. "Leon, Sim, fix Baldy there so he doesn't talk so offensively." The two thugs jumped forward, knives suddenly in their hands, their movements quick and deadly.

As a knife came lancing toward his belly, Haakon grabbed the man by the wrist and yanked him forward, sidestepping the knife and almost disjointing the man's shoulder with the violence of the move. His knuckles crunched against a shaven temple and the man dropped. Jemal took out the second man with a neat, surgical incision inside the elbow. The fat man's other cronies began their attack but Rama was instantly among them, her claws slashing too fast for any possible defense. Then Jemal had his powerblade under McTeague's chin.

"Call them off," he said quietly.

"Cut it!" McTeague yelled.

The fighting stopped as both sides quickly withdrew from the sudden brawl. Haakon stepped up to McTeague, whose head was canted unnaturally high, the skin of his neck and chin growing reddened and blistered by the proximity of the powerblade.

"You and your mob will leave us alone, got it?" Haakon ordered. "If you give us any trouble, I'll kill you. If I hear that you're trying to incite anyone against us, I'll kill you. If any of us dies or is hurt accidentally, I'll kill you. Are you getting the picture, McTeague?"

The fat man started to nod but thought better of it. "Got you," he said.

"Then get out," Haakon said. Jemal removed his blade but did not put it away just yet. McTeague jerked his head toward a side cave and his followers began making their way toward it, many of them nursing injuries. A woman dressed in partial armor started to walk past Rama; the Felid slashed out and down with the claws of one hand, opening four parallel wounds that streaked from the woman's forehead to her collarbone. The woman fell back, screaming.

Haakon leaped in front of the Felid and shoved her away. One of McTeague's followers helped the wounded woman up and led her off. "What the hell was that for?" Haakon shouted. "The fighting was over!"

Rama smiled and began to lick the blood from her claws. "I did it because I wanted to. Because I like it. And you're a fool. We should have killed them all. Now we're locked up in a prison with deadly enemies. Your years in the slammer should have taught you better."

"If we were in for life, it'd be different," Haakon said. "But we're not. Don't you realize Lopal Singh will know about everything we do here? If we start out killing people, he could think we aren't desirable immigrant material."

"And don't put your hands on me again, ever," Rama hissed.

Haakon stepped in lightly. His first backhander came so swiftly that even Rama's reflexes couldn't save her. The steel bracelet slammed into the side of her head and sent her down. She had her feet under her before she hit the floor in a move that was almost an optical illusion, and then she was coming back up, claws out and teeth bared. The claws came from both sides but Haakon was already inside them, his elbows blocking her wrists. Then the other bracelet cracked into her chin and she went down again. This time she landed on her back and stayed down.

Immediately Haakon regretted it. Not here, in front of the others, and not now. It was the savagery of the pits again, reasserting itself; the need to establish dominance at once and without question. He had thought he'd put it all behind him but she was too much, even for his control.

Nobody helped Rama to her feet. She would have killed the first to touch her. Her smell was acrid and angry, but she seemed composed and voiced no threats. After shaking herself all over in a truly catlike manner, she took up the lead to her sled.

"Let's go," Haakon said.

They entered the nearest tunnel. It was an odd combination of nature and architecture, with chunks of rock and crystal protruding from the smooth walls. Some of the crystal glowed, providing light.

"Hey, spacers, need a guide?" They looked around for the source of the voice. Finally Haakon spotted it; what appeared to be a boy was seated on a rock outcrop just overhead.

"That's the second such offer we've had of late," Jemal said.

"But I mean it," the boy said.

He jumped from the outcrop, doing a forward flip as he came down, landing lightly on the heavy pads of his heels. His toes were as long as fingers, the big ones opposed and prehensile. He appeared to be about sixteen standard, with a wide, lipless mouth fixed in a toothy smile. His temples were shaved, the remaining hair colored a bright orange. Big gold hoops hung from his jug-handle ears, and he was dressed only in an embroidered vest and shorts. From the back of the shorts protruded a long tail, furred on its upper surface. Haakon classified him as a variant of the Singeurs:

human stock grafted with monkey genes for the early no-grav ships.

"Come on, I'll show you where you can sack and stuff." He turned and they followed his waddling gait. He carried his tail high in an S-curve, its length decorated with several jeweled rings. "First," he said, stopping before a side tunnel, "keep out of these places marked with yellow panels." Above the entrance a rectangular flash-plate blinked.

"Why?" Jemal asked.

"Because they'll take you to places you don't want to go. Whoever built this place never heard of Euclid, nor Einstein neither. Just keep away from them. We call them spook tunnels."

"What is your name, little one?" Soong asked.

"Oh, some call me Ape and some call me Four-hands and some—"

"But what is your real name?" Soong persisted. A throat-sac swelled beneath the boy's chin and he emitted a high-pitched, gobbling screech.

"I don't think you could pronounce it," he said.

"Probably not," Haakon agreed. "What do you prefer to be called?"

The boy pulled himself up to his full meter-and-a-half height. "Alexander," he said.

"A most euphonious name, fraught with historical significance," Soong said.

Alexander led them through a short side tunnel that opened onto one of the balconies six stories up. Haakon peered over the edge and saw the dock where the shuttle had been. He looked back through the short tunnel where he could see, on his own level, the tunnel that was now six floors below.

"Hold it," Haakon said. "What just happened?"

Alexander's face erupted in a toothy grin. "I knew that would throw you. It's one of the spook tunnels, but it's safe. There's no stairs here, nor no lifts nor grav tubes. Just these little short spook tunnels that take you from one level to another. Look here." He pointed with a toe at a large numeral six painted on the floor. "You just look through these lift tunnels for the floor number you want. They ain't laid out in any order anybody's ever been able to figure out. You just got to learn the layout."

They passed people on the balcony, dressed in the same motley as McTeague's mob. The planetoid didn't seem heavily populated. Chambers opened off the balcony, many of them having names painted over or beside the doors, often along with admonitions such as "Keep Out" and "Intruders will be slain without mercy." Others were more enigmatic: "I love Vegan and give good multiphase." Graffiti abounded on the walls, much of it bizarre: "O ye of the floating world, know that flesh and smoke are one" and "Deep down inside, aliens are still aliens" and "In thy orisons be all my sins remembered." Many of them were in scripts unfamiliar to any of the *Eurynome* crew. Soong paused before one written in Han characters.

"What does it mean?" Mirabelle asked.

"Roughly translated, 'In the time of Duke Ling, a wise man discovered the universe within the walls of his prison cell.' "

They went on without stopping until Alexander pointed out a row of doorways with no writing beside them. "These have never been occupied. Here you can all bunk close together," he said.

Haakon picked out a door and went inside. The room was roughly square, about five meters on a side and three meters high. He tossed his pallet on the floor. It was rolled into a cylinder twenty centimeters long and ten centimeters

thick. On the floor it hissed and unrolled, inflating itself
into a man-sized mattress and sleeping-bag combination,
weatherproof and suitable for extreme temperatures. His
other possessions he left in his bag. Alexander came in and
eyed the doorway, which was just a rectangular hole in the
stone. "If you got no blanket, maybe we can scare something up to cover the door."

"How come you're helping us, Alexander?" Haakon
asked.

"Does no harm to do favors," the boy said. "Besides,
that job you did on McTeague probably made you a lot
more friends than enemies. I wish you'd killed him though."

"Next time," Haakon said. "Now, why are you here?"

"Aw, I got here as a stowaway. They thought that
looked suspicious or something, so I'm here until they
decide what to do with me."

"That was all you did, was it? Just stowed away? And a
committee of dedicated malcontents has you stashed here
for fear of you?" Haakon bent a slightly quizzical gaze
toward the monkey-boy. Jemal and Soong came in.

"Truly," Soong said, turning to them; "this one must
have been a very paragon among stowaways to have in-
spired such trepidation. That even such a brute as Lopal
Singh should regard him as dangerous bespeaks much."

Alexander lowered his eyes and broke into a rueful grin.
"Aw, that ship I stowed away on, I kind of lifted a few
things. I had to live, you know."

"Petty pilferage?" Jemal asked. "A thief with five
manipulative appendages. The mind boggles."

"Well, maybe it wasn't so petty. I stowed in the Number Six hold of a drone freighter working the Twenty
Planet route run by the Blue Circle Line. Number Six had
to have air, see, because it transported live plants and
fauna. It also had lots of small luxury and techno items:

jewelry, chips, thimbles for navigation computers, stuff like that. We'd stop at some little port and the unloading crew would come aboard. I'd strike a deal for some of the stuff they wanted but wasn't being shipped to their particular planet, see?''

Jemal nodded. ''That's the kind of drive and initiative that has spread humanity triumphantly throughout this arm of the galaxy. How did you get caught?''

''The whole line relocated to the Cingulum when Bahadur annexed some of their homeports. One minute I was getting my stuff ready for sale on Omega Omega Upsilon Rho slash Two, the next I was looking down some beam rods in the Cingulum.'' He shrugged expressively with his entire body, tail included. ''It's the breaks.''

Mirabelle came in, now wearing a one-piece armorcloth coverall in deference to her new hostile surroundings. ''Her majesty is sulking in her cell. That was a mistake, Haakon. You should have left her alone or killed her. You'll have cause to regret that blow.''

''I know it,'' Haakon admitted, running his hand over his bare scalp. ''That woman is excessive.''

''She is valuable though,'' Soong said. ''She has great charm when she wishes to employ it, and in close combat she is worth many trained warriors.''

''Why'd you let her pose as the master of the ship?'' Jemal demanded. ''I don't see we've gained any advantage by it.''

''It's inconvenient,'' Haakon said, ''but to the authorities it'll make more sense. She's the one on their files as a big operator. She's the one with all the connections among the Bahadur smugglers, and with the police and government. If a pack of cons pulls a breakout and steals a ship and goes into business for itself and she's among them, who's going to end up in charge? If we had come in here with her in a subordinate position, Lopal Singh's cop antennae would've stood up and quivered.''

Haakon felt Jemal's elbow in his ribs and followed his friend's gaze to where Alexander was standing, a look of great attentiveness on his face.

"Hey, don't mind me," Alexander said. "Just go on with your conversation. I find all this just fascinating." He gave them a great, ingratiating grin. Mirabelle put an arm around his narrow shoulders.

"Of course," the technothief said, "you would never repeat anything you hear in this place, would you?" She smiled radiantly and with a certain fetching deadliness.

"Me? Are you serious? Do you know what they *do* to snitches in this place?" He assumed a look of unbridled horror. "They tie them to a rock, see, and then they—"

"You may spare us the no-doubt fascinating details," Soong said. "A simple assurance of confidentiality will suffice."

"Oh, sure. You can bet your life on it."

"Good," Haakon said. "You've already bet yours. Now where do we eat around here? Surely they haven't just stranded us to let us starve?"

"No, they feed us. If you want to call it that. I've had better though."

"You lived pretty well in Number Six, did you?" Jemal quizzed.

"Better? I lived like a king! They had a synthesizer that could make anything. And there were lots of raw materials around to throw into it too: plants, minerals, chemicals— everything right there for the taking."

"You must have come close to bankrupting Blue Circle Line all by yourself," Jemal noted.

"They could afford it," Alexander contended. "Come

on, let's round up the cat-lady and I'll show you where you can eat.''

Rama had marked the entrance to her cell with four parallel scratch marks. Haakon examined them closely. They had scored the hard stone to a depth of at least a centimeter.

"She must have those claws tipped with durasteel," he mused. "Hey in there, the kid's going to show us where we eat. Want to accompany us?" He was answered by a hiss and a wave of nostril-burning scent.

"Guess she don't want to go, huh?" Alexander asked.

"She's a picky eater," Haakon answered.

A brief walk and two spook tunnels later they entered a high-ceilinged room with tables of many designs scattered haphazardly about. Alexander showed them a long stone shelf along one wall where, at irregular intervals, trays of food appeared, seemingly out of nowhere. They stared intently but never seemed to be looking at exactly the right place to see a tray materialize. It was obviously a variant of the spook-tunnel phenomenon.

Jemal took a sampling of the food.

"Pretty fancy trick. Too bad the food's such slop." It was the kind of reconstituted protein and carbohydrate that ships or armies resorted to when all fresh or preserved provisions gave out: a shapeless, colorless, tasteless mass that would maintain life and health but did little for morale.

They took their trays to a low table surrounded by scruffy cushions and sat down. "I don't figure the original inhabitants of this place programmed it to turn out human-style food throughout eternity," Haakon said. "So this must be provided by the present management. Am I right?"

"Sure," Alexander said. "But don't ask me where they leave it so it winds up here. I been all over this rock and never seen any kind of kitchen or lab or anything.

Maybe they land it some other place on the rock, but I doubt it."

"Then where do you think it comes from?" Mirabelle asked.

"I think they put it in a transmitter setup on another of the little worlds here in the Cingulum and it ends up in this room."

"Matter transmission across vacuum?" Soong queried. "It's been deemed impossible. Many experiments have failed over the years. I don't believe that any mass above a few grams has ever been transmitted, and that only over a few meters under laboratory conditions."

"Yeah?" Alexander challenged. "You ever seen anything as weird as the spook tunnels? They work."

"Reprimand accepted," Soong acknowledged.

"He's right," Haakon said. "Whoever built this place had scientific resources we've never dreamed of, and no respect whatever for any of the laws of the physics we accept."

"And are these odd conveyances also used to transfer information?" Soong asked Alexander. Haakon shot Soong a sideways look, momentarily puzzled by the question.

"Information? What do you mean?" Alexander asked, his look open, his bewilderment genuine to all appearances.

"The gentleman who greeted us upon our debarkation, McTeague, seemed rather well-informed of our circumstances prior to our arrival." Haakon mentally kicked himself. The excitement of the clash and the mind-bending phenomenon of the spook tunnels had driven the fact from his mind. Fine intelligence officer he was these days.

"Oh, that. To tell you the truth, I don't know. I figured he got it from some shuttle pilot or crewman. There's no rule I know of says they can't talk to us cons."

"Detainees," Mirabelle corrected. "We haven't been

convicted of anything, or even charged. That means we're detainees, not convicts."

"Pure as methane snow, that's us," Jemal confirmed.

"When was the last shuttle here prior to our arrival?" Soong persisted.

"Three, no, I guess it was about four days standard before," Alexander replied.

"Then news of us couldn't have arrived in that way," Haakon said. "Do you know of any signal-receiving gear in this rock?"

"No. But that doesn't mean much. I'm not exactly privy to the counsels of the big wheels around here, if you know what I mean."

"Such waste of talent," Jemal said.

"Where's the guy in the metal suit?" Alexander asked. "Is he a robot, or a cyborg, or a man, or what?"

"He claims to be a man," Haakon said. "We're not really sure. In any case, he can't eat this kind of food. He brought along his own rations."

"You sure got a weird crew," Alexander said, scratching the back of his head with the tip of his tail. Then, almost shyly: "Say, look, I'm pretty handy aboard ship. When they turn you loose, if you could put in a good word for me, well, I sure could use a berth. You wouldn't regret it."

Haakon had been expecting it. "I don't think you'd want to space with us."

"Hey, I know what you're thinking," Alexander protested. "But I wouldn't steal from you. That was just to stay alive and not too uncomfortable, you know?"

"It's not that," Jemal said. "It's just that we're under certain, well, difficulties that might make it extremely hazardous for anyone else to travel with us."

"I'm not afraid of danger," Alexander claimed, puffing

out his bony chest. "I've been in plenty of tight places before, I can handle myself."

"Beyond question," Soong said. "Still, this is something that can be neither discussed nor debated. Be assured that, were our circumstances otherwise, you would be our first choice as crewmate."

Obviously sceptical, the boy lapsed into silence for the rest of the meal.

FIVE

The Council sat at a broad, circular table in an undistinguished Cingulum worldlet. The room was little more than a cavern but it had no visible entrance, exit or opening of any kind. The Council members were of various sexes and ages. All were human, although some were of genemanipulated types. All were air-breathers. The logistics of multi-species life-support had defeated the best efforts of the various human resistance movements and governments in exile. The Cingulum was strictly for air-breathing humans.

Since the early days of planetary colonization, humans had been altered to varying degrees to cope with the varying conditions of hundreds of worlds. The hundred or so humans now around the table were a fairly representative group. The majority had few, if any, differences from the basic human stock, but many genetic adaptations were not external. Some might have been mistaken for aliens. Relations among the various types were not always tranquil. Friction between standard humans and the assorted neo-humans had replaced the ancient antipathies between races. Not much united these humans except a common enemy.

Dominating the table was the huge bulk of Lopal Singh. He was as massive as it was possible for a human to be while enjoying good health and a long life span. Smallest were the Janids, standard in appearance but under one meter in stature. A few were animal-gene grafted, types from the early days of genetic experimentations. Most of the nonstandard types, though, were limited and planet-specific.

The meeting was nearing its end. Reports had been given, projects discussed, security examined. Sann Tredegar, chairman of the Council, asked for any final reports or comments. Tredegar's enormous eyes were adapted to the dim light of his homeworld. He wore filters to protect his eyes since most of those present were accustomed to Sol-type light ranges.

"I have one more matter to bring to the attention of the Council," said Lopal Singh.

"The Chief of Security has the floor," Tredegar said.

"The members of the Council will recall that in my report of new ships arrived since our last meeting, I mentioned one *Eurynome*. It is crewed by persons claiming to be refugees from Bahaduran oppression. That they have been kept imprisoned by Bahadur is almost certain. Whether their offenses were political or merely criminal remains undetermined. They have been placed in Coventry until their disposition is settled. One of them, the supposed leader, is a notorious gang-leader and fence; another is a technothief. Two are former officers of Delius, another an intelligence officer of Han who was probably an assassin. There is also an engineer in a very elaborate prosthetic suit; he seems to have no record."

"They sound worthy of investigation," Tredegar said.

"However, that is your department. Why do you bring it up before the Council?"

"I think that this crew may be suitable for undertaking an exploration of Meridian," Lopal Singh said.

"Must we sacrifice another expedition to that place?" demanded one of the diminutive Janids.

"What sacrifice?" This from Tagus, a man with a saturnine face and blue skin showing a faint patterning of scales. "We have too many refugees as it is. I read your report on this *Eurynome*, Colonel Singh. These people are probably spies for Timur Khan. If not, they are common criminals. Why not give them a choice: go into Meridian, or stay in Coventry forever."

"Why do you think these people are suitable?" asked a furry Goswanan.

"They seem intelligent," Lopal Singh said, "and they have an ideal cross section of skills. There is a saying about Felids having nine lives, and the man called Haakon has endured years in the Bahadur pits. Such a man can live through almost anything. Also, I don't trust them. I think they're lying about the Felid being their leader. She's the logical one, but I feel that the real leader is the hairless convict, Haakon. It is the reason for this deception that I am trying to discover. In the meantime, an expedition to Meridian will keep them occupied and neutralized."

"Neutralized," said a gray-skinned female from Serengeti. "That is uncharacteristically evasive of you, Colonel Singh."

"I mean just that," Lopal Singh said. "They will be unable to do us any harm for a while. If I thought there was no possibility of their returning, I would not recommend the action. I truly feel that this group may be able to do it."

"I agree," Tagus said. "At least I agree that they should be sent. I don't recommend that we let them take their own ship, however. I've seen it. It's a royal yacht with the armament of a light cruiser. It would be an invaluable addition to our naval forces."

"If we keep that ship," one of the Janids pointed out, "our captains will be cutting each other's throats for it."

"It can be stripped of its luxurious furnishings before commissioning," Tredegar said.

"Let's not get ahead of ourselves," Lopal Singh cautioned. "The ship is theirs when they return from Meridian with a full report."

"Spoken with more than a little optimism," said Tagus. "What ship of ours can be spared for this expedition? It must be eminently expendable, and in our situation, little that we have classifies."

"Admiral Roque?" Tredegar turned to face a squat Nereid.

Roque fidgeted for a moment. Although his face was capable of little expression, he was embarrassed to be addressed as admiral. He had once been a brevet commodore, later skipper of a freighter. Put in charge of the Cingulum's motley fleet and tagged with the rank, he still felt like someone fantasizing himself in a grandiose role. "There's an old scout craft, the G-102. It came in with an ore freighter. Must be a hundred years old, or more. Not good for much anymore. Was scheduled to be scrapped and replaced. We could give them that."

"I don't want to send them in with a vessel that will fail them," Lopal Singh said.

"It's solid," Roque assured him. "Just old and a little slow. Not up to the modern craft is all. Not many comforts either. I'd sure trade her for that spacegoing whorehouse they came in."

Eventually the vote was taken in favor of Lopal Singh's project.

*   *   *

"What's this Meridian?" Haakon asked. He was sitting on his pallet, arms wrapped about his knees. The rest of the crew were crowded into the little room as well. Lopal Singh's vast bulk blocked the door.

"It's the great puzzle of the Cingulum. It's a worldlet like this one, but even stranger. The people who created the Cingulum could do things with space and time that were in defiance of anything we think we know about natural law. These rocks are honeycombed with paradoxical phenomena, like the spook tunnels here in Coventry. There are places in the Cingulum where you can step through a doorway into another worldlet. Coventry is one that has none big enough to transfer a human."

"We were speculating on where the chow came from," Haakon said.

Lopal Singh nodded. "Exactly. The biggest mystery is Meridian."

"Why is it called that?"

"For reference. It was picked to be the 'center' of the Cingulum. All distances and placements are measured from Meridian. It's a plain, featureless rock on the outside, just like all the others."

"And inside?" Haakon asked.

"Ah, that's the question. There's one entrance, a cave mouth just large enough to accommodate a small scout ship. Six teams have gone in; three in ships, three in pressure suits. None have come out."

Haakon was silent for a moment. He was beginning to get the picture. "Reports?"

"Only for a few minutes after entering the cave. You'll hear what we have. I'm afraid it's of little use. Apparently no two of the probes experienced the same thing after entering."

"Unmanned probes?" Haakon asked.

"Numerous. Never a thing after they entered."

"And you want us to be probe number seven? Are you serious?"

"Only if you want to go."

"And if we don't?"

Lopal Singh looked about. The rough stone walls were depressingly monotonous. "The spook tunnels are briefly fascinating," he said, "but I suspect that Coventry could quickly become boring. Several years of it could be more than a man of intelligence and spirit might be able to bear. Of course it may be that your prison experience has hardened you to such things."

Haakon glared at him. At least the NeoSikh had the grace to lower his eyes. In him, it was an admission of deep shame. "If we'd known that we were just exchanging prisons, we wouldn't have come here. We'd heard that the Cingulum stood for resistance to Bahadur. We expected to be welcomed as fellow freedom-fighters."

"Spare me your indignation, Haakon. The Cingulum has unfortunately acquired a reputation as a refuge from *any* law, not just Bahadur. You've met McTeague and others like him. If we allowed it, criminal scum like that would control this place."

Haakon was, of course, perfectly aware of all this. Still, just now his best bet seemed to be to play on the big man's conscience.

"The Council doesn't trust you, Haakon," Lopal Singh went on, "I don't trust you either. If you undertake this mission, it will go a long way toward allaying our suspicions. In any case, you would have your ship back and we'd let you leave."

"If we return. What makes you think we'd have a better chance than the others?"

"Because of the hardships you've already survived. I know what the Bahadur pits are like, and you came through them in one piece. We're not sure that recording instruments will function within Meridian. The technothief can bring back a report. You have a good Tesla man. As for the Felid—" He shrugged. "They're hard to kill, and I think she'd be little loss in any case."

"Now to the crux of the matter," Haakon said. "Just why are you people so desperate to find out what's inside Meridian?"

Lopal Singh regarded him levelly. "Does this mean that you are ready to volunteer? If it does, I'll tell you. There can be no backing out once you've been briefed."

"Have I any choice? What the hell, count me in. I can't speak for my shipmates though. We'll have to take a vote."

"By all means. I think they've all been in Coventry long enough to have acquired sufficient dislike for the place."

Tredegar looked at five tough, intelligent faces and a metal mask. Not a starry-eyed idealist in the lot, and that was all to the good. He found himself agreeing with Lopal Singh: If any team could come back from Meridian, this one could. Some of them anyway. Whatever their virtues, group solidarity and loyalty to one another did not seem to be among them.

"We know absolutely nothing about the race that constructed the Cingulum," Tredegar began, "except that compared to theirs, our knowledge of mathematics and physics is laughably primitive. They left behind them the Cingulum itself, and a pack of puzzles and paradoxes that have us going half-crazy trying to figure them out. It is almost as though they were teasing us."

"Surely," Soong said, "you have not sent several expeditions to their death in a spirit of pure scientific curiosity."

"Hardly. Some of us, myself included, believe Meridian to be the key to all of this. We think that the original Cingulans left it behind as a vault, a repository of their knowledge, waiting for a people advanced enough to enter it and pry out its secrets."

"Obliging of them," Jemal said. "Do you know any reason they might have done this, aside from posthumous generosity?"

"Who can guess their motives? Still, if the answer to their powers is to be found, it must be in Meridian. I strongly suspect that whoever gains possession of those ancient secrets will thereby become immensely powerful. It could mean safety for the Cingulum. Someday soon Bahadur will move against us. If we lose our freedom and Bahadur gains the Cingulum, well, I leave to your imagination what will become of humanity; just let someone like, say, Timur Khan Bey be the first to wield such powers."

Tredegar scanned the faces of his audience. Haakon, Jemal, Soong and Mirabelle wore thoughtful expressions. Rand's mask was unreadable. Rama was sharpening her claws with a metal file, apparently too absorbed in her task to listen.

Tredegar continued. "You will now wish to hear the recordings from the other expeditions to attempt Meridian."

"Hear?" Haakon echoed. "No visual images?"

"None, I fear. We lost visual contact the instant each expedition entered the cave, and audio contact mere seconds after that." He touched a plate on the desk before him. "This was the first try. They went in aboard a small scout ship."

The voice reproduction was clear but slightly muffled: *"Just rock walls so far. Proceeding dead slow. Instrument readings—peculiar. Are we still on visual? Making a star-board turn now. Cave opening up and a bright light ahead.''* Then another voice: *''Hey, that's a sun! How did we—''*

"That was the end of the transmission," Tredegar said. "This was the second team, also in a scout."

Once again a slightly muffled voice: *"Floor angling sharply upward. Walls are brightly colored with lots of glowing crystal. It's like a genie's cave. Do genies live in caves? Maybe it's bottles or lamps. Anyway, I think I see the genie now. I'm getting the hell out of—''*

"And now the third. A crew of two this time, in a small open ore sled." The recording consisted of about fifteen seconds of hysterical laughter.

"The next team went in wearing pressure suits with umbilical rescue lines attached. I don't think you really want to hear half a minute of uninterrupted screaming. The lines came back released. They had cut themselves loose."

"Or somebody did it for them," Jemal commented.

"Yes, there is always that intriguing possibility. Next went two men in pressure suits with permanently attached cables." He touched the plate again.

The recording was brief: *"Uh, the walls are making faces at us."*

"This time the cables came back with the ends white hot and fused. The last expedition was by a single person, a herm from Testament."

"It is to be wondered at that you could even find one to go by this time," Soong said.

Tredegar looked at him, his face unreadable behind his eye filters. "There are some truly dedicated people here in the Cingulum. There were more volunteers, but the Council put a halt to expeditions after this one."

"I am abashed," Soong said. "Please go on."

The herm's voice was melodious: "*It's dim but there is light. It's like a sea twenty meters down. There seem to be things drifting about, but they're indistinct. Wait—I see movement ahead; it's—*" There was a sharp intake of breath, then: "*Leviathan! Leviathan!*"

"What shape did the cable come back in this time?" Haakon asked.

"It did not come back. It was pulled in, along with a large chunk of the rock to which it was secured."

"Count me out," Rama said, her filing now finished. "This is a suicide mission and you know it."

"So we get a choice of suicides," Haakon told her. "You go with the rest of us."

Lopal Singh, until now lounging in the back of the conference room, looked up sharply. Rama seemed about to rebel; then she broke into her carnivorous smile.

"Well, why not? I always wanted to die in an interesting fashion."

"You'll get your chance," Haakon told her.

"Of course," Tredegar said, "you will be given drugs to combat hallucinations."

"Forget it," Mirabelle told him. "Hallucinations don't burn through cables or tear rocks loose. Whatever's in there is for real."

"What was that last word the herm used?" Soong asked.

"Leviathan," Tredegar explained. "It's a name from the ancient Hebrew holy book, in which it seems to refer to some sort of sea monster. Later, in the Western Middle Ages, it was the name of a demon prince. Still later it was used to refer to the whale."

"What's a whale?" Rama asked.

"A big seagoing mammal back on Earth, now extinct," Jemal said. "Any of the possibilities seems daunting."

"Why won't you let us take *Eurynome*?" Rama asked. "She's perfect for exploration, and she has armament fit for shooting our way out of anything."

"Anything?" Tredegar queried blandly. "I doubt it. In any case, your ship is too large to enter the cave. The ship we will give you should prove adequate."

"Have your skippers drawn lots yet for who gets *Eurynome*?" Haakon asked. "Never mind. How about armament?"

"I rather doubt that conventional weapons would be of any use to you. Besides, we don't want you to go about destroying anything in there. You may take sidearms if you insist, but this is not a military adventure. What we want is a report on what is in there, and a safe way in and out. You will stay no longer than required to determine those things, then return. Any dismantling will be done by our own scientific teams. Is that clear?"

"Do you think we'd want to hang around for the sights?" Jemal asked.

"Let's just say that peculiar things happen in there," Tredegar answered.

"Have any others disappeared within Meridian prior to your six attempts?" Soong asked.

"We don't know. There was a fair amount of exploration when the Cingulum was first discovered, and there were disappearances, but there always are. Frontiers naturally attract people who are desperate, greedy or just reckless, and they are often in obsolete ships. We've searched such records as exist from those early days, but nothing definite has turned up."

"I have a suggestion," Rand announced.

"I hope it's a good one," Haakon said. "I've heard nothing but depressing news so far."

"Let's back in. We'll have our nose pointed at the

entrance and our tubes pointed at Leviathan, or the genie, or whatever it is.''

"I second that," Jemal said. "A speedy exit seems to be of the essence.''

"Carried," Haakon said.

"When do we go?" Mirabelle asked.

"It's up to you," Tredegar said.

"Let's make it soon," urged Jemal, "before we lose what nerve we've got left.''

"I want to see the ship first," Haakon said.

"Then if you will accompany me," Tredegar invited.

"Are we really going to take this thing into that cave?" Rand demanded.

"Quite a comedown from *Eurynome*," Jemal agreed.

C-102 was a scout stripped to the bare essentials. The frame was a flattened rectangle, the hull transparent for maximum eyeball visibility. Crew quarters were rudimentary and storage space next to nonexistent. It was designed for short hops from a mother ship. Control was in a sphere situated amidships, with the crew's chairs gimbal-mounted so that the optimum observation angle could be reached no matter the relative position of the craft.

"You're spoiled already," Haakon said. "Not long ago you'd have jumped at a chance to get your hands on a craft like this. A lot poorer than this, for that matter.''

"I was desperate then.''

"You think we aren't desperate now?" Mirabelle asked. She turned to see Rama entering with her sled in tow. "Why don't you leave that stuff here? There's little enough space as it is.''

"Only a fool trusts his possessions in the hands of strangers." The Felid looked to a corner where Haakon and Jemal had stacked their overstuffed spacebags. "Those two know I'm right, not so?"

Haakon shrugged. "Bring it if it makes you feel better. You could get along with about ten percent of that stuff though."

"Why should I deprive myself?" She grounded her sled and punched a pressure plate to release a bunk from the wall, which she hopped into before it was fully inflated. "Tell me as soon as anything interesting happens."

They went through an inventory checklist. "We have stores for six months," Mirabelle reported.

"Roughly five months, thirty days, twenty-three hours and fifty-seven minutes in excess of our life expectancy once we go in," Jemal commented.

"Always the pessimist," Haakon said. "You're getting old."

"I'd like to get a lot older," Jemal muttered.

"Everything seems to be in order," Soong reported.

"Well, why hang around?" Haakon said. "Let's go." He punched his orders into the computer and the display lit up with the coordinates for Meridian. "Tredegar?" he called.

"Here," came the voice from the commo grille.

"We're going to go in as soon as we get there. Meet you at Meridian. Out."

The worldlet might have been Coventry or any of hundreds of others in the Cingulum. The cliff they faced was, to all intents and purposes a natural feature, as was the cave in its face. True, worldlets this tiny should not have either the water action or the volcanic forces that would ordinarily produce such caves, but it certainly appeared natural.

Nearby hovered several vessels of the Cingulum's security force. "I don't suppose you'd consider making a break for it?" Mirabelle asked.

"What do you think they're waiting for us to do?" Haakon replied, gesturing toward their escort. "I'd love to, but we don't dare risk it. Besides, I want *Eurynome* back."

"When will you commence entry?" Tredegar asked over the commo.

"Just about immediately," Haakon answered with great imprecision.

"Then good fortune to you all," Tredegar said.

"All our prayers go with you." This from Lopal Singh.

"Get fucked, you overgrown ape," hissed Rama. She added an obscenity so complex it required three languages to complete.

"Hear, hear," Jemal said.

"My sentiments exactly," Mirabelle added.

"Duke Ling could not have put it better," said Soong.

Rand made a sound that might have been a laugh. Haakon smiled. It was the first time they had all been in such agreement. Well, it was a start.

"Rand," Haakon ordered, "back us in. Dead slow astern."

Thus, tail first and in a borrowed ship, the merry crew of *Eurynome* entered Meridian.

PART II

SIX

They were ready for anything. They scanned the rough walls, looking for signs and portents, wonders and terrors.

"So far it looks remarkably like a cave," Haakon reported. "Hey, Tredegar, you still got us on audio?"

"Yes, but we lost visual contact as soon as you entered." The voice had the same muffled quality they had heard on the earlier recordings.

"Proceeding astern," Haakon said. "Nothing to report so far. The cave seems to be flat and straight, opening up a bit now—hold on, something's changing. The floor is angling downward and there's some sort of light source. Are you still hearing me, Tredegar?"

"Yes, but faintly," came the response as though from a great distance.

Abruptly the cavern widened and the light source became clearer. The light was white and diffuse, wreathed in mist that filled the part of the cavern they were entering.

"Looks like fog," Jemal hazarded.

"Fog can't exist in a vacuum," Rama said.

"You don't say. I think it's been established that this place doesn't go by the rules; so it's fog until we find out what it really is," Haakon said. "Hey, Tredegar, are you still hearing me?" No answer. Two more tries produced no response. "I guess we're on our own now," he said.

"It's clearing up ahead," Soong reported. The mists thinned to reveal a bright sun shining in a clear blue sky.

They regarded this unexpected turn of events for several seconds before Mirabelle articulated what they were all thinking: "Uh, this just isn't right."

"Is it not amazing," Soong said, "how your thoughts mirror my own with such precision? I daresay our ship-mates have very similar thoughts."

"Rand," Haakon said, his voice tight as though a great hand were squeezing his chest, "get us out of here. Ahead dead slow."

The craft came to a stop and smoothly reversed direction, reentering the mist. As it closed around them, Haakon said: "I saw land in there. Hills covered with vegetation far below us. Anybody else see that?"

"I saw it too," Jemal said.

"I saw big flying creatures off to starboard," Rama said. "Like huge birds, or perhaps flying reptiles. There was no scale to judge by, but I think they were bigger than this ship."

"I didn't see them. I was looking down," said Mirabelle, "and I saw a river winding through a valley with a dendritic drainage pattern. I cound be wrong, but I could just make out an ocean on the horizon where the river split into a delta. It was almost at the skyline, so I can't be sure."

"I saw the flying creatures also," Soong confirmed. "At least one of them looked as though something was riding it."

"You know," Jemal said, "that's a lot to find inside a tiny worldlet like this. Any bright explanations?"

"We know from the other expeditions that this place generates hallucinations," Haakon said.

"Damned thorough hallucinations," Rand said. "I scanned that ground with infrared and UV. It read just like a normal, Earth-type planetary surface, river and all. And I saw something else. There were stars out beyond that sun. I don't think they were any that could be seen from the Cingulum."

"Did we get any instrument readings?" Rama asked.

"They've been deteriorating since we entered," Haakon reported. "I don't get a thing now." He looked around at the fog. "We've been in here a lot longer than the first time. What's happening?"

"I don't even want to guess," Jemal said. Then their stomachs did flip-flops as their chairs swung wildly on their gimbals. Suddenly the attitude of the ship was radically skewed.

"Right us!" Rama yelled, and Haakon worked the attitude controls frantically to rotate the hull around until they were once again sitting upright.

"What the hell happened?" Jemal demanded.

Haakon removed one of his steel bracelets and let it go. It thunked solidly to the deck. "Gravity just took hold of us. Right about Earth normal, I imagine."

"The fog's thinning again," Mirabelle pointed out. Gradually the mists cleared. Once again they were in a region of blue sky. Beneath them a vast river wound through a valley toward a distant sea.

"Damn it, Rand," Haakon barked, "I told you to get us out of this place!"

"I reversed us, Captain. Navigation's your job. Don't feel bad though, I've been scanning on UV; there's been no trace of that cavern since we first emerged from the mist.''

"You might have said something," Haakon said evenly.

Rand gave a remarkable, metallic shrug. "Why be the bearer of bad news? You were all going to find out anyway."

"Thoughtful of you," Jemal commented. "What do we do now, Hack?"

"I've never run into a situation quite like this before," Haakon said. "Not to be ducking my responsibilities or anything, but I'm wide open for suggestions." He gazed about and met nothing but blank, bland stares. "Just as I thought," he said. "Well, this is a scout ship, isn't it? So let's go scouting."

"At least we'll find out how solid these illusions are," Soong concurred. "Let us by all means get a closer look."

"Gaah," came a voice from nowhere in particular. "What's going on out there?"

"Just what we were wondering," Jemal said. "Speak, O thou apparition."

"Get me out of here!"

"Where's here?" Haakon asked, but then Rama was tearing her straps loose. She darted to her sled and began ripping bundles apart, exposing something that looked like a jeweled snake. She yanked hard on it and a squalling figure exploded upward, scattering bags and boxes all over the interior. Rama held Alexander dangling by his tail as though he weighed no more than a kitten.

"Hey, easy on the tail, cat-lady. I can't scratch my back without it."

"Alexander," Jemal sighed, "you're letting this stow-away compulsion of yours get entirely out of hand."

"Drop him, Rama," Haakon ordered. She complied. "I

hate to say it, kid, but you've probably just pulled your last such stunt."

"How come?" The monkey-boy looked around. "You know, somehow I always pictured royal yachts looking a lot fancier than this." Then he looked through the transparent hull and saw the blue sky, the green land and the river. "Hey, I know I wasn't in there *that* long!"

"It's a long story, and you aren't going to like it." Haakon said. He rubbed his hands over his face and his slick scalp. "Now, strap in and shut up. I'm taking us down."

Below, the undifferentiated mass of verdure began to define itself into individual trees. They could see ruffling disturbances of the vegetation as small animals rushed in panic from the descending craft. Of the animals themselves they could see nothing.

"Can anybody identify the trees?" Haakon asked.

"The ones along the river look rather like palms," Mirabelle said. "Up in the hills—I don't know for sure. I see a big clump that could be pines, but others seem to be hardwoods."

"That's an awfully Earthly sounding collection of flora," said Jemal.

"It is not at all uncommon for vegetation on Earth-type planets to bear some superficial resemblance to those of Earth. I think that when we get a close look at these, we will find that the resemblance is rather slight."

"Anybody here ever been to Earth?" Haakon asked. There were no affirmative replies.

"I haven't either," Haakon continued, "but I've been on several terraformed planets where they used Earth flora and fauna, and those down there look just exactly like palms to me."

He lowered the vessel to treetop level and cruised over several acres of the "palm" grove.

"They're palms, all right, but they're all wrong." Everyone's attention turned to Alexander.

"Say on," Jemal told him.

"Well, see, where I was raised, on Hanuman, we sort of specialized in palms and other tropical trees."

"That figures," Haakon said. "So you know real Earth palms when you see them?"

"Sure. We had every kind that ever evolved on Earth, and some that were gene-manipulated. But those down there, look—see those tall, skinny ones with the little bushes of fronds on top? Well, those are Hawaiian Royals, but they got *bananas* hanging off them. And some of them have dates and coconuts, and they aren't on the right kind of tree. It's like somebody's painting pictures of trees and they know what they look like but not how they work."

"You think that's a mystery?" queried Jemal. "This place has no business being a planet at all. Let's worry about the damned trees after we find out whether it even exists outside our own heads. Hack, can we trust the instruments as far as an atmosphere reading?"

"I think so. Some of them are back to normal, but if the compass is right, this place has no magnetic poles."

"That's impossible," Rama said. "To develop along Earth lines like this, it must have a nickel-iron core and rotate at a minimum speed and—" She let her protest trail off. "So what? This place is fifty kinds of impossible."

"One thing's for sure," Jemal said. "We're not in Kansas anymore."

"I was on Kansas once," Alexander said. "Dull place. Nothing but grain fields everywhere."

Jemal sighed. "Do the young no longer study classical

literature?'' Then, ''What about it, Hack? Do we dare try a landing and exploration?''

''Hell, why not? Let's start at that clearing up ahead. That way we can get a look at the river and the vegetation both. I'll bring us down far enough from the nearest bush so we'll see anything that gets close. Armor up, everybody.''

They pulled on singlets of armorcloth and tried on the helmets that were racked by the airlock. Alexander could not find a suit designed for a tail. ''Guess I'll just have to take my chances,'' he said.

''Then you'll stay aboard until we know more about the place.''

''Let him go if he wants,'' Rama said. ''He's nothing to us, and he committed suicide by joining us anyway.''

''What does she mean?'' Alexander asked.

''You'll find out all too soon,'' Haakon said. ''But for now you stay aboard until we've cleared the way.''

The little ship settled to ground on a bare patch of sandy soil fifty meters from the riverbank. A hundred meters away the tree line snaked, waving in a steady breeze. There were no animals in sight, but they could see the bones of something that in life had massed about as much as a standard human.

''That river must be at least three kilometers across,'' Mirabelle observed. ''It must drain a whole continent.''

''When we go out,'' Haakon instructed, ''keep part of your attention overhead. Remember those birds or whatever it was Rama and Soong saw. Big flyers like that are almost always predators. Rand, you stay here with Alexander.''

''No argument,'' said Rand.

''Rama,'' Haakon continued, ''you go out first. The rest of us will cover you from the platform.''

''Why me?'' she demanded.

''Because you're the fastest. If you're attacked or

threatened, you stand the best chance of getting back aboard alive.'' To his amazement, she accepted without demur.

The ship extruded its platform and ramp. They filed out onto the platform and sniffed the alien air. It was full of the smell of plants, living and dead. There were noises from the trees: buzzings and clickings and squawkings that sounded perfectly fit for the surroundings. That was peculiar. None of them had ever stepped out for the first time on a new planet without encountering smells and sounds that seemed entirely unprecedented. Even the most Earthlike of them gave sensory impressions that caused momentary shock and required a period of adjustment for new arrivals.

This planet was different. It seemed almost like coming home: a paradoxical phenomenon, for, although they were all genetic Earthies, none of them had ever set foot on the ancestral planet. And yet the similarity was illusory. And they knew it. It was so internally inconsistent that it didn't even bear thinking about.

Rama strode down the ramp with her feline glide. Her weapons were strapped about her person. She didn't bother to keep one in hand because she could reach and use any of them so quickly that the time lapse would be nearly irrelevant. In any case, millions of years of evolution had proven that the greatest of all survival traits was the ability to run and hide, and she wanted all limbs available for that purpose.

She walked across the sandy ground, toward the skeleton that lay a few meters away. Her eyes scanned the tree line and the sky. She searched the sand for lurking predators. The soil seemed too firm for tunneling beasties, but that meant little. The dangers of alien worlds were often things without precedent. Every few seconds she turned to scan the river. She knew of many predators that lurked in water, only to dart out to seize prey on land. Then she studied the skeleton.

"Not much but a spine, rib cage and skull. Limbs are gone, if there were any. Probably carried off by predators or scavengers. Marks of small teeth."

"What does the skull look like?" Haakon asked.

"About the size of a big dog's. You know what dogs are like, don't you?"

"Sure," Haakon said.

"Nasty things. This thing has vegetarian teeth, all at the back of the jaws, so it must be a grass-eater. Two eyes, right where you'd expect them to be, big nostril hole with a bone septum. When it had a nose, there must have been two nostrils. A couple of bumps far back on the skull, probably supports for horns or antlers, I'd imagine."

"Anybody see any grasslands around here?" Haakon queried.

"Just trees and sand so far," Mirabelle answered. "That doesn't necessarily mean anything. It might have been dragged here by whatever killed it."

"Not dragged," Rama said. "Flown. There are big bird tracks all around. Three toes front, one back. Big, deep claw indentations. It was a predator, all right. Each track is about a meter across and pressed about five centimeters into the sand. It's pretty firm sand too. It must have been heavy."

Jemal gave a low whistle. Oddly it was both disquieting and comforting at the same time. Nothing *that* big had ever evolved on Earth. Nothing that flew, in any case.

"Why the small teeth marks then?" Jemal asked.

"Scavengers," Haakon answered. "Jem, you go over to the river and see what you can see. We'll keep you covered, but be ready to sprint."

"You don't have to tell me that," Jemal said. He

descended the ramp and walked slowly toward the river, a
beam rifle cradled in his hands. He had nothing like the
cat-woman's speed, and he wanted to be ready. A line to
his power-pack would yank the weapon tight against his
belt if he had to drop it quickly. He approached the huge
stream with utmost caution.

"It looks almost like an inland sea," Jemal reported.
"No visible current. That's about standard for one this big
when it's not at high-water stage. Wide mud flats out
there, covered with small tracks. Looks like small-bird or
maybe reptile signs, but damned if I'm going to go down
for a closer look." Then: "Something big is surfacing
there." He pointed to a spot about two hundred meters out
where the water was roiling and thrashing. Abruptly a
gigantic, rounded bulk was breaking the surface.

"Jem, be ready to run," Haakon ordered.

The monster kept breaking surface endlessly, growing
higher and longer. Much longer. All at once two spouts of
spray shot a hundred meters into the clear air, fountaining
gracefully at their tops like giant flowers, then ceasing
abruptly. Across the wide expanse of water they could
hear a sound like a monstrous steam valve opening up.
The beast rolled on its side, exposing a pale belly, in
contrast to the gray-green upper part, and a jaw full of
jagged teeth that seemed to run a third of its length. To the
rear of the jaw was a single tiny eye. At least it looked tiny
on the vast creature. The eye appeared to be at least two
meters across.

Then the thing rolled over and dived beneath the surface,
meter after meter in seemingly endless succession. Finally
a huge, horizontal tail broke surface and waved for a
moment, before slapping the water with a report like a ton
of high explosive and disappearing beneath the surface.

The sense of size, grace and raw power was utterly breathtaking.

"That," Jemal said in a strangled voice, "unless I miss my guess, was something very like a whale."

"Whale, my butt," Haakon snorted. "That thing must have been three hundred meters long. No whale ever grew that big."

"If I remember my Melville correctly," Jemal said, trying to make up for his jitters by sounding pedantic, "the whale was not a river beast. And the only big one with teeth was the sperm whale, which threw up a single spout. The only one with two spouts was the toothless right whale. Anyway, the birds grow big here, so why not the whales? If the design is a little wrong, it's only to be expected in a place where bananas grow on the wrong kind of palm." He was jabbering on, trying to relieve his nerves.

"You're getting talkative in your old age, Jem," Haakon said. "Now come back to the ship. You too, Rama."

"The question," said Soong when they were reassembled on the ramp, "is not that the birds and whales and palms are wrong, but rather why are they here at all? I think we are in agreement that this is not an hallucination, are we not?"

"I wouldn't count on it," Haakon said, "but we might as well proceed on that basis. Suggestions, anyone?"

"I have one," Rama said. She yanked her helmet off and fanned her striped mane. "Let's stop trying to figure out the mechanics of this place and concentrate on how to get off. We don't know where we are, and this isn't a deep-space craft anyway. We must have come here through some kind of interplanetary spook tunnel. They seem to lead both ways, so let's find it again and get back to the Cingulum."

"I'll second that," Jemal said. "There's one bright spot in all this though."

"I'll be glad to hear it," Mirabelle said.

"I'll bet Timur Khan's little execution device won't work here," ventured Jemal, smiling for the first time in far too long.

"What's that?" Alexander asked, suddenly all ears.

"You'll hear about it later," Haakon told him.

"Birds coming!" Rand shouted.

They looked upward. In their preoccupation with the river monster they had forgotten to scan the sky. Ten immense birds were circling high overhead.

"They look a little like eagles," Jemal said, "but no eagle has wings that big in proportion to its body. That figures. Think of the weight they're supporting." Then he added: "They're descending."

The birds were circling lower, not beating their wings but soaring gracefully, ever lower, left wings tilted slightly below the right. Then they were cruising a few meters off the ground, circling the ship.

"There are riders on them," Mirabelle said. They could all see that now. Abruptly the birds cupped their wings, ceased forward motion and settled gently to the ground. They left off their lockwork movements and began preening their feathers and grooming their wings. In contrast to the long wings, each had a stubby body, about three meters long, and broad, fan-shaped tails. Their legs were short and stumpy, ending in the vicious talons of a bird of prey; their heads were a meter long, mostly hooked beak. All were of a single color, but the colors ranged from space black to metallic red, blue, yellow or green.

The birds, though, were of secondary interest. What drew all eyes were the riders. They appeared remarkably human: small, skinny and primitive. They were dark-skinned, but little more was apparent from the sixty meters that separated them from the ship.

"From what I can see," Jemal said, "these folks won't be much use in helping us get away from here. Those spears they're carrying have stone heads."

One of the riders dismounted and approached the ship fearlessly. As it neared, they could see that it had lank, stringy black hair to its shoulders, interwoven with small pieces of bone and colored beads. Feathers the same color as its mount's, bright red, slanted from its temples past its ears. It wore only a leather belt holding a crude stone knife and ax. It had small, pointed breasts but male genitalia. The face was human, oddly birdlike, and its feet, while human in conformation, had clawed toes.

"I think its a herm," observed Mirabelle.

"We'll need a closer look to determine that," said Haakon. "I think those feathers grow from its scalp."

"Breasts and hair and feathers just don't go together," Jemal said, then shrugged. "So what else is new around here?"

"It's a gene-manipulated species," Haakon said, "although I've never heard of this one. In any case, it'll speak an Earth-based language. Get the translator going."

It was not needed.

"Who are you?" it said. "Why are you here? Did Xeus send you?" The first sound of its last word was a gutteral click.

"We don't know who Xeus is," Haakon answered, having difficulty with the click sound. "We are lost travelers trying to find our way home. We mean you no harm and we will leave if you wish. But if you don't mind, we'd like to know a little about where we are."

Without a word the native turned and walked back toward its fellows, most of whom had by now dismounted.

For primitives they were displaying remarkably little interest in the presumably unprecedented appearance of a spaceship in their midst.

"You'd think they'd act a little awed or something," Jemal said, slightly miffed.

"They ride on eagles," Haakon pointed out. "They see three-hundred-meter whales every day and God knows what other wonders. They may find us boring."

One of the "eagles," a bright yellow one, opened its beak wide and regurgitated the carcass of a deerlike animal, largely digested but much of its skeleton and hide still intact.

"Now we know why those bones were here," Rama said. "Let's leave this place. We won't learn anything from these little beasts."

"Don't be hasty," Haakon cautioned. "We're in no rush, and this place disturbs me. I want all the information I can get before we undertake any action."

"Xeus," Soong said, reproducing the click perfectly. "The word stirs some memory, but I can't bring it to the surface."

"How did they degenerate so badly?" Mirabelle asked. "After all, human gene-manipulation hasn't been used for all *that* long. It's plain they're not true aliens, not with those bodies and speaking an Earth-based language."

"I was wondering that myself," Haakon said. "But I've heard that it doesn't take people long to revert to the primitive when they're stranded and isolated. Maybe an immigrant ship put in here during one of the wars. If all the technologically skilled people were killed, the survivors might reach this stage in four or five generations."

"You think the immigrant ship was carrying gigantic whales and eagles?" Jemal needled.

"And Royal Hawaiians with bananas?" Alexander put in.

"I was trying not to think about that," Haakon said. "In any case, primitive or not, they know more about this place than we do. If there are spook-tunnel openings around here, they might know about them. Maybe they have places that are taboo; that'd be a good place to start."

"Might I point out," Soong said, "that these people fly. They may know of places high in the atmosphere where birds and riders have disappeared."

"Right," Haakon agreed. "So we'll hang around for a while."

The native finished its conference and returned to the foot of the ramp. "This is Eaglefolk territory," it said, spreading its arms in a sweeping circle to take in the sky as well as the land.

"Eagles," Jemal said. "It called them eagles."

"What else?" Mirabelle asked. "It's obvious they used eagle or hawk genes. I've seen a hundred different beasts called 'horse' and only a few of them looked much like the parent stock. I guess it's easier to use the old name than make up a new one."

"More flyers coming," Rand reported suddenly. "And I don't think these are on birds."

A commotion began among the Eaglefolk; the one who had been conferring raced back to his mount. The birds spread their massive wings and began to lurch skyward, their riders waving weapons and shouting shrill war cries.

"Nothing that big should be able to take off from the *ground*," Jemal said, shaking his head. "With wings that long, they should take off from cliffs or need a half-kilometer run to get airborne."

"What have we here?" Rama said, "an inter-tribal war?"

"It's not just rival tribes," Rand said from inside the ship. "Come and look at this." He was standing with

Alexander by a viewer, tapping the plates to follow the action overhead.

The others crowded around in time to see him zoom in on one of the new arrivals. It was not a bird, but a reptile. Its wings were long and ribbed, with tiny vestigial claws at the joint where the slender ribs fanned out to support the wing membrane. The thing had a long tail ending in a flat, paddle-shaped rudder. Its neck was about two meters long, with a triangular, big-eyed head that bore a jagged crest. It tilted slightly to reveal the rider, whose legs clamped its body just ahead of the wings.

"Hey," Alexander said, "I never seen a genesport like that before."

It was not as human-looking as the Eaglefolk, but the parent stock was unmistakable; arms and legs were in the usual place, the torso was longer than a human's and seemed to be more limber. The neck was longer as well. The head was small in proportion to the torso, the face triangular, with wide, sharp cheekbones and a small pointed chin. The eyes were large and had vertical pupils divided into three round segments connected by narrow necks. It was covered with silvery scales. Most startlingly, a mass of beautiful silver hair covered the top of its head and trailed behind it in the wind.

"Bird people with feathers and lizard people with scales," Jemal said, now numbed by oddities, "both of them with hair. What pack of happy genetic loonies designed them?"

"One can only speculate in the absence of solid data," Soong said. "In the early days of genetic experimentation, many things were tried. It was not uncommon for them to be carried out in secret, on remote worlds—"

"Oh, be quiet and let's enjoy the fight," Rama said, gazing upward through the transparent hull. Her whiskers were abristle and little growling sounds escaped from her throat as she hungrily watched the battle aloft.

"It's like those old vids they used to put on ribbons," Haakon said. "I mean back on Earth. Which war was it, Jem? The one where the flyers rode flimsy little machines and dueled?"

"I think it was that series of wars in the first half of the twentieth century. They called it dogfighting, but I don't know why."

"Will you two shut up!" Rama hissed. Her claws were out now, making blows at imaginary enemies. High above, birds and reptiles were circling for position, darting in to slash with vicious claws while their riders threw missiles or stabbed with long lances.

"The eagles are outnumbered by at least half," Mirabelle said.

"But they are better flyers," Soong observed. "They are more maneuverable and can turn more tightly."

For all the excitement, it didn't seem as though a great deal of damage was being done. Some of the mounts showed wounds from claws and bites, and there was a steady shower of drifting feathers, but nobody seemed to have been killed so far.

"Hey, look at this!" Alexander said. He had zoomed in on an especially ferocious fight, in which bird, reptile and riders were circling and twisting so rapidly that their movements were hard to separate. It seemed that the ideal position was above and behind the foe, and each was trying to gain the advantage while denying it to the other.

Abruptly the eagle grasped one of the reptile's wings in its claws. The reptile froze for an instant, and in that time the bird's rider leaped astride the reptile, one arm around the lizard-man, the other wielding a stone knife. The eagle rider yanked backward as it stabbed, toppling both riders from the reptile. Apparently the move was deliberate.

The crew tore their eyes from the screen and gaped upward to see the two tiny intertwined figures hurtling down. They writhed and struggled for a few seconds, then separated.

"Hey, look!" Alexander said again, pointing. The eagle was in an astonishing power dive, seeming to be perfectly vertical, beating its wings to gain speed. Its rider was no more than forty meters from the ground when the bird spread its wings, brought its tail down and turned the dive into a looping pullout, somehow snatching its rider in passing. The unfortunate lizard-man continued to fall, landing with a sickening thud ten meters from the ship.

"Good thing it didn't hit the ship," Rama said. "We'd never have cleaned the mess off."

"You Felids give whole new meanings to the word 'imperturbable,'" Jemal told her.

Overhead, the riders were breaking off engagement, apparently satisfied now that there had been a fatality. The reptile riders fled along the coast; the Eaglefolk descended toward the ship. They circled for some time at the height of a few meters, waving weapons and singing exultantly.

"Pretty poor victory," Rama said. "Only one enemy dead."

"Not unusual for primitives," Jemal commented. "War to annihilation is rare at the precivilized stage."

When the birds landed, the spokesperson approached again. This time it was walking with a slight strut. From one bloody hand it dangled a long silver mass of hair.

"Scalped the bugger on the way down," Jemal noted. "Now that's real presence of mind."

The red-feathered being waved the scalp at them happily. "You brought us luck!" it shouted.

"Always glad to be of assistance," Haakon said. "Now, if you wouldn't mind, we could use a little information."

"Who are you?" it asked, as though no violence had transpired. "Why are you here?"

"We're from the Cingulum," Haakon replied. "We're here because we don't want to be, and before you ask again, we don't know who Xeus is."

"Strange," the being said, looking perplexed. "Xeus sends the most odd things. Perhaps he just didn't tell you he sent you." It seemed happy with that explanation. Then: "You must talk to the Ancestor."

"Whose ancestor?" Haakon asked.

"Ours. Ancestor-of-us-all, Ancestor-who-rides-the-Rukh. Ancestor knows most things. We will take you to the Ancestor. Come with me."

"Ah, I don't think your birds will carry our weight," Haakon said.

"Weight? Eagle catches the great watersnake! Eagle flies off with horn-beast! Your weight? Come. Eagle will carry you in his claws. Will not squeeze hard."

"I'm afraid not," Haakon said. "We can't leave our ship. It's taboo."

"Taboo?"

"Yes. We are bound to it for now. Our spirits would be most displeased should we leave."

"Oh. Kapu. I understand." It stood in thought for a while, droplets of blood running down the long silver hair to stain the sand. "I will talk to the Ancestor. You stay here till the sun comes up tomorrow. Maybe the Ancestor will come on the Rukh to see you."

Without further ado the little being turned and walked to its bird. With a flapping of wings and raising of dust, the aerial armada lurched into the air, circled twice and flew inland.

The sun was low now, sinking below the just-visible bank on the far side of the river. "I don't suppose anyone would like to go take a closer look at the reptile-man," Haakon said. There were no volunteers. "Then let's go inside, have something to eat and discuss our situation."

Wearily they sat on the craft's skimpy furniture while Alexander, now a self-appointed steward, hustled some reconstituted rations.

"How long since we entered the tunnel?" Haakon asked.

"Subjective time, about five hours," Jemal reported. "Real time?" He shrugged.

"This place bends classical physics into some truly baroque configurations," Soong said. "We may not even be in the same time frame we were in when we entered."

"Those eagles," Jemal pondered, "and the dragons, or whatever it was the lizard-men were riding."

"What about them?" Haakon asked.

"Look, there's been plenty of experimentation with human and animal genes. The results are beings like herms, and like Rama and Alexander here."

"It's resulted in some truly superior personages," Rama said complacently.

"I'll pass on that. In any case, I know of some attempts to create fabulous creatures like that through gene manipulation. None of them were very successful. As for those eagles and those dragons, *nobody's* genetics are that sophisticated."

"I am inclined to agree," Soong said.

"Maybe the dragons are indigenous," Mirabelle hazarded.

"Not a chance," Jemal said. "They look too much like dragons. Even though such creatures never existed on Earth or anywhere else I ever heard of, one look and we know what to call them. They're archetypal creatures right out of our own mythology."

"They didn't breathe fire," Haakon pointed out.

"Maybe there are some things even the most skillful genetic engineers can't do," Jemal said.

"Should we stay around to meet this Ancestor?" Rama asked, cutting across the situation. "It must be some withered ancient of those little savages. What use could it be to us?"

"We've got nothing better to do tonight," Haakon said. "Might as well wait until morning. Who knows? Maybe this Ancestor has all the answers."

This speculation received a chorus of snorts and groans. He dodged a few thrown objects and lowered his bunk, where he crawled in and cradled his head in folded arms. It had been a long, eventful day. The light bothered him. "Lights out!" he ordered. They were extinguished and he gave a contented sigh. Even here there were advantages to being captain.

SEVEN

The crew took its time throughout the morning, making observations, recording instrument data, all of it highly questionable, and generally wasting time in waiting for something to happen. Alexander, now let out without a suit, found a fallen palm. Triumphantly he pointed out the snaky mass of hairy, animal-looking roots, studded with starlike masses of crystals along their length.

"See?" he said. "Told you they wasn't no real palms."

The others were not so jubilant.

"I was ready for gene-manipulated Earth plants," Jemal said. "But this is nothing of the sort. It's alien all the way through. No technology ever existed that could twist alien DNA—or whatever it is that alien cells use—into Earthly forms of life."

"No Earthly technology, maybe," Haakon agreed. "But we know that whoever made the Cingulum had access to rules we've never heard of. Maybe they made this place too." They were sitting in the shade of the ship, watching the river and hoping to see the awesome river "whale" again, but no one would admit it.

"How could that be?" Jemal demanded. "From what they told us back in the Cingulum, all evidence said that the people who built it probably disappeared before life ever evolved on Earth. How could they have developed a fancy for Earthly life forms, real or mythical?"

"I don't know. It's—"

"Birds coming," said Soong from the platform. All eyes turned skyward. This time there were eleven fliers. Ten were eagles. The eleventh dwarfed them all. It had at least three times the bulk of any of the other birds.

"Ancestor-who-rides-the-Rukh," Soong said quietly. The others said nothing. They were getting a little past wonder. "That must be the Rukh. The name is familiar to me, and it has just now returned to my memory."

"The giant bird ridden by Sindbad," Jemal said.

"The same. A coincidence of design is just marginally acceptable. But a coincidence of names?"

He let the thought trail off as the birds circled for their landing maneuver. The Rukh, meanwhile, circled overhead. When the others were down, it settled slowly, its wings barely moving. Then, with an astonishing absence of sound, it landed.

How to describe it? The thought sped through their minds. Next to it, the magnificent eagles seemed shabby. Its form was not that of an eagle or a hawk. If anything, it somewhat resembled a raven. But no raven had ever had such colors. The feathers of its head might have been made of pure gold. Its wings were so black they seemed to need stars. Its back was greener than emeralds, its tail a volcanic eruption of red. Those were only the major color groups. Others chased about its huge body with a variety and intricacy that were painful to the eye.

Even in this stupendous creature certain elementary laws of physics seemed to hold. It was a little like a raven, but its proportions were not quite those of the Earthly bird. The head was smaller in relation to the body, the body itself rounder. The beak was more hooked, the tail long and wide. Like the eagles, it had short, stumpy legs.

The mount had everyone so enthralled that for several moments no one took notice of the rider. Once they did, they had eyes for nothing else. It was a herm. Not an equivocal herm like the Eaglefolk, but a genuine, human herm of the type developed less than two centuries earlier. The other riders rushed forward, some of them crouching, others climbing atop them to form a human pyramid for the Ancestor to descend.

Once on the ground, it was obvious that the herm was well over two meters tall. She (the herm was plainly of the female type) strode toward the ship. Herms were customarily beautiful. This one was staggering. Her skin was black, her hair golden. Despite her patent femininity, her male genitalia were fully developed. She wore only a few strings of bone and bead jewelry. Stopping at the base of the ramp, she regarded them with cool, steady eyes like silver coins.

The crew of the G-102 descended the ramp, almost unconsciously. Not spoken among them was a feeling that this person should not be made to look up to anyone.

Haakon reached the ground first and stood before the herm. What should he do? Kneel? Bow? For a wild instant he wished he were wearing a skirt so he could curtsy. He settled on what his military academy had termed the "archaic-Germanic military obeisance." It consisted of a heels-together, slightly stiff, slightly inclined bow. It could, under the proper circumstances, be combined with a hand kiss, but that didn't seem warranted here. It took a nice piece of judgment to keep his eyes from descending too low; the herm was taller than he, and a bow too deep might appear as though he were ogling her incredibly perfect breasts. He heard a gust of repressed chuckles behind him. Later, he thought.

"Welcome," the herm said. The voice was as perfect, as godlike, as the body. Neither truly male nor female, it was husky, contralto, and infinitely enticing. Unlike Rama's pheromones, which worked only on males, the herm's attractions were irresistible to both sexes.

"On behalf of my crew, I thank you for your welcome," Haakon said. "I'm Captain Haakon, late of the Delian service, and these are my crew." He made brief introductions. He had the glimmerings of an idea of who this was, but he was unwilling to articulate it just yet.

The herm looked them over. Behind her a line of ten Eaglefolk stood, clutching weapons. They, who just the day before had seemed such proud, self-assured warriors, now were little more than subservient bodyguards. The subservience did little to blunt their vigilance though. They seemed to be ready to skewer and cook on an instant's notice.

The herm stepped up to Rama, raised a hand and stroked the Felid's face. Rama purred and exuded a slight, musky scent, not one of sexual excitement but of contentment as she rubbed her face against the hand. Her shipmates regarded the development with undisguised amazement.

"This one is beautiful," the Ancestor said. "Your name is Rama, little one?" The tone was not condescending, although the herm towered over the big Felid.

"It is," Rama acknowledged, licking the herm's hand with a raspy tongue.

The Ancestor turned to Haakon. "You are beautiful too," she said. "In a hairless sort of way." She swept her gaze over the rest of the crew. "To be sure, none of you is unattractive." Her eyes rested for a moment on Mirabelle, then passed on to Alexander. "Of course there are limits, even to my rather generous aesthetics."

The monkey-boy looked crestfallen, but she cupped his chin in her hand and tilted his face up to meet her silver-eyed gaze. "Some qualities, though, transcend mere aesthetics. There are beauties beyond mere beauty." This statement, unclear as it was, brought a blush to Alexander's ears.

"Hey, lady, I'm not—"

"Yes, he is," Haakon said. "Though it may not seem so to him. And now, my lady, would you care to come into our ship? I fear we have few comforts to offer, but what we have is yours."

The herm nodded graciously and signaled to the guards to wait outside. They complied uneasily. Haakon, for his part, eyed the Rukh apprehensively.

Inside, they managed to arrange furniture so they could sit in a rough circle, facing one another.

"My children say that you have questions you wish to ask of me."

"That is true," Haakon said. "First, though, do you have a name we can call you by?"

"I am the Ancestor."

"Yes, but didn't you have a name before that?" Haakon persisted.

She frowned. "No."

"How long have you been here?" Haakon asked.

"I have always been here."

"But did you not once live in a place called Testament?"

Her frown deepened, as though she were trying to dredge up something long forgotten. "The word seems familiar, but I don't remember where I might have heard it."

"Does the word 'Leviathan' mean anything to you?" Soong asked.

She smiled, revealing a dazzling set of teeth. "Of course. Leviathan is the great river beast, the water god. There is nothing else under the sky like Leviathan."

"I can believe that," Haakon said. "Ancestor, we come from—well, it's a far place, so far that there is no way I can express it. We want to return. We hope you can help us find our way back."

"Can you not just go back the way you came?"

"I'm afraid not. Tell me, do you know of places where people have simply disappeared? Are there places where your eagles have flown and simply winked out of existence?"

She regarded him steadily. "Is that how you came here?"

"It is. Do you know what this thing is that we're sitting in?"

"A flying ship? I cannot say how I know that. It's as though I had been in one before, although I know I haven't."

"Well, we flew into a sort of invisible gate and emerged high over your territory. When we tried to return the way we had come, the gate was gone. We must find another or we are stranded."

The herm was silent for a moment. "I know of these places of which you speak. I am afraid I cannot help you though. They appear, and for a few moments you can see another place, as though through a door. If anything goes through that door, it travels to that place beyond. But it never lasts for long, and I have never heard of two such instances occurring twice in the same spot." These words cast a pall over the proceedings. Then: "You must go to Xeus."

"Who is this Xeus? One of your eagle riders asked us if we were sent by Xeus."

"You don't know Xeus?" the herm asked incredulously. "Xeus is God."

"Ah, well," Haakon temporized, "it has been our experience that the aid of the gods tends to be of an insubstantial nature. We really need something a bit more concrete."

"I don't understand," the herm said. "Xeus will help you, if only you can reach him. It is his way."

"Are you saying," Soong asked, "that Xeus is an actual person, whom one may find and speak to?"

"Not a person; a god. He can do anything."

"Have you actually seen him?" Mirabelle asked.

"Yes, of course. Who would want a god one could never see?"

"Who indeed?" Jemal said. "What is Xeus like?"

"How does one describe a god to one who has never seen one?" the Herm asked.

"A problem that has faced many visionaries," Soong commented.

"His form is human. At least he has taken human form when I have seen him. Tall and golden he is, and shining like flame."

"How does he arrive?" Haakon asked. "In a ship? Does he fly?"

"He appears," she said. "I awake and he is there. When he has done all he has come for, he simply vanishes."

"Meaning no indiscretion, but just what *does* he come for?" Haakon persisted.

"Many things. Sometimes he advises me about things of importance to my people; sometimes he gives us new rituals to perform. Sometimes he comes just for sex."

After a short but painful silence, Jemal said: "To

be expected, of course. Gods are known to favor only the fairest of mortals. You are mortal, aren't you?''

"Surely. Are you?"

"All too mortal, I fear," Haakon replied. "That being the case, we'd like to get home before our allotted span is up. Have you any way of summoning Xeus for a conference?''

"I should say not!" she said, shocked. "One does not summon a god like some errant tribesman. You must go to him. If he finds your petition worthy, he may help you."

"Is he the kind of god who is unfailingly helpful?" Soong asked hopefully.

"Not always," the herm said with a rueful grimace. "For instance, he created the Dragonfolk just so my children would have someone to fight. I wish he had not done that, but one cannot question a god. He said that my children were growing too numerous and this would be an interesting way of reducing their numbers."

"Ecologically minded rather than merely arbitrary then," Mirabelle said.

"But possibly sadistic," Haakon added.

"Sounds like my kind of god," Rama commented. "Tell me, dear Ancestor, how may we find this Xeus and prove ourselves worthy of his attention?''

"You must follow the river north, toward its headwaters. Xeus lives there, and there you will find him . . . if you live."

"How can we prove ourselves worthy?" Haakon asked.

She gave him a look of calm appraisal. "Xeus will give you ample opportunity to show what you are made of."

After the formalities of leave-taking, the herm boarded the formidable Rukh and departed, trailed by her faithful "children." Haakon, followed by his crew, went back inside the craft and began searching in the ship's banks for information.

"So, you think this creature is the herm from Testament who was the last before us to attempt Meridian?" Soong asked.

"I'm almost sure of it," Haakon answered. Then the readout came up. Haakon read the relevant portions aloud: "Berengaria Lavoisier, fifth-generation herm from Testament. Subaltern in the Fourth Legion of the Host of the Trinity during the wars with the Serene Powers. Promoted to captain in the Host of the Holy Spirit just before the collapse. Fled to the Cingulum due to religious persecution two years after the occupation of Testament by Bahadur." He punched another plate and a holo formed. They were looking at a herm, black-skinned and golden-haired, with silver eyes.

"Close," Jemal said, "but not quite." It was true. The herm in the holo was beautiful, but without the godlike glamour of the Ancestor.

"The height's wrong too," Rama pointed out. "This says that Lavoisier was one point six seven meters tall. The Ancestor is at least two point two. I was looking up at her, and I'm one point nine."

"Also, the time element's a little skewed," Mirabelle said. "Look at the date of the expedition. She couldn't have been here over three months standard."

"Time means nothing in this place, and that's the same herm," Haakon insisted. "Look at that holo. If you were going to start with that person and make her into your absolute human ideal, what would you do?"

"Assuming I had godlike powers," Jemal mused, "I'd stretch her a little and expand a bit here and there for truly heroic proportions, reshape the face a bit, maybe make the hair a tad more luxurious. In fact, I think I'd turn this one into something resembling the Ancestor.''

"Her memory of her former life seems to have been wiped, if your theory is correct," Soong pointed out. "The people of Testament are of a very strait-laced religious sect. This pagan creature remembers nothing of that, nor of space technology, although certain phantom memories must have remained. The feeling of having been in a spacecraft before, for instance.''

"Do you think this god Xeus is real or imaginary?" Mirabelle asked.

"I think he's real," Haakon answered. "A god? No, unless you accept a primitive's definition of the term. If he's one of the race that built the Cingulum, then he can probably do things that really do look like miracles. However, most of what we've seen involves card tricks with space-time, or peculiar genetics. Even if they made this whole planet, it seems to behave according to most of the conventional rules.''

"Except for having no magnetic poles," Rama said dryly.

Haakon heard some suppressed chuckles. One of the chucklers was Alexander. The other was Rand. "Something amusing?" he asked.

"It'll have to wait," Alexander said. "After dark tonight, I'll show you.''

"Show me what?"

"We don't want to ruin the surprise," Rand said. "Something I and the kid saw last night after the rest of you were asleep. Believe me, it'll change your ideas about this place.''

"Great. Just as I was formulating some I could live with," Haakon said. "Okay, everybody strap in. We've accomplished all we're going to by hanging around here. Let's head north and talk to a god.''

They took the G-102 up to treetop level and began to cruise, keeping their speed low to get a good look at the planet. For kilometer after kilometer they saw more of the semitropical riverside vegetation. Once in a while startled animals would break cover and run. Twice they saw whole herds of animals on the move across plains several kilometers distant from the riverbank. Magnified image showed these to be large mammal-like creatures of some sort, but little else was apparent.

As they continued along the river, the behavior of their instruments grew increasingly erratic. Data readouts collapsed into incomprehensible gibberish and the image screens faded, flickered and went blank with greater frequency.

"You know," Jemal said, "if the drive or the anti-grav starts to go on us, we're finished." He was a little pale.

"We have a choice," Rama said. "We can poke along like this forever, or we can gain altitude and make the highest speed we can. I say we waste no more time and take our chances with a power failure."

"I would advise in favor of caution," Soong put in.

"Me too," Mirabelle added.

"Since when did democracy blossom among us?" Haakon asked. After returning Rama's sullen glare for a moment, he said: "As a matter of fact, I agree with Rama."

"Then why are you not climbing and putting on speed, you hairless and unattractive creature?"

"Because," Rand butted in, "that's what he's been trying to do for the last twenty minutes."

"Right," Haakon said. "This is our top speed and maximum altitude for the moment."

"What?" Rama demanded. "This will take forever!"

"Would you rather walk?" Haakon asked.

"We'll be reduced to that if our power failures increase much more," Soong pointed out. "In light of that, I suggest we not travel directly over the river as we have been doing. If we must set down, land is the place to do it."

"If the anti-grav goes all at once," Mirabelle said, "a splash-down might be a little easier on us than hitting the ground."

"Hey, folks," Alexander said, "I realize I'm not exactly a member in good standing with this crew, but I gotta point out that old Leviathan could swallow this ship without a burp. What say we stick to land?" He smiled encouragingly.

"Right," Haakon said. "From here on in we travel over land at treetop level. And we don't travel after dark."

"This could turn out to be a long, dull trip," Jemal said.

"Long, yes," Soong concurred, "but far from dull. This place seems designed to sustain a lively interest."

As dusk closed in, Haakon turned away from the river and searched out a suitable landing site. It did not take him long to find what he wanted: a grassy hill free of large vegetation, where anything hostile could be seen from a long way off. He tried to scan the tree line with remotes, but they were useless.

"We'll button up for the night," Haakon said. "That way nobody has to stand guard. We should be safe . . . unless there are land animals as big as Leviathan."

"There might well be," Mirabelle said helpfully.

"I don't want to hear about it." Haakon went to the dispenser and drew a mug of strong tea. He had to hit it twice to make it work.

"Hey, boss," Alexander said, "can we wake you up tonight to show you our little surprise?"

"Sure," Haakon answered. "Go ahead. Make my misery complete. That's what a captain's for."

*   *   *

He awoke with rock dust stinging his nostrils. It took him a moment to realize that his bed was too soft for the pits and that someone was shaking his shoulder. In the pits they used a vibro-whip.

"Get up, Hack." It was Jermal's voice. "You've got to see this."

Haakon swung groggily out of his bunk. The interior lights were out but there seemed to be a flood of illumination from somewhere. He followed Jemal toward the lock.

"The view's better out on the platform," Jemal told him. Vaguely he could see the shapes of the others, standing outside.

"My orders were to button up for the night," Haakon said peevishly. "Why are you—" Then he saw it.

A planet was looming above the horizon. Not a moon, but a planet, complete with oceans and continents. About a quarter of its arc had cleared the horizon already; this was the source of the illumination he had half-noticed earlier. It seemed uncomfortably close.

"Uh-uh," he said. "Not possible. That's way too close. It should be tearing this planet apart. Earthquakes and tsunamis and volcanoes and everything."

"You think that's something?" Alexander asked. "Look over there." He pointed several degrees to the left of the rising planet. Another one was beginning to clear the horizon. If anything, this one was even closer.

"All right," Haakon demanded after a pause for adjustment, "how many?"

"We counted fifteen last night," Alexander said. "They're not all this close. Some were so far out we could barely see them, but they were planets all right. There was one looked like it was nothing but ocean, and another one all red, like it was just desert, but there was life on it."

"How could you tell?" Haakon asked dully. He was growing weary of impossibilities.

"Because part of it was in nightside and there were lights showing. Only big cities could make that much light."

"Did you see lights on any of the others?" Mirabelle asked.

"Not for sure," Alexander said. "But when a planet's mostly water, about all you see is clouds anyway. The desert place had a real clear atmosphere."

"I tried them on infrared and UV," Rand said. "I didn't get anything really conclusive. My sensors aren't of astronomical quality. I think I saw signs of civilization on a couple of them, but I can't be sure."

"If we're stranded here," Rama said, "I'll go mad. This place is insane and I'm going to end up that way myself." In the dim light her slit pupils had expanded to huge black disks.

"It's entirely possible that we're already crazy," Jemal said. Other planets were already poking above the horizon.

"They're not even on the same plane," Haakon said. "Are there no rules at all around here?"

His rhetorical question went unanswered.

By midafternoon of the next day the ship was moving at little more than a walking pace.

"I hope everybody brought along good hiking boots," Haakon told them. "I think we'll all be needing them before tomorrow."

"I hate to say it, boss," Alexander said, "but I ain't so good at walking." He held up a handlike foot for inspection. "See? Built for climbing, not for walking."

"I guess we'll just have to leave you to guard the ship if we have to proceed on foot," Haakon said.

"Well, I could *try* to keep up," Alexander said, alarmed.

Haakon grinned. "I thought so."

"You can leave me with the ship," Rama offered. She snuggled back into her bed of fragrant, expensive silk rugs. "I hate roughing it."

"You can't fool me," Jemal said. "I've seen you eyeing that jungle. You want to get out there and hunt down small animals to torment, kill and finally eat raw." She hissed at him.

That night they admired the drifting, impossible planets once more. The next morning the ship would not move.

EIGHT

The morning was spent in making preparations for their trek. There was a great deal of griping and grumbling over the prospect. The only one maintaining much equanimity was Haakon. As far as he was concerned, anything was better than breaking rocks in the pits.

"I'm too old for this," Soong said. "I'm a poet and philosopher, not an explorer."

"And an assassin," Haakon reminded him.

"That too. An occupation for a gentleman, I assure you. But this? Mere drudgery, fit only for those not suited to scholarly pursuits."

Soong fussed with his pack irritably. It was a bad sign. If the preternaturally calm Soong could be so ruffled, what might be expected from the likes of Rama?

Rand sat despondent, his small pack of necessities beside him. Of all of them, he had the least to carry along. The concentrated nutrients he required took up little space, and clothing was no problem.

"What's the matter, Rand?" Haakon asked. "You're weatherproof, unlike the rest of us. You're mostly motorized, so this won't even be much of an energy drain."

Rand looked up with his blank, metal-masked stare. "We've been losing power in everything since we got to this crazy planet, and losing it faster as we've come upriver. What if the next thing to go is my prosthesis? Have you considered that?"

Haakon was caught up short. He hadn't considered that, and he should have. The welfare of his crew was part of his responsibility. "You stay here with the ship then."

Rand vented an extremely peculiar sigh. "No, I'll go with you. I'm good for only about another year without Galen treatment, so getting back is paramount. Besides, I don't want to be left back here alone. Don't worry, I'm just feeling a bit of self-pity."

"Suit yourself," Haakon said. "But if you feel any systems failing, you're going to have to come back here immediately, and we may not be able to spare anybody to come back with you."

"I'll chance it," Rand said.

Mirabelle was uncommonly despondent, for her. She had been down ever since the encounter with the herm. After her skill as a technothief, the thing she was proudest of was her great physical beauty. Meeting the Ancestor had been ego-bruising.

Haakon walked over to her. "Cheer up," he said. "She had divine intervention. You came by your looks naturally."

Mirabelle glared at him for a moment, then smiled. "How do you know?" she demanded.

"My female intuition," he said.

He went over to Jemal and Alexander, who were making up packs. At least the kid seemed cheerful enough. That was a pleasant change. He was young enough to consider this an adventure instead of the forlorn last effort of a group of doomed people.

"You getting about ready, Jem?"

Jemal nodded.

"How about you, kid?"

Alexander looked up at him and grinned. "A monkey's always ready to take to the jungle, boss. Just let me at them trees and then stand back."

Haakon grinned back at him. "That's what I like to hear, even if you're lying."

He helped Jemal strap down a last piece of equipment and decided to stop stalling. Now for the worst part. He went over to Rama, who was spitting and swearing at her anti-grav sled, which refused to work. She could be smelled half a kilometer downwind. She bared her teeth when she saw him coming.

"This wretched device isn't functioning," she said. "I won't be able to bring along any of my things!" She gave the offending raft a clawed kick that left gouges in the metal but bruised her toes. She swore all the louder.

"Tough," Haakon said. "You'll have to get along with a bag and pallet like the rest of us. And I'd suggest you take better care of your feet. You're going to need them."

She turned on him murderously. "You got us into this, you bald idiot! And I haven't forgotten what you did to me back in Coventry. I'm going to repay you."

He faced her down. "I didn't get you into anything, cat-woman. Timur Khan had you picked up because you're a thief. You came along on this expedition because you didn't want to die, just like the rest of us. However, if you feel you have any disputes to settle, I'm at your disposal.

I'd rather settle with you now than worry about my back later on."

She relaxed a little. "Let's not, just yet. We still may need each other eventually. As soon as I know I don't need you though, you're mine. But don't worry about your back. That's not my style."

Oddly enough; he believed her. It was not that Felids weren't treacherous. In that respect they were at least as awful as ordinary humans. But they were creatures of pure style, and Rama had adopted a style of peculiar honor. Even though she was a criminal, her courage was unquestionable. And although she was vengeful, she met her enemies face to face.

"Get packed then," Haakon said. "Take nothing but what you can carry comfortably. We move out within the hour."

The final debate was about how to make the start. They had a collapsible boat that would carry all of them, plus such gear as they had to take.

"The boat will be easier than walking," Haakon pointed out. "The motor's not working, but we've got paddles. We'll make better time on the river if we stick close inshore, where there's little current."

"We'd be a snack for Leviathan," Mirabelle demurred.

"You saw the size of that thing," Haakon said. "It has to keep to mid-channel, where the water's deep enough for it to dive. The water's too shallow inshore. We'll never go more than fifty meters from shore if we can help it."

"I don't like the idea of traveling on water," Rama said uneasily.

"Me neither," Alexander added.

Haakon sighed in disgust. Spacers. They'd dare the most hazardous voyages in suicidally rickety ships with perfect equanimity, but faced with the outdoors and a little physical effort, they fell to pieces. "How about you, Jem?"

"I'm with you, Hack. Whatever you decide. I don't like to walk either."

"Soong?"

"Whatever we choose, we face unknown dangers. I advise we conserve energy to the greatest extent, and that means travel by water until it proves too hazardous or too rigorous."

"Rand?"

"It's all the same to me. If I go in, I'll sink, but I can walk to shore. Whatever's quickest."

"Good," Haakon said. "That makes it unanimous. We take the boat."

As they picked up the light, transparent craft and carried it to the shore, Jemal cocked an eyebrow at Haakon. "Unanimous?"

"When the captain gives an order, it's unanimous," he said complacently.

They piled their gear into the boat and climbed aboard gingerly. Their first efforts at paddling succeeded only in letting them drift farther downstream. None were experienced on the water. Haakon and Jemal were trying to dredge up half-forgotten memories of small-craft classes from their military-school days. None of the others had even that much to draw on. Eventually they managed to get the boat to spin end-for-end. It was pointless, but at least they weren't losing ground. By dint of trial and error they contrived to get one of the ends pointed upstream and keep it there. Fifteen minutes of hard paddling brought them back even with the ship.

"Tell me again, Hack," Jemal puffed, "about how this boat's going to save us time and energy."

"It'll work out," Haakon insisted grimly. "We just have to get it under control, that's all."

"I think I'm getting seasick," Alexander groaned, his face green.

"We're not at sea, you idiot," Jemal said. "It's probably those bananas you've been eating. Just because they look like bananas doesn't mean they eat and digest like bananas. You saw what the roots looked like. You've probably poisoned yourself. Serve you right too."

"Give me that thing," Rama said, holding out a hand to Mirabelle. Mirabelle handed over her paddle, which she had been wielding ineffectually in the bow of the boat. The Felid had been sitting in the center, as far from the water as possible. But her patience, never very strong, was becoming exhausted. Mirabelle moved aside and Rama knelt in the bow, critically examining the paddle. Then she dipped it in the water and raked backward. The boat shot forward in a swift surge. As she continued to rake the boat began making real headway. Unfortunately it was also heading out toward midstream. Haakon left his post in the stern and turned the rudder over to Jemal. He climbed into the bow next to Rama and began to ply his paddle. The boat straightened out and made steady progress upstream.

"That's more like it!" Jemal said. "We just keep our two strongest paddlers up front. The rest of us can steer and criticize."

"You'll take your turn, you malingerer," Haakon said. He was already sweating profusely. In spite of himself, he felt better than he had in days. A good workout was what he needed. It was what they all needed. Anything was better than sitting around brooding on their problems, of which they had plenty.

In spite of Haakon's reassurances, they kept their eyes

peeled for Leviathan. They also watched for eagles, dragons and any other horrors that might appear.

"Hey, look!" Alexander cried suddenly. Curled in a wretched ball against the bottom of the boat, he was pointing downward. Something was going past about two meters below. It was long and snakelike, as big around as a man's thigh, with a small, serrated fin along its spine. They watched about fifty meters of its length go by before its tail came into view—little more than a flat, vertical paddle with fins.

"I wish we had seen its head," Soong said.

"I'm glad we didn't," Alexander protested. "What we saw was bad enough."

"At least it didn't seem hostile," Haakon said.

"Not many things do until they eat you," Mirabelle pointed out. "I'm having second thoughts about this whole boating idea."

"You had second thoughts about it before we started," Haakon said. "I overruled them. I still do. Now, somebody spell me and Rama up here. Everybody takes a turn working the bow paddles."

Mirabelle and Soong took the next shift, while Haakon and Rama moved amidships. The technothief and the assassin were not able to keep the pace for very long. Haakon had expected that. They were all going to have to get broken in to the vicious labor.

By the time Soong and Mirabelle were exhausted, Alexander was sufficiently recovered to take a paddle, with Jemal as his mate. To Haakon's surprise, the monkeyboy proved to be an extremely powerful paddler, and Jemal had difficulty in keeping up with him. He was not quite as strong as Haakon or Rama, but his power was far out of proportion to his size.

The sun was only beginning to lower when Haakon began looking for a suitable campsite. He spotted a promising piece of ground and pointed to it. "We're going in over there." He turned the tiller and the paddlers changed direction to swing the nose of the little craft around. There were no complaints from his crew. They were all exhausted and wanted only to rest.

The boat nudged ashore and they piled out, lifted the craft and carried it ashore, where they unloaded it and inverted it over most of their gear. Then they unrolled their pallets and collapsed on top of them.

"Don't get too comfortable," Haakon ordered. "We have to get the tents up, and some of us are going to gather firewood."

"Firewood?" Mirabelle exclaimed. "What for? Our rations are self-heating, and God knows it's plenty warm around here."

"A fire might scare away unwelcome animals," Haakon insisted. "Besides, it's traditional. When you're in the woods, you build a fire. I think there's a rule about it somewhere."

They groaned, but Alexander and Soong got up and gathered a few armloads of dry wood. They didn't have to go far; there was wood everywhere. When it was all piled in the center of the campsite, Haakon took out his beamer, dialed it to lowest power and turned it on the wood, which immediately burst into flame.

"Beats rubbing two sticks together," Jemal said.

Rama wrinkled her nose at the smoke. "Filthy stuff," she said. "Why do some people like it?"

"Some think it's romantic," Jemal told her, stretching out on his pallet. "You're just spoiled. You're used to air that's been filtered and cleaned and laundered and purified until your lungs think they've gone to heaven. If you'd been breathing rock dust as long as Hack and I, you wouldn't mind a little smoke." The breeze wafted some of the smoke over him and he broke into a coughing and sneezing fit that left his eyes red and watering.

"From now on we set watches," Haakon said. "Everybody stands one watch each night, sixty minutes per watch. If things start to look really dangerous, we'll use two people on each watch."

As he finished speaking, there came a bloodcurdling screech from the forest.

"What the hell was *that?*" Alexander demanded.

"Probably just a local tree frog," Haakon said. "Then again it might be something getting set to gobble us up. Keep it in mind while you're on watch. Now, let's tackle those tents."

The two big dome-shaped tents required little more work than the pallets, but they needed to be staked down against the possibility of a high wind. They were standard emergency equipment on any ship but, as was the case with most emergency equipment, none of the crew had had any experience with them since their earliest days as spacers. Inside, the tents were unexpectedly roomy and comfortable. Rand, Rama and Mirabelle tossed their pallets into one; Soong, Jemal, Haakon and Alexander took the other.

They broke out the rations and ate, trying not to think of what might be lurking outside the circle of firelight. The tents had interior illumination that was still working, but nobody had thought to bring along an outdoor lamp. There was little talk. The paddling had left them numb with fatigue.

Alexander had first watch, but Haakon and Jemal sat up with him. Jemal was too keyed up to sleep, and Haakon still wasn't certain of just how responsible the monkey-boy was. He was the youngest of them all, and his history wasn't one to inspire confidence. He liked the kid, but that wasn't the same thing as trusting him. They made a little circle around the fire, talking idly and once in a while throwing another stick into the flames.

"At least is *smells* like real burning wood," Alexander said. "Could be worse. Hey, boss''—he turned to Haakon—"how long do you think this trip's going to take us? I mean, it'll be fun for a while, but I can already see that the novelty's going to wear off pretty quick."

"Point A," Haakon said, ticking points off meticulously on the fingers of one hand, "I have no way of knowing, because I don't know the distance involved or the terrain to be covered. Point B, I've never gone to seek an audience with a god, and I suspect I'm not alone in that regard around here, so I don't know what the god in question will consider a sufficient pilgrimage. Apparently he has preferences that we'll have to go along with. Point C—and this is the really important one—it doesn't matter worth a damn whether you or anybody else enjoys this expedition. Whether it turns out to be a pleasant vacation or terrible hardship, we have to go through with it because we have no choice. It'll take as long as it takes. Period."

"Okay, that's all I wanted to know," Alexander said. He picked up a mug of hot tea and sipped from it.

"We're going to have to start trying the local food supply pretty soon," Jemal said. "These survival rations won't last many more days. At least we know the bananas are okay."

Alexander grinned ruefully. "The dates aren't bad either."

"You tried the dates?" Haakon asked.

"Yeah, they're fine. Just like at home."

"Then since you're so anxious to be a guinea pig,"

Haakon said, "you can try out everything from now on. I hope you're not vegetarian."

"No." He looked at Haakon with alarm. "Wait a minute. I'm not eating river snakes or dragons or anything like that."

"Don't worry," Haakon said. "You get hungry enough, you won't be nearly so picky."

The next morning the crew broke camp and started upriver without difficulty. Most of them were sore, but at least they had the boat under control now. The river was placid, and there was no noise from shore. It seemed like an idyllic day for a cruise. The idyll lasted for almost an hour.

The sun was still low in the east—and that was the direction the attackers came from. Rama's ears were the keenest, and she turned to face the odd buzzing noise, squinting into the sunlight. "What's that?"

The others paused to see what she was staring at. The buzzing became a loud drone; then at least a hundred flying creatures swooped over the tree line, making straight for the boat.

"Head for shore!" Haakon shouted. They paddled frantically, trying to get solid ground under their feet before confronting this new threat. It was no use. The flyers closed the distance with easy speed. Against the sunlight no one could make out what they were, but it was obvious that they weren't eagles or dragons. They gave off an impression of long, jointed bodies that tapered sharply to the rear, but there were no visible wings.

The first one zoomed overhead, causing everyone to duck and giving them a fleeting look at it. It was an insect, its wings apparently transparent and moving so fast that they were all but invisible. Then the others were roaring overhead. They were about three meters long from their globular heads to their blunt-pointed tails. Like most things on this planet, they were far larger than they had any right to be, and like at least two of the other flying species, they had riders.

The riders, like the Eaglefolk and the Dragon riders, shared human qualities with those of their mounts. They were exoskeletal, compound-eyed bipeds with arms, hands and weapons. Haakon could see their spears.

"Don't anybody fire unless they attack," he ordered. "And keep paddling."

But no one was paying any attention. They were holding their weapons nervously, watching as the insects went into a turn that should not have been possible. Then, they were heading back. Somehow they looked far more menacing than the eagles or the dragons. Their appearance, their sound, their very aspect, spelled pure malevolence.

"I think they're dragonflies," Jemal hazarded. "Four wings and capable of unique aerobatics."

"Another violation of the square-cube law," Haakon said. "Here they come. Their weapons are primitive and we're armored, so don't shoot unless you have to."

The bugs were speeding toward them, now no more than two meters above the surface of the water. When they were within five meters from the boat, they pulled up suddenly and soared overhead. Spears rained down on the little craft. Shouts and curses proclaimed several hits. Haakon looked to see if there was any damage, but the armorcloth seemed to have preserved everybody's skin. The impacts were painful, however.

Jemal picked up a two-meter spear with a bone tip that lay in the bottom of the boat and waved it angrily at the insects. "You dumb bastards! We've done nothing to you! Get the hell away from us before we fry you!"

Snarling and spitting, Rama grabbed up a beam rifle. She was giving off her fighting scent and appeared to be perfectly insane with rage. She raised the rifle and drew a bead on one of the bugs.

"No!" Haakon shouted. He was making his way toward her when the next attack hit. The leading bug slammed into him from the side, its legs seeking to grip his body while its wings fanned the air deafeningly. He tried to push himself loose from the stubby legs, but the awkward angle did not allow him to bring his greatest strength to bear. To his horror, he felt himself being lifted from the boat.

The sounds of the fight grew fainter until all he could hear was the beating of wings. He twisted his head around and stared into an utterly alien face looking down at him. The huge compound eyes took up most of the head, situated above mandibles that worked sideways. The bug chittered at him and raised a bone club, bringing it down with crushing force against his shoulders. With all the strength he could muster, Haakon brought the side of his fist against the mount's head. The armored skull was immune to his blow, but he caught the edge of an eye. The creature screeched and Haakon felt the grip of the legs loosen momentarily.

Then the club descended again, striking with sickening force, sending waves of pain streaking from his shoulder and down his side. Here Haakon's years under the whip were in his favor; he did not allow pain to distract him. This time his fist crunched fully against the compound eye. The mount screeched again and lurched sideways. The legs let Haakon go—and he was tumbling through the air.

He struck the water with his back, knocking the breath

out of himself. Reflexively he tried to draw air into his lungs. It was a mistake, as he was now several meters below the surface of the river. He fought down panic, forcing himself to relax. He had to regain his orientation or he'd try to swim straight for the bottom. His downward motion ceased and he opened his eyes. Bubbles rose from his clothing and he began to follow them. They would be rising toward the surface, unless they were as perverse as everything else in this impossible place.

To his great relief, his head broke the surface a few seconds later. He coughed and sputtered and shook his head to clear the water from his ears. When he had his breath back, he looked about for the boat. It took him several seconds to spot it. It was far upstream, and when he realized to his horror that he was well out toward the middle of the river, he began swimming frantically for shore. He began to realize that taking the river route was not one of his better decisions, and he sincerely hoped he would live long enough to regret it properly.

The battle seemed to be continuing around the boat. He saw several of the insects burst into flame and fall to the river. Then there was a buzzing behind him and he twisted around in the water. An insect and a rider, possibly those he had just escaped from, were skimming right above the surface, heading straight for him. He grabbed at his belt and tried to yank his beamer loose.

It proved to be unnecessary. A pair of narrow jaws about three meters long broke the surface and snapped shut on bug and rider. Haakon had an impression of hundreds of needlelike teeth closing with a crunch. Then the jaws disappeared, along with the prey. He didn't know whether to be relieved or terrified, and he decided he was both. He tried to swim toward the boat, but he seemed to be caught in a current that was sweeping him downstream. He spotted something bobbing in the water—a pack, apparently knocked overboard during the battle. It was buoyant, and he grabbed on to it, kicking his feet behind him. It was easier than swimming and enabled him to keep his head high in order to see where he was going. His whole body tingled in anticipation of those terrible jaws closing on him. And then there was Leviathan. No. The monster would never take notice of anything as small as he.

He saw a head break surface not far away. It appeared to be human. Kicking his way toward it, he shouted: "Hey! Over here!" The head turned to face him and he saw the striped hair, now dark and plastered sleekly to the head, and the twitching whiskers. Rama! She saw him and swam toward him with long, powerful strokes. When she was near enough, she reached out and put a hand against the pack. She was breathing heavily and he could smell her rage.

"We've got to get ashore," he said. "I just saw something with jaws so big you could stand up in them; it snapped one of those bugs right out of the air."

They spotted the nearest piece of shore about a hundred meters away and began swimming toward it. He craned his neck to see where the boat was, but he could not catch sight of it. With a hollow sensation in his stomach, he realized that it had probably been sunk.

"This pack must've been knocked overboard," Haakon explained as he paddled. "I grabbed it and used it as a float."

"It didn't fall," Rama said. "I was knocked overboard by one of those things, and the monkey-boy threw it to me but I couldn't catch up to it. There are a lot of little currents and eddies around here." She looked about for more bugs. There were none. "They must have had enough.

If you'd let us open fire at first, we might all be together now.''

"Nag, nag, nag," he said. "Is that all you ever do?"

"It's better than worrying about what's below us right now," she said. He began to kick harder.

They stumbled ashore, bedraggled but relieved. There was a narrow, rocky beach before them and beyond that, dense forest. Haakon noted with astonishment that the sun was still low in the east. The whole frantic action had occupied only a few minutes. He picked up the pack and slipped his arms through its carrying-straps. Shrugging it onto his shoulders, he began walking upstream. Rama followed.

"Keep your eyes open for the others," he ordered. "And scan the water for any more debris. We're going to need all our gear."

"You think I don't know that?"

They saw no more signs of their companions as they made their way along. Within a few minutes they were standing on a point of land where the river current split. Haakon looked down the other side and saw nothing but water. The shoreline was visible on both sides. They were on an island.

"Damn!" he said. "How did we come past this island without noticing it?"

"Haakon," Rama said, "you may be a great spacer pilot, but as a river pilot, you're an utter failure."

"Let's head back downstream on the other side. The boat may have drifted this way."

Wordlessly the Felid followed him. At its extreme downstream end, the island was within a hundred meters of the shore. A narrow, vegetation-covered spit of land angled out into the current from the shore just below their position. They had passed around the spit in the boat, never realiz-

ing that they were going around an island. There was no
sign of the boat or their shipmates. They might have been
swallowed up by the river. Or by one of its creatures.

"Ready for another swim?" he asked Rama.

"Swim if you like," she said. "I think I'll build a
raft. I'm not curious to get a look at what lives down
there."

He stared at the murky water. She was probably right.
"A raft it is then," he said. "Let's go look for some
wood."

"There's no rush now. I'm going to dry my clothes
first."

Unself-consciously Rama peeled out of her clothes.
Haakon sat on a nearby rock and watched with interest as
he tugged his boots off. He had never seen a naked Felid
before. As it turned out, she looked much like an ordinary
human woman, only bigger and more muscular. Most of
the difference was in the head, hands and feet. Her small,
round breasts were high-set, the black nipples in dramatic
contrast to her white skin. A double row of vestigial
nipples ran down her ribs almost to her human-looking
navel.

As Haakon undressed, Rama watched him with equally
frank interest. She seemed to approve of his rocklike
physique. "Not bad, for an ape," she commented. She
spread her clothes on a rock to dry and fanned her mane
across her shoulders.

Haakon opened the pack to see what they had. Its seal
was intact, its contents dry. Inside he found a rolled-up
pallet and sleeping bag, a powerblade, a small music unit
and a book full of incomprehensible figures. The pack had
probably belonged to Mirabelle. He touched a button on
the music unit and heard the strains of an odd, wailing
melody, set in a style he failed to recognize.

"That'll do us a lot of good," Rama snorted.

"I'll admit I'd have preferred some rations," Haakon said.

"You get a fire going, dear one," the cat-woman said. "I'll get the rations while our clothes dry."

Naked and barefoot, she darted silently among the trees. Haakon almost called out for her to be careful, then shrugged. Nothing he could say was likely to affect her behavior, and she seemed to be capable of looking after herself.

He gathered firewood, of which there was an abundance, and ignited it with his beamer. It burned merrily, and as he stared into it, he thought of the previous night. Already he was missing Jemal and Alexander. Hell, he even missed Soong and Rand and Mirabelle.

By the time he had a good bed of coals ready, Rama returned, swinging a pair of chunky, rodentlike beasts in one hand. She dropped them to the ground next to him.

"I killed them," she said. "You clean them."

"That's fair," he admitted. He took up his powerblade and began carving up the creatures. Rama stood at a distance to avoid the inevitable stink of burning hair and hide. He was no expert, but the powerblade allowed for speed. Haakon skewered some of the meatier parts on sticks and set them to cook over the coals. He examined the heads of the creatures, but he was no zoologist. They were just furry rodents to him. They had big front teeth and their paws seemed to be adapted for digging, but that was as much as he could figure out.

"You're more of an outdoor type than you let on," he said to Rama.

"It's in the genes," she replied with a shrug. Although her clothes were dry, she made no move to put them back on. Neither did Haakon. The sun felt good. In any case, he had been kept without clothing for so many years that he scarcely noticed their absence. He picked up a skewer and sniffed at it.

"I guess this is as good a time as any to see if the local animals are edible," he said. "We'd have had to find out eventually in any case." He returned the skewer to the fire. "I'll wait till it's better done though."

"Not me," Rama said. She took up one of the rawest-looking pieces and tore at it.

"Better let it cook longer," Haakon advised. "There might be harmful microorganisms in it."

"I'll take my chances," she said. "You wouldn't want to be around me if I were reduced to eating ruined meat. It does bad things to my temper."

In the marshy area between the island and the mainland they located a stand of something that might have been bamboo. The tall reeds ranged from finger-thin to twenty centimeters in girth. Haakon cut a supply of the larger ones with the powerblade while Rama searched for vines strong enough to bind them into a raft. The task of raft-building took until late afternoon, and when it was finished, they stood back and examined the float critically.

"Well," Rama said, "at least it won't have to carry us far." She climbed aboard the rickety raft and Haakon shoved it off. He clambered aboard and began poling toward the shore. They stayed on their knees, unwilling to risk capsizing anything so unsteady.

Ten meters from the island, Haakon's pole stopped touching bottom and they were adrift. The impetus from his last thrust kept them heading toward the farther shore, but they were slowing. Then something bumped the bottom of the raft.

"What now?" Haakon said, drawing his beamer. The bump came again, this time harder. A form broke surface next to the raft, a black-gray bulk with a squarish head.

"Don't shoot yet," Haakon cautioned. "There may be another kilometer of it down there."

The head, as bulky as Haakon's body, turned to regard them with mournful eyes. Its mouth was cleft in the center, and a mass of vegetation, apparently dredged from the river bottom, hung from it. The thing munched placidly as it watched them.

"It looks harmless," Haakon said.

"Nothing that big is harmless. I'm just glad there's nothing riding it for a change."

"I wish Jem were here. He could tell us what this thing's a distortion of." His mind went back to long-ago classes in Earth and Xeno zoology. "I think there was something called—a manitou? No, a manatee. A mammalian browser, extinct about the time space travel began."

"Don't tell me, let me guess the rest. Back on Earth they didn't grow this big. Am I right?"

"I don't know, but it's a safe guess. Whoever plays with genetics around here is sure hell on size."

Haakon probed with his pole once more, hoping he wouldn't poke some sensitive part of the beast's anatomy. The pole touched ground again as they drifted past the animal. It seemed to lose interest in them and slowly sank beneath the surface. He poled faster, and within a few minutes the raft nudged the shore. They scrambled off as though it were on fire.

"What now?" Rama asked.

"We keep going upriver. That'll be where the others are headed."

"If they're alive," she said.

"We have to go on the assumption that they are. If they

aren't—'' He shrugged. "Then we carry on alone. We're not going to get off this planet until we find Xeus."

"Why are you so sure this putative god can help us?"

"I'm not sure at all, but if you have a better plan, I'll be glad to hear it."

"I have none. Let's go god-hunting." She shouldered the pack.

"That's us," Haakon said, grinning. "Holy pilgrims."

NINE

Alexander was scared. Not dry-mouthed, panicky scared like he'd been when the bugs attacked, but just plain all-around scared. He'd been alone before, but never under such circumstances. Never on an alien world, and never *marooned*. He wished one of the others would show up. When the bug with its spear-wielding rider had swooped down on him, he'd decided quicklike that he wasn't all that afraid of the river and he'd dived in. He'd made shore without looking back, scrambled up the bank and into the trees. When he'd worked up enough nerve to go back for a look, there had been nothing to see: no boat, no shipmates and, blessedly, no bugs.

Now he started trudging slowly upriver. He didn't like to walk. He wasn't built for it. He did not, however, see any options open to him. He wished, above all, that he was back in Hold Six. He sighed at the memory. Now there'd been a spacer's paradise. He thought of himself as a spacer even though his travel had been

141

unofficial. He had little use for petty distinctions like that.

He heard something moving in the brush nearby. Immediately his monkey genes took over and he scrambled up the nearest tree. He found a comfortable branch and waited, his heart hammering madly. As usual, when he got scared, he got hungry too. Noting one of the banana palms nearby, he ran out to the end of his branch and snatched a few. Returning, he sat with his back against the trunk and peeled a banana with his feet. He stuffed it into his mouth and scanned the ground below for whatever it was that had made the noise. It sure tasted like an ordinary banana.

A couple of chunky beasts came out into the clearing under the tree and rooted around. They had short hair and thin legs ending in tiny hooves. They didn't look dangerous, but he knew that vegetarians could be plenty vicious. He'd just wait right here until they went away.

He wished Haakon would show up. He liked the captain, and felt safe with him. He liked Jemal too. Hell, right now he'd settle for the cat-lady, and she scared him half to death. At least she was human, sort of.

One of the animals below raised its head and snorted. The other started and they looked around nervously, then charged for the brush. Alexander looked down to see what had scared them away. He heard more noise. Something was coming toward him. The new arrival strode into the clearing and stopped, leaning wearily against the base of the tree.

"Hey there," Alexander called. She was dirty and her hair was straggly and wet, but Mirabelle looked beautiful to him. He was so happy he could have wept.

"Alexander?" she said, searching the foliage overhead.

"Here." He descended branch by branch, dropping several meters at a time and grabbing limbs with hands and feet to control his fall. Just for joy he did a double somersault on the last drop and landed right in front of the technothief. To his great delight, she grabbed him in a fierce hug. No doubt about it, she was a real mammal.

"Have you seen any of the others?" she asked.

"Would I be here alone if I had?"

"Same here. I went into the river when the boat overturned."

"It sunk, huh? Well, it wasn't worth a damn anyway. What do you think we ought to do now?" He was anxious to be relieved of any further responsibility for his future actions.

"I guess we walk upstream. That's supposed to be where Xeus is."

He canted his head at a quizzical angle. "Do you really believe in this Xeus character?"

"The expression 'believe in' implies a factor of faith," she said pedantically. "On the other hand, 'believe' implies a well-reasoned adherence to scientific thought. That is, you believe something for which there is sufficient evidence to merit belief. Now in this case we have neither the kind of divine revelation that brings about a 'belief in,' nor do we have proper empirical evidence to warrant even a provisional belief in the existence of this putative Xeus. So, to answer your question, no, I don't 'believe in' Xeus. However, at present I have no other options for my future activities and therefore choose to follow the extremely slim possibility of finding the hypothetical Xeus."

Alexander continued his sideways-upward gaze at her, replete with doubt and irony. "You know, lady, much as I like you, I think you could get boring as hell."

She broke into tinkling, musical laughter. "Now you know how a technothief thinks and speaks. We're bigger sticklers for precision of utterance than lawyers are. Don't worry, most of the time I talk like a real human being. Look, our chances here are two: slim and none. Let's take the slim chance and head toward where we were told Xeus is. One thing we know for sure: This place obeys no rational rules. So at the risk of sounding professional again, rational objections don't qualify. If there's Leviathan and the Rukh, then maybe there's Xeus too." She smiled down at him so radiantly that he felt all warm inside.

"Sure," Alexander said. "You know, it's kind of like a dream." His face twisted into an unfamiliar, thoughtful mold. "I mean—I don't know the right way to say it, but it's like, I don't know, but this place goes by dream rules, right?" Her hand dropped to his head, ruffling his coarse hair and sliding down his neck to his shoulder, the gesture not seeming sensual, but encouraging. "I mean, when you dream, anything can happen. Here anything can happen. So maybe here the kind of stuff you can dream can be real. Maybe if we can dream Xeus, we can find him." His face screwed up into a forlorn knot. "Hell, I wish I could talk like you or the captain or Jemal. I know what I want to say but I ain't good with words."

She smiled at him, and the smile was not the slightest bit patronizing. He would have caught something like that in a second. "Alexander, you have a fine way with words. They express your soul, and that's what words are for. We all saw that when we first met you. Even Rama did, although in her weird, feline way she'll never say it."

He actually felt himself blushing. "I'm not educated like you and the captain, or Jemal or Soong, nor maybe even like Rand and the cat-woman. I ain't good with words. But I'm good with my hands and feet and tail. I can see and hear and smell things real good. You know, people like you all, people who are big and pretty and educated, you kind of make me feel—kind of, I don't know—" He hunched his shoulders and waved his hands and tail in an attempt to express these unaccustomed thoughts.

"Intimidated?"

"Yeah, I guess that's it." Then he added hastily, "But that don't mean I don't like you a lot."

"I'm flattered," she said with genuine sincerity. "So let's not act like you're some kind of subordinate or inferior being. We're equals, shipmates, fellow spacers. I think that your special traits and adaptations will keep us alive a lot better than my academic training. My kind of education earned me a cushy living back in the civilized worlds." She looked at him with a mischievous grin. "It ain't worth shit here. Lead on."

Somehow her words made him feel better than he'd ever felt before. Was she conning him? Screw that. She was his *shipmate,* for God's sake. You had to trust your shipmates. He searched the jungle roundabout with ears and eyes and nose sharpened by renewed urgency. After all, he was helping a shipmate who maybe wasn't as good as he was at this kind of thing, just like he knew she would look out for him on one of those big settled worlds, where it was all cities and police and rules that he'd never be able to adjust himself to.

Nervously, to pass the time, he found himself talking about irrelevant things. Mirabelle was as serene as ever, but she was more than happy to keep up with his babblings, maybe to relieve her own nerves. He liked to think that anyway.

"You know, that cat-woman—" he said, "—she's something that makes my tail twitch, you know what I mean? She's bigger than most humans I ever seen, except maybe for old Lopal Singh, and she's tough and strong and smelly, but you know what? She makes my tail twitch. Maybe you don't know what that means among us Singeurs, but it means we're attracted to somebody. It's screwy, but as much as she scares me, I'd like to jump on her like a laser on an atom in a Tesla engine." He looked back over his shoulder at her, but for the moment she held her counsel. He babbled on. "I ain't seen nothing on a dozen worlds that scares me like that woman does, but I'd like to get into her spacesuit, you know? Does that make me some kind of weirdo?" He felt like an absolute fool saying these things, but his nerves were right on top of his skin and crawling; he had to say *something*.

"It's her genes, Alexander," Mirabelle said, pushing fronds away from her face. "We're all human, although some of us have grafted, non-human genes. Humans like cats, but we're also a little repelled by them. The connection goes back to the first evolution of both species. We respond to a cat's sensuality and intelligence; we're repelled by their bloodlust and ferocity. Humans are bloodlusting and ferocious too—in a different way. Rama likes to hurt things, but it's an innocent, primitive sort of viciousness. It's not the twisted, perverted sadism that we're familiar with, not at all like the way Timur Khan is, for instance."

"That guy. I'd still like to get the story on him and you people."

"I'll tell you tonight if we find a quiet place to bed down. But getting back to Rama. She's attractive because she's designed to be. I'll have to admit, she is beautiful. Even I find her seductive. Does that surprise you?"

"It sure does. She hates your guts!"

"Hate with Rama isn't human hate. It's a conditioned response. No, not conditioned but built into her genes.

She's hostile to me because she sees in me a rival for power and position."

"Well, maybe she's beautiful," Alexander said, "but I've never seen *anything* as beautiful as you."

She smiled again. "Thank you. But my beauty is as artificial as hers. We've been gene-manipulated in different ways. Plus that, she has those pheromones."

"You mean the way she makes smells? Jeez, sometimes she could drive me out of a banana tree, but other times she makes my tail—well, you know."

"Exactly. It's the mating of human and cat qualities that's made the Felids feared everywhere."

Alexander mused for a while. "That woman," he said at last. "She's the captain's, ain't she?"

"That's right," Mirabelle replied. "It's been that way since she showed up on *Eurynome*. I don't think either of them has caught on to it yet, but you did, and so did I. Probably the others too, except perhaps for Rand. Who knows how to figure *him* out? God, what a mating that will be, when it happens."

"I'll say!" Alexander chuckled and slapped his tail against the ground. "That woman'll turn the whole perfume factory on for that! I hope I'll be close by to sniff it."

She slapped him gently on the back of the head. "Keep your senses on our surroundings," she reminded him. "And keep your tail ready to swing from a limb. We aren't out of danger here, you know."

Sobered, he did as he was told. Still, he felt a whole lot better. Now he felt like he was a little bit in control of the situation. Here was Mirabelle, and she was counting on him. He didn't understand a lot about this place, but maybe she did. She made people like the captain and the cat-lady seem more like real people. Somehow that made the whole situation seem a little easier to take. He didn't know just quite why that was, but it did. He was satisfied with that. Come right down to it, he just had to be.

"You mean this Timur Khan guy has explosives implanted in your *heads?* Explosives he can set off at any time? That's awful! It ain't right. Nobody should be able to do things like that to people." Alexander was genuinely shocked. He and Mirabelle sat in a small clearing, a pile of fruit between them. There were plenty of easily climbed trees nearby.

"Timur Khan doesn't worry about right and wrong," she said. "He cares only for power. But now you know why we didn't want to take you with us. How would you like to be in our ship in deep space when all our heads exploded?"

He looked a little sick. "It just ain't right," he muttered. Then he firmed up. "But I don't care. I'm still with you. I'll go where you go, even if it means getting stranded."

"That's brave of you."

"Naw. It's just that I feel right with you people. I never felt that way before with anybody." Then he brightened. "Hey, I tell you what. Let's go find Timur Khan and kill him!"

"I'd love to, but I'm sure he's protected himself from that possibility. He'd be a fool not to with a bunch as hard-bitten as our crew, especially with Soong a trained assassin. Whatever else he is, the man's no fool."

"I guess you're right. It's fun to think about it though."

"Fine. You think about it and let's get some sleep."

He had made comfortable beds, using springy brush topped with a thick layer of feather-soft ferns he had found growing by the river. They hadn't dared to build a fire, but the night was warm and they wouldn't miss their bedrolls, now floating down the river. Alexander rolled into his bed and watched as Mirabelle stood and peeled out of her coverall. Her faint, starlit silhouette looked firm but incredibly voluptuous.

"No peeking," she said.

"Can't help it if I got good night vision," he answered. He wished it were a damn sight better.

She chuckled softly and her bed rustled faintly as she stretched out. "Good night, Alexander."

"Good night," he said. His tail twitched.

Alexander scanned the clearing from his position on a low tree limb. The clearing was no more than a hundred meters from the river. He and Mirabelle had been on the move for three days now, and this was their established tactic. Whenever they came to a clearing too big to walk around conveniently, Alexander would climb to a high spot and observe it for a while before they crossed. He could hear nothing now but a murmur of wind over grass and the chittering of local insects.

"See anything?" Mirabelle's voice was quiet, but she could make it carry.

"Been a hell of a fight out there, not too far back. There's blood and trampled grass, some burn spots like someone coulda used a beamer. You think maybe we should go around this one?"

"We need a closer look at the signs. If those are beamer marks, it means some of our people ran into trouble here."

"Yeah, that's what I was thinking. Okay, I'll go first. You keep in mind where this tree is in case we have to run for it. We get more than halfway across and we gotta run, head for the other side. I see a big tree over there with blue and red flowers on it. It's got some low branches, and there's a coconut tree right next to it I could reach if we have to stay there a while.''

She grimaced. "I hope I never have to eat coconut again. Or bananas or dates, for that matter.''

He grinned. "If you'd kept ahold of your beamer, we coulda been eating steak.''

"Don't think about food just now. Think about trouble instead.''

"I been thinking about nothing else for days. Trouble, danger, you name it.''

Alexander stepped out into the clearing, his eyes darting nervously from side to side, nostrils flared to test the breeze. He felt naked and exposed, wishing he were back in the relative security of the trees. Not that anyplace around here was all that safe of course.

He came to an area of trampled grass, where the ground had been torn up by something big and heavy, with claws. There was blood scattered around, and the burn marks on the ground and nearby plants looked symmetrical enough to be from a beamer.

"How many were there?'' Mirabelle asked.

"At least a dozen, maybe more, plus some kind of big animal. Look, see those footprints? A whole bunch of them were barefoot. And at least three were wearing boots.''

"Do you think the ones wearing boots were ours?''

"Most likely. You seen anybody else around here in boots? And look here.'' He pointed to the faint imprint of a shod foot. "This one's different from the others. Kind of a honeycomb-pattern tread. I bet that's Rand.''

"Can you tell which the others might be?'' she asked.

"Not for sure, but the feet are kind of small and the stride a little short for the captain or Rama. Maybe it's Soong and Jemal.''

"I wish we had some instruments for testing this blood,''

Mirabelle said. "It could be from any of them, or even from the animal."

"Whatever did the bleeding did it no later than this morning. It's still wet, and it ain't turned too brown yet. And we don't want to mess with that animal."

"Can you tell what it was?"

"Just that it walked on two legs and dragged a big tail behind it and had about a five-meter stride. It went off that way." He pointed inland.

"Did the others go with it?"

"Looks like it. Not as many tracks though, and none of the booted ones. Maybe they were being carried. I hope so, because if they weren't, it means that monster ate them right here."

"Perhaps some of them were riding on it. People and beasties seem to form bonds in this place. Can you tell if it was a bird or reptile or mammal or what?"

"Four-toed track, three toes forward and splayed out, one in the back. Claws on the tips of the toes. I dunno, looks like a big bird or lizard track to me, but around here, who can tell? Let's just keep out of its way." He looked up at her. "Well, what now?" She just stared back at him silently. He looked down at the ground, fists on hips, elbows stuck out. "Yeah, I guess you're right," he said at last. "Come on."

With Mirabelle following, he set off on the trail of the monster.

TEN

"I still don't believe this," Jemal said.

"Why not?" Soong asked. "You've had all day to get used to it. Even the bizarre becomes acceptable after the passage of sufficient time."

They sat on the ground, their hands tied behind them. Next to them lay Rand. To conserve power, the engineer had put his metabolic functions on maintenance level for the night. He was probably asleep, or somewhere near that state.

"Maybe I'll be able to buy this tomorrow then," Jemal said. "Tonight's too soon."

He looked at the circle of natives sitting around the fire. Just beyond the flames he could see the legs and belly of the thing that had brought them here. The light didn't reach high enough to illuminate its head or its tiny forelegs.

"A *dinosaur!*" Jemal said in protest. "A goddam dinosaur! And not just any dinosaur either. A genuine *Tyrannosaurus rex,* the most clichéd dinosaur of the lot."

"Actually," Soong said, "it might be the very similar *Mongolian Tarbosaurus*, but I take your point. Somehow, though, I doubt that the historical beasts were quite like this one." From where they sat, they could hear its stomach grumbling; the sound woke disquieting thoughts of what it might be digesting soon.

The natives were a bit of a disappointment. Unlike the bird-people, the dragon-people and the bug-people, they looked like ordinary human beings. Their color was hard to judge because their bodies were completely painted, but their hair ranged from dirty brown to dirty black, and there were both blue and brown eyes among them. They weren't ordinary humans though. Ordinary humans did not ride dinosaurs. On the ground near the beast was a long contraption of wood and leather. One broad strap would go around the Tyrannosaur's neck, and a loop at the far end encircled the base of its tail. Other straps and cords fastened around its body. When the thing was in place, as many as nine people could ride on the monster.

"Here it comes again," Jemal said. The dinosaur had been shifting restlessly from one huge foot to another, and now it walked around the fire and strode over to them. The natives paid it no notice. The creature, which massed many tons, moved almost noiselessly.

When it reached them, it bent low, raising its tail slightly to counterbalance the weight of its leaning body. As the massive head lowered within the level of the firelight, Jemal sucked in his breath. The thing was just too fearsome to get used to, even though it went through this ritual several times each hour. The head was two meters long, most of it consisting of massive jaws studded with teeth twenty centimeters long. The eyes were mounted well to the sides of the skull under flaring wings of bone covered with thick pebbly skin. It had to turn its head sideways to look them over with one eye to make sure they hadn't moved too far and that their bonds were still tight. Even more disturbing than the creature's size and ferocity was the cold intelligence in that gaze. This was not the brainless, lumbering dinosaur of popular legend. It was a reasoning being, although its intelligence was undoubtedly not of the same sort as a human's.

They had been observing it through the day, ever since their capture that morning. The natives had never spoken to the beast, but it always seemed to do what they required of it. Or maybe the dinosaur was giving the orders and the people were responding. It wasn't clear, except that humans and reptile shared some bond of communication.

The three crewmen had been crossing the clearing when the natives had risen silently from high clumps of grass and advanced on them. Soong had drawn his beamer and burned the ground before them, but the natives had merely spread out. One had grabbed at Jemal and had been cut by a powerblade. Jemal had lost his beamer in the river. Then the Tyrannosaur had stood up. It had been lying in a slight depression, surrounded by tall grass. With its head out of sight, they had taken it for an outcropping of rock. Standing, its head was seven meters from the ground. Soong trained his beamer on it.

"Not a chance," Jemal had said quietly. "Not with a hand beamer. Even if you kill it, it'll swallow us before it knows it's dead."

They had handed their weapons over. The natives had taken them in phlegmatic silence, like men performing a tedious chore. They hadn't made any attempt to communicate; they had picked up the three men like so much baggage and tied them into the bizarre dinosaur saddle.

The man who had been cut bound up his bloody wounds with no show of suffering.

Now the monster straightened, its head disappearing into the obscurity above the firelight. It seemed satisfied with its inspection. Jemal scooted on his bottom until his back touched the nearest tree trunk.

"They just picked us up," he said, not for the first time. "It's like they were sent to get us."

"Yes," Soong said, "but by whom?"

By whom indeed? And what kind of being had human-dinosaur teams as lackeys? A nut landed on Jemal's head and he grimaced. That was all he needed. Probably the rest of *Eurynome*'s crew were dead; he was trapped on an impossible world, prisoner of humans and dinosaurs; his only companions were an assassin and a talking tinshop; a little bomb was planted in his head, a sadistic, maniacal tyrant holding its control; and now a nut had fallen on his head. He could just cry.

Then another, bigger nut fell on his head. That was too much. He looked up into the tree. Somebody was hanging from a branch by his tail up there, with a handful of nuts in one hand. He nudged Soong with a foot, raising his eyes and eyebrows skyward. The assassin looked up and caught sight of Alexander. He smiled, but neither made a sound. Alexander made a circle of forefinger and thumb, the ancient human sign that everything was under control. Jemal sincerely doubted it, but he was willing to play along if the monkey-boy could just get them out of their predicament. He made frantic mouthings of "Who else is with you?"

Alexander held up a single finger, then made a very ancient cursive gesture of both hands, indicating the body of an extraordinarily voluptuous woman. Jemal risked a low *meow* sound and Alexander shook his head vigorously, holding both palms cupped almost at arm's length from his chest. Jemal looked at Soong.

"It's just the kid with Mirabelle," he muttered. "I wish it were Hack. Even the cat-woman would be better."

"You are difficult to please, my friend," said Soong. "I myself am overjoyed to find that any of our comrades are alive at all."

"Don't get me wrong," Jemal said. "I like the kid, and anyplace else I'd take Mirabelle over any number of Felids. It's just that Hack's an old friend, and as much as I detest her, I think Rama's a good person to have guarding your back in a tight spot."

"In the absence of the persons of our choice," Soong said, "I suggest that we accept this unlooked-for reunion with our shipmates in a spirit of becoming modesty and gratitude."

"God," Jemal fumed, "can't you ever express a thought without a lot of pompous bullshit?"

"I express myself in a concise and economical manner," Soong said primly. "I would think that you—"

"Hey, you two!" Alexander said in an urgent whisper. "Can you shut up for a while? Look, I got a powerblade. I can be down and slit your ropes before your buddies there catch on. Can you pick up Rand and fade back into the brush? If you can't, we'll have to leave him here."

Jemal looked at Soong. "Do you think we can carry him? I hate to leave a shipmate behind, but if he can't carry his weight, which looks considerable, better that two of us get away than all three stay in custody."

"I think we can carry him," Soong said, lying with an arm pillowing his head, as though murmuring pleasantries before going to sleep. "In any case, we need not go far before returning his various circuits to full power."

"That could take a while," Jemal said. "In any case,

he doesn't move at really high speed even at full power.''
He sighed. "Hell. I guess you're right. Can't just leave
him here, can we? Okay. When the kid cuts our ropes, I'll
grab the arm and leg on this side, you grab the ones on
your side, okay?''

"Exactly my thought," Soong replied.

"Then we light out for the forest like stripe-assed apes,
right?''

"I could not have put it better myself," said Soong.
Shortly Alexander was behind them and there was a faint
crackle and a stench of burning hair as the ropes were
severed. After that the monkey-boy went quickly back up
into the tree. Nobody seemed to have noticed a thing.
Quietly, naturally, as if it were the most natural thing in
the world, Jemal and Soong each grabbed an arm and a
plated thigh of the Tesla specialist, stood up . . . and ran.

For a moment there was a stunned quiet. Then the
natives leaped to their feet, yammering. With somewhat
more deliberation, the Tyrannosaur lurched to a standing
position and stared into the forest. It gave vent to a
wheezing, honking call before stumbling forward to smash
into the tree line. For a few seconds all was pandemonium,
and during those seconds Jemal and Soong made their
escape.

"I hope that thing doesn't have good night vision,"
Jemal panted. Even though their burden was surprisingly
light, carrying it between them made running awkward.

"Put me down and turn my power up!" Rand ordered.

"Are you kidding?" Jemal demanded. "We're stopping
for nothing." He fiddled with the controls at Rand's belt.
"Okay, you're on. When we drop you, you better hit the
ground running, because I'm not slowing down." They
flopped him over and let him go. After a few stumbling
steps, Rand had his stride and was keeping up.

"What happened back there?" demanded the metallic voice.

"Simple," Soong said gasping slightly now as he tried to push vegetation out of his way without slowing down. "We were held prisoner by savages and a dinosaur until the monkey-boy dropped out of a tree and cut us loose. We've been running ever since."

"Anything else you want to know?" gasped Jemal.

"I'm sorry I asked. Where are we headed?"

"Away," Jemal said. "Now shut up and run!"

They crashed through the brush, wheezing and terrified. Jemal caught a low branch across the chin and fell backward, landing with the wind knocked out of him. Then a pair of hands were beneath his armpits, yanking him to his feet. Dazedly he wondered which of his companions was helping him, and then he saw that it was Alexander. He wondered briefly where the kid had come from.

Minutes later Jemal came across Soong, collapsed next to Rand in a small clearing. In relief he sank down beside them.

"How far behind us are they?" Soong asked when he had his breath.

"I don't know," Jemal managed. Alexander dropped from a tree limb and walked over to them.

"Where've you been?" Jemal asked.

"I been keeping up with you in the trees. It's lots easier going up there. You don't need to worry about the big lizard and his friends. They took a wrong turn just after you left. Guess they don't see so good in the dark."

"Why didn't you say something then?" Jemal asked, choking on rage.

"Actually, you was kind of fun to watch, stumbling around like that. Why ruin the show?"

"You little half-ape bastard," Jemal said. "Just wait

until I can stand up again. I'll strangle you with your own tail. I'll cut your lungs out and fry them with—''

"That's gratitude for you," Alexander said. "Next time I'll just let the damn lizard eat you. A couple days later I'd trip over you someplace in the jungle and I'd look down at that pile of lizard shit, and you know what I'd say? I'd say: 'Hey, Jemal, you sure ain't changed much.' '' He fell all over himself laughing and Jemal started crawling toward him with a murderous look on his face.

"Will you people quiet down!" hissed Mirabelle. She stepped into the clearing. "A tracking satellite could hear you from a low orbit." She walked over to Jemal and kicked him hard in the ribs. "Leave Alexander alone. He just saved your neck. He's in better shape than you are right now, and in case you hadn't noticed, he's the one with the powerblade."

Jemal groaned. "This hasn't been my day."

Alexander sat on a limb, leaning back against a trunk, his head cradled in interlaced fingers. He was enjoying the fading remnants of the nightly planet show. A really spectacular green orb was just disappearing beyond the mountain range to the north. His companions were still sleeping on the ground below. They'd told him to wake them at first light, but it wasn't quite bright enough yet. He'd found this spot the previous night. It was on a spit of land extending out into the river and surrounded by marshy ground that looked too soft to be crossed by the dinosaur or anything else of comparable size.

"Hello."

Alexander had the powerblade out and humming so fast that he was surprised to find it in his hand. The voice had come from somewhere in the tree—a voice he'd never heard before. He strained to see in the dim light. There was something out there on the end of the branch.

"Who the hell're you?" he demanded, heart hammering.

"Why, I am the archetypal messenger."

"Arche . . . what? Come on, talk simple or I'll have to wake up my educated friends to interpret. Matter of fact, that sounds like a good idea anyway." He called down: "Hey, we got a visitor! Wake up!" The snoring below didn't break rhythm.

"You needn't bother," the visitor said. "They won't awaken until I leave."

"Is there some point to all this?" Alexander asked. "I mean, this is dramatic as hell, with you out there where I can't quite see you and my friends sleeping real peaceful-like down there, but wouldn't it make more sense to just come walking in when it's light and declare yourself?"

"You astonish me!" the messenger reproved. "Have you no sense of style? Are you so mean-souled and plod-ding that you've lost the love of mystery?"

"Look, mister, all I want is a soft berth on a good ship, and I think that goes for my friends too. We want off this place and back to real space, where real rules apply. This never-never land is driving us nuts."

"If you want those things, they must be earned."

Alexander stared hard. The light was growing and the shape at the end of the limb was taking on form and a little color. It was male, like the voice, and he was sure dressed funny.

"Are you Xeus?" Alexander asked.

The messenger laughed merrily. "Oh, gracious goodness, no! I am merely his messenger."

"Well, what say you deliver your message? My butt's getting sore from sitting on this limb."

"Peremptory, aren't you?" the messenger sniffed. "I

always said that no good would come of cultivating you people. Oh, very well. You are to ascend the peak called the Fang, in the range called God's Teeth, if you would meet with the great Xeus.''

"How're we to recognize this Fang?" Alexander asked. "There's a whole bunch of mountains up north." Then another thought occurred to him. "Wait a minute. What about the other two who were with us? We haven't seen them since—'' but the messenger was no longer there.

Alexander woke the others and told them what had happened.

"It seems to fit with everything else that's happened since we got here," Jemal said. He seemed to be over his anger of the night before, but Alexander kept a low branch handy just in case.

"Could you see much of what he looked like?" Mirabelle asked.

"It got light enough to make out a little. I never seen anybody dressed like that. He was light-skinned, no beard or mustache but bushy side-whiskers. His clothes were some kind of cloth. It looked awful old-fashioned, all wrinkly and creased like it was made out of real plant fiber or animal hair. He had tube pants on and little leather shoes that looked shiny. The coat was real funny. Up on the chest it had flaps that turned back like this''— he made descriptive hand motions —"and down below there was two taillike pieces that hung below the branch. His shirt looked white and he had a puffy scarf kind of thing stuck into it, with a pearl or something jabbed in the middle of it. He had a shirt collar with long points that just about touched his ears, and he was wearing white gloves and a vest with a little chain across his belly. And you think the rest of him was funny-looking, wait'll I tell you about his hat.''

"Let me guess," Jemal said. "Was it tall and almost cylindrical, but flaring a little at the crown, with a slightly rolled brim? And did it look like it was made of a rough, nappy substance like felt?''

"You saw him too?" Alexander asked suspiciously. "I thought you was asleep.''

"What you're describing is a Western gentleman of about the Byronic period, say early nineteenth century. Earlier the pants would've come to just below the knees. Later the hat would have been made of silk.''

"If Xeus really sent him," Mirabelle said, "he must be absolutely nutty for theatrical trappings.''

"We already knew that," Soong said. "Witness what we've seen so far: a mixture of the historical, the mythical and the utterly alien.''

"I don't think he was really there," Alexander said. "I think he was some kind of projection.''

"Why do you say that?" Jemal asked.

"Well, he sure looked solid, especially the way his coattails hung down over the limb, but he was sitting on the same limb as me and I never felt anything when he appeared nor when he went. It ain't all that big a limb. I would've felt anything a tenth of that weight on it.''

"Good point," Mirabelle said. "Now we know Xeus is probably watching us if he has instruments of such sophistication.''

"Real comforting," Alexander said.

"I suppose that mountain range to the north must be God's Teeth," Rand said. "But how are we supposed to know which one is the Fang? He didn't leave us a map, did he?''

"Haven't you figured out how this place works yet?"

Jemal asked. He pulled on a boot. "We march to that range and we look for the tallest, ugliest, meanest, most unclimbable peak anywhere to be seen. That'll be the Fang."

Nobody challenged his logic.

ELEVEN

Haakon moved as quietly as he could. He had fallen into a rhythm of movement, based on the limits of his vision. He would scan ahead and listen, and when he was satisfied that there was no danger, he would move forward cautiously. Then he would halt, watch and listen again. It was natural to this environment, where a constant lookout was necessary to survival. On a civilized world one could just amble along any old way, with body on autopilot and brain in neutral. Here it would be fatal.

Rama was behind him. He couldn't hear her and he didn't look back at her, not wanting to take his attention off his surroundings for even a second. She had the beamer. She was faster with it than he was, and also more accurate. Not that he was any slouch, but he figured that since he was point man, he would be more likely to get into trouble than she, and she would be better at shooting the trouble off him. That was the idea anyway. He wasn't really sure of her loyalty yet, but he had to display a certain amount of trust or there could be no cooperation at all.

Rama ducked soundlessly beneath a branch Haakon had pushed aside. Her eyes were slitted and she was listening in all directions. They'd seen nothing of the others, but that didn't bother her. She could get along without them just fine. All she wanted was a ship away from this place, to take her back to her beautiful *Eurynome*.

Then she remembered Rand, the Tesla man. She was no engineer. Maybe she needed him after all. Probably Haakon too, since she wasn't a pilot. With such a ship and with those two in suitably subordinate positions, she would have the nucleus of a really potent gang. Actually Soong might not be a bad man to have around either. He was, after all, a trained assassin, and it often paid to have one of those among the membership. But not Mirabelle. She could think of no earthly use for Mirabelle. Certainly the woman was a splendid thief in her own right, but Rama preferred to deal in fine goods such as jewels and art works and other desirable commodities she could touch and see and smell for herself. Technical data seemed so drab and boring, however valuable.

She watched Haakon as he went before her. He really wasn't too objectionable, for an ape. He moved well; he was strong and quick; and he didn't stand around dithering when there was immediate action to be taken. And he was certainly tough. He had to be, to have survived so long in the Bahadur slave pits. She shuddered involuntarily at the thought of how close she had come to going into those pits herself. Not that she wouldn't have survived too, but she couldn't stand to think of having all her beautiful hair stripped off, probably her claws surgically removed as well. Worst of all, the confinement of prison. Felids never made good prisoners, and she was wilder than most.

No, there was no doubt that Haakon was a good man, for an ape. The problem was that he would make a fine lieutenant, but he was boss instead. That she didn't like. She was born to lead and he just wouldn't acknowledge it. Then she remembered how he had struck her, and a low growling started in her throat. She took a close sight on his broad back and considered a quick, silent rush with claws out. Not to kill him of course; he was too valuable. For that she could use the beamer. But just to teach him a lesson.

"Don't even think it, you whisker-nosed bitch," he said.

Damn! The man really was acute, she had to admit. "You couldn't have heard me," she said, not even trying to protest innocence.

"I smelled you. Same smell you always put out when you're about to attack."

She fumed. That was one place where the geneticists had gone wrong. The smells were fine for lovemaking and for most other things, but they made it impossible for a Felid to hide its emotions.

The exchange didn't cause them to relax their caution. Every few steps they scanned the branches overhead. From time to time Rama would stop and turn, looking back along the way they had come. Cautious as they were, the next inhabitant they encountered still took them by surprise.

Haakon was stepping around a knee-high rock when it unfolded. He whirled with the powerblade out and jumped back to give Rama a clear shot at whatever it was. The rock continued to unfold—until finally they saw a short, man-shaped creature little more than a meter tall. It had been sitting on the ground with its face against its knees, its long arms wrapped about itself. Its skin was gray, and except for parts of the face, it was covered with mossy, gray-green hair. It blinked at him with shiny black eyes.

"Who the hell are you?" Haakon demanded.

"Why should I tell you?" it said in a voice that might have come from the bottom of a well. "This ain't your forest, is it? No, this is my forest, so let's hear your name first."

"What have we found?" Rama asked, amused.

"I don't know, but he doesn't want to cooperate," Haakon said. "You *are* male, aren't you?" Except for the beard, there was nothing visible to indicate sex.

"Of course!" The little man looked offended. "How about you?"

"Same here," Haakon said. He nodded toward Rama. "But she's female. See? We're making progress already. Now, since this is your parlor, my name's Haakon and this is Rama, and we're looking for somebody called Xeus. Know where we might find him?"

The mannikin clapped his hands and capered about. "Want to find Xeus, do you? In trouble, are you? Hee, hee!"

"Look, homunculus," Haakon said, his patience wearing thin, "it tickles me no end that you find us amusing, but we'd like some answers."

"Let me burn his toes some," Rama said, fingering the beamer. "I'll bet we learn everything he knows by the third toe."

The little man waddled over to her and looked up. Standing at his full height, the backs of his knuckles touched the ground. "Burn our toes, will we?" he said merrily. Then, with the tiniest flex of his huge feet, he sprang to her shoulders, wrapped his long arms about her head and planted a huge, wet, slobbery kiss on her lips. She fought mightily to tear him loose, but even her great strength was insufficient. Then he jumped away, leaving her squalling and rubbing at her mouth with her sleeve.

"Disgusting creature!" she screeched. "I'll kill you! Where are you?" She looked about wildly, but the dwarf had disappeared.

"Before you kill him," Haakon said, "where's the beamer?"

She looked numbly at her empty hand, then turned on Haakon, snarling. "What were you doing while I was being attacked, you bald person? What use are you? I'd be better off alone."

"I was looking out for real danger," he said, carefully keeping his voice level and his face serious. Inside, it was another story altogether.

"After all, surely you're equal to the threat posed by a little hairy, one-meter male human."

She radiated a scent fit to flatten trees and her claws came out; her hair stood on end and she hissed. She was about to go into one of the legendary Felid conniptions and Haakon wondered whether he might have gone too far. He looked for a good tree to climb.

"Hee, hee." The voice came from somewhere nearby.

Rama's hair slowly lowered and her scent abated. When she spoke, her voice was quiet but her claws were still out. "Where are you?" she demanded.

"Behind you."

She whirled . . . and froze when she saw him holding the beamer. From within his beard he produced a stubby little pipe and stuck it in the hole in his whiskers where his mouth presumably was. Flicking the beamer to lowest power, he lit his pipe with it. When the weed was going properly, he tossed the weapon back to Rama. She turned it to full power and pointed it at him but Haakon snatched it away from her.

"Hold your temper," he told her. "We still want some answers from him."

"I've had none from you yet," the dwarf said, puffing contentedly. "Names'll do for a start. Mine's Troll."

"It fits," Haakon said. "I'm Haakon. That's *Captain* Haakon, of the *Eurynome,* currently on detached service for the Cingulum."

"I got the Haakon part," Troll said. "Ain't sure what a captain is, nor a eurynome, nor a cingulum."

"Not important at this juncture," Haakon said. "The lady is Rama."

Troll smiled up at her. "Pleased to meet you." She fumed.

"Now we're really getting somewhere," Haakon said. "Since you're feeling talkative, how about telling us where we are?"

Troll took his pipe from his mouth and made a sweeping circle with its stem. "This here's Troll's Wood." He replaced the pipe and puffed.

"I'll try to keep it simple. How do we find Xeus?"

Troll pointed with his pipestem again, this time to the north. "Go that way."

"How far?" Haakon asked patiently.

Troll shrugged. "Can't say. Old Xeus ain't nailed down to one spot. He lives up that way though."

"Thanks," Haakon said. He turned to Rama. "Let's go." They started to walk away.

"Up in them mountains," Troll said after them.

Haakon stopped and turned. "Mountains, you say?"

Troll nodded, puffing away. "Big range called God's Teeth."

"God's Teeth. Thank you. We'll keep an eye out for a big mountain range." He cocked his head at Rama and walked away again.

"Peak called the Fang," Troll called after them. Haakon stopped and turned again.

"The Fang. We'll find Xeus there?"

Troll shrugged once more. "Dunno. Might not be at home."

"Of course. Then we'll just have to sit on his doorstep. Thanks again." They moved away and when Rama looked back, the little man was gone.

They continued their cautious progress until late afternoon. Before they halted for the evening, they could see a mountain range looming in the distance. As had become their custom, Haakon built a fire while Rama hunted. She came back with something that might have been a sort of pig except that it had a pair of stubby tentacles flanking its snout. It tasted fine though. They bedded down for the night and when they awoke the next morning, Troll was squatting by the embers of the fire.

"What are you doing here?" Haakon asked, surprised.

"You might find him easier was I to go along with you."

"Why would you want to help us?" Haakon asked.

"Life gets boring," Troll answered.

"I can believe that, you small, hairy and ugly creature," Rama said. Turning to Haakon, "You don't intend to let this smelly thing accompany us, do you?"

"Things might go easier with a guide," Haakon pointed out.

"I don't trust him," she protested.

"You don't trust me either," Haakon said. "And since I don't trust you, that makes us all even."

"But you and I are stuck together," she said. "Why compound our miseries with this unnecessary being? It is of doubtful use and of no aesthetic value whatsoever."

"Don't mind her," Haakon said to Troll. "It's just one of her fetching little ways. She really likes you, but she's too shy to admit it."

Rama hissed at them both, then walked down to the river to wash herself.

"How did you know how to use a beamer?" Haakon asked when she was gone.

"That thing I lit my pipe with? Just seemed like the right way to use it."

"And you never used one before?"

"Never even seen one before. Want some grub?" He held out a fiber-net bag of fruit and tubers and a couple of fish that were still wiggling.

Haakon took one of the fish by the tail between thumb and forefinger and held it at arm's length, eyeing it doubtfully. "I'm not sure I can scale this with a power-blade."

Phlegmatically Troll produced a little knife of flaked stone from inside his beard. With a few astonishingly swift and practiced motions, he scaled and gutted the fish. With equal facility he whittled a pair of forked sticks and propped the fish over the coals with their bellies spread open. While Troll built up the fire, Haakon examined the little knife. It seemed to be made of obsidian, beautifully flaked to a feather edge. It was fragile but would cut with more precision than a powerblade or steel. Troll tossed the tubers into the bed of coals and peeled some of the fruit.

"Have you ever seen Xeus?" Haakon asked.

"Nope. Always wanted to though. I hear he knows all sorts of things. Maybe I can ask him something."

"Like what?"

"Dunno. I'll think of something, I expect."

Haakon pointed at the tubers in the coals. "What are these?"

"Taters."

"How can we tell when they're done?"

"You'll know."

Rama returned from the river, looking displeased to find Troll still there. She brightened at the food though.

"So you are going to let him travel with us?" she asked Haakon as she tore into a fish.

"He's a free man or whatever. He can go where he wants to. If that happens to be where we're going, who're we to stop him? Besides, I think he can vary our diet agreeably." As though to confirm this, the tubers popped amid the coals, splitting open and exposing a puffy mass of starchy white pulp. Troll took one from the fire, brushed the ashes from its peel and began to eat it, peel and all.

Haakon tried to imitate him but had to drop the tuber when it scorched his fingers. When it had cooled sufficiently, he brushed it off and bit into it. Although it burned his tongue, it was delicious, a little like fresh-baked bread and something else that he couldn't identify. He wondered if this was another copy of something that grew somewhere out in the real universe. Rama nibbled daintily at one of the tubers but didn't share Haakon's relish.

When they were finished, Troll doused the fire and cleared away the remains of their breakfast, carrying them down to the river. When he tossed them in, swarms of little fish obliterated the scraps within seconds. He scattered the fast-cooling ashes, and when he was finished, only an expert tracker could have seen that there had been a recent camp. Haakon nodded his approval. Troll was going to be handy to have around.

They resumed their northward progress, moving faster now because Troll led them on the best paths, cutting away from the river. His stumpy legs carried him as fast as their long ones, and he was just as cautious as they were.

Once, in the early afternoon, he halted them and faded from the trail. They followed him wordlessly into an outcropping of rock on a nearby slope and crouched there without speaking.

Rama's impatience got to her at last. "What is it?" she whispered. Troll inclined his head so slightly that the motion was barely discernible. She looked in the direction he indicated, and froze.

A hundred meters away a massive, reptilian head was looming above the treetops. It turned from side to side, looking over the whole forest with a dreadful air of intelligence and purpose. Even from a distance they could see the thing's teeth; it was no plant-eater. They stayed hidden and watched it for an hour, until it was out of sight. Then they waited for another hour before finally relaxing, massaging stiffened and cramped muscles.

"What was it?" Haakon asked.

"Big lizard," Troll said.

"Even I saw that. What kind of big lizard?"

"Can't say. Keep out of their way myself, every chance I get."

"That thing wasn't just cruising for food," Rama said. "It was looking for something, or someone."

"Could be," Troll answered. "Only saw its head though. Couldn't see was there anyone riding it."

Haakon looked at Rama. "Who rides a thing like that?" He was certain he already knew the answer.

Sure enough, Troll said: "Big-lizard riders."

Haakon groaned. "Describe them."

"Like you two. Uglier. Painted up."

"Those lizards—" Rama said, looking a little pale, "—do they get any bigger?"

"Lots bigger," Troll assured her. "That 'un wasn't very big at all."

He led them back to the trail and they followed him very, very quietly.

As they traveled, Haakon tried to draw the grunting, monosyllabic little man out, but he didn't get much for his efforts. Troll's urge to communicate was spotty at best; his curiosity was haphazard; and his motives were murky. It was that last factor that worried Haakon. Just why was Troll tagging along with them? Boredom, as he claimed? Maybe, but it seemed unlikely. Was he, like the Ancestor, another of the explorers sent by the Cingulum to probe Meridian? Again maybe, but which one? Without the G-102's memory readings, he had no data to figure on. Troll's familiarity with the beamer argued for that interpretation, but anybody who could create Leviathan and freak banana trees and dinosaurs could certainly build a dwarf with a few selective memories and skills. In any case, he wasn't taking the little man's presence as lightly as he pretended. He'd lived too long to be that gullible.

Three days of exhausting travel brought them to the foot of the mountain range called God's Teeth. Along the way there had been some narrow escapes, and twice more they had encountered the patrolling dinosaurs. Each had slightly differed from the others, but all were big toothy carnivores.

They found no sign of their companions. By mutual consent Haakon and Rama had said nothing to Troll about the others. It seemed like a sensible precaution since there might be some danger to their friends in letting the little man know of their existence. His motivations were still suspect.

Haakon looked along the crests of the range. They were impressive but not quite what he'd expected here, where everything seemed to be outsized or otherwise outrageous.

"Which one's the Fang?" he asked Troll.

"Oh, them there's the little mountains, the baby ones. On past them's the big ones. Daddy of 'em all's the Fang. You'll see him from the top of these."

"Somehow I knew you'd say that. Ready for a little climb, m'dear?" he asked.

Rama shrugged resignedly. "Having no choice, yes. It seems I must endure your company a little longer. Anything has to be better than this riverside jungle."

Haakon winced. "Never say a thing like that."

Troll nodded sagely. "It'll get lots worse."

"Have you ever been up there, little man?" Rama asked.

"Nope. Most places're worse than Troll's Wood though. I heered these mountains got things in 'em to curl your hair and freeze your blood." Then he loosed one of his inappropriate chuckles.

"Merry little soul, aren't you?" Rama said. "Tell me, just who does a solitary sort like you hear these things from?"

"Others," Troll replied. And that was all he would say on the subject.

They camped and rested for the remainder of the day. On the next day they began their climb. Within an hour they had passed out of the near-tropical vegetation of the river bottom and into a towering forest, where the trees were far more widely spaced. They were gigantic, making the biggest trees of the lowland seem puny by comparison. Their branches started more than a hundred meters up and interlaced so thickly that little sunlight got through, leaving clear ground below, almost free of underbrush. It made the going easier, although the land was steep, and it made them nervous that there was so little cover should they be attacked.

Once, during a break, Haakon paced around one of the bigger trees. It took him seventy paces to make the circuit. The tree was covered with thick, soft, grayish bark. He rapped it with his fist and his hand sunk in to the wrist. He returned to his companions.

"I know it's getting to sound a little repetitious," he said, "but the trees should be getting smaller as we climb, not bigger. The soil is thinner on mountainsides, and those trees must need tremendous roots."

"It's just like the palms, and you know it," Rama said. "It's not a tree; it's something twisted to look like one. Down below it there must be another tangle of snakes and crystals. This place is so frightening that your brain insists on interpreting things as they seem while you're still trying to make it all fit into your old nature lessons. Nothing here is what it looks like, including him." She gave Troll a nod. "You'd do well to keep that in mind."

Haakon was annoyed, but he knew she was right. The trees, the animals, they all *looked* so real, so natural, albeit exaggerated and out of place. He had to keep reminding himself that they were all part of somebody's incomprehensible game. He had a sneaking hunch that the gamester was somebody named Xeus.

Troll looked back and forth from one to the other in puzzlement. "I'm Troll," he said, "and them's trees. What's so hard to figure?"

"Either you know, little man," Rama said, "in which case you'll keep up your pretense, or else you're as ignorant as you sound and it would take us much, much too long to tell you about it."

She and Haakon stood up to resume their climb and Troll arose to waddle along beside them, shaking his head philosophically at the strange doings of the aliens.

The light was dimming a little and they were looking for a good campsite near a stream when they came across the statue. It was carved of a green, jadelike stone in the form of a squatting, vaguely froglike creature. It was about chest-high to Haakon. It wasn't truly froglike, but the squatting posture made it seem so, and the flat, triangular head added to the illusion. Framing the lips, however, was a squirmy mass of tentacles, and it had what might have been atrophied wings on its back, a real peculiarity on something clearly not designed to fly. It gripped the edge of its short pedestal with massive clawed toes. Most peculiar of all was the smoke coming from its flared nostrils.

"I never expected it to happen so soon," Rama said, looking from the statue to Troll. "I've finally seen something uglier than you."

"Where's the smoke coming from?" Haakon queried of nobody in particular. "Troll, have you ever seen anything like this?"

"Nope," Troll said, shaking his head. "Don't like it neither. Let's don't stay here tonight."

"That suits me," Haakon said, "but first I want to examine this thing." He looked all over it but could find no entrance where material could be introduced for burning. "The smoke must be coming from below," he announced at last. "Come on and help me tip it over." Troll backed away, shaking his head, but Rama put her shoulder to the statue and they struggled to tilt it.

"Why do people persist in making things as hideous as this?" Rama said, gasping explosively with the effort. "I've seen art galleries full of this kind of ugliness. Are we Felids the only true lovers of beauty?"

"Hold it right there," Haakon said, sweating profusely, "I think I can get down and see under it now."

"Better look quick," she managed to strain out between clenched teeth. "I can't hold it long."

He flattened and looked under it and saw only blank stone. Then he shoved himself away as the statue came crashing back down. Rama caught a noseful of the smoke before she could spring back and was coughing and sneezing as she rubbed her hands together, trying to get some blood back into them after the strain. "Curiosity satisfied?" she said at last.

"No," Haakon replied. "I still can't figure where the smoke is coming from."

"From some pit in hell, I think," she said. "It smells awful! Let's get away from here."

"Not a bad idea," Haakon concurred. "We might have just profaned somebody's pet idol."

"Bright of you to think of that so quickly," she said.

They walked on for another half-hour before they found a good spot to camp and began to arrange their bedding. Troll waddled off to find dinner. The little man could always come up with something where the other two would have hunted helplessly for hours and found nothing.

"Do we dare start a fire where it's so open?" Rama asked. Her voice sounded a little odd, but he couldn't put his finger on it just how. "There's whoever made that idol to consider too."

Haakon gathered wood. "Hell, I'm tired of skulking, and that statue's probably just one of Xeus's little jokes anyway. Maybe he'll come to us if he can see us from a distance."

He drew his beamer and flashed the wood into flame, relishing his sense of recklessness. He sat near the fire and Rama sat uncharacteristically close to him. When she looked at him, he saw that her pupils were dilated into enormous disks. He squinted at the lowering sun. It was too early for that; her eyes should still be slits. Then he caught the scent and it threw him back to the day they were first boarded by the Cingulum picket-ship. Surreptitiously, but desperately, his hand stole into his pocket, searching for his nose filters. Faking a sneeze, he stuffed them in behind his shielding palm.

"You know, you're not so bad for an ape," Rama said, purring loudly and rubbing herself against him.

Then he caught it. "The smoke! It was that damned smoke from the idol! You caught a snoot full of it and it's made you horny! Well, maybe another time, but this isn't it, and I don't care for chemical inducements."

She rammed two claw-tipped fingers into his nostrils and they emerged with the filters impaled on their tips. Flipping them away, she wrapped a python-powerful arm about his shoulders as her other hand yanked down the fastening of his coverall. "What's wrong with chemical inducements, Captain, darling? They're a specialty of mine."

Then the wave of overpowering pheromone hit him and, lacking any choice, he cooperated with the inevitable.

An hour later Troll came back to the campsite with his bag full of oversized nuts and a medium-sized furry animal over his shoulder. "Beasts is wary hereabout," he said. "Had to roam far." He dumped his burdens and sniffed suspiciously. "Smells funny here." Then he caught sight of Haakon, whose visible parts were covered with claw marks; he looked quickly at Rama, who was unmarked but bore a look of intense smugness.

"Looks like you two been fighting and she won, hee, hee!" He went into transports of mirth.

"Something like that," Haakon said. "What's for supper?"

Later, settling back to sleep with a comfortably full stomach but hurting everywhere else, he heard her whisper in his ear: "Not bad, for an ape."

TWELVE

"You took advantage of me," she hissed at him the next day as they resumed their climb. "You took advantage of my drugged state and ravished me."

"Took advantage of you!" he exclaimed, trying to keep his voice low so that Troll, who trudged ahead, would not hear. "*Your* drugged state! How about that brew of aphrodisiacs you hit me with? You stuck your fingers up my nose halfway to my esophagus to snag my filters out so you could land on me like a she-boar in heat, you randy alley cat! Is it my fault that that stone frog's smoke lit you up like a whorehouse sign?"

"Are you referring to my pheromones, you odious primate? Those are perfectly natural body chemicals that help to raise my race above yours!"

"You weren't complaining about it yesterday!" he yelled quietly. "You were pretty enthusiastic, as a matter of fact, even though you clawed me half to ribbons."

"Enthusiastic!" she shrieked, all restraint gone. "That

smoke had me so ripped I'd have told Troll he was a lover worthy to couch a goddess! And as for those scratches, a male of my race would have considered them affectionate love pats and responded in kind, unlike you, you clawless, fumbling, awkward idiot!''

The exchange might have gone on for some time had they not been attacked at that moment.

The attackers did not, for a change, arrive on animals, mythical or prosaic. Instead they were in bizarre machines. The first came cruising low between the trees, weaving in and out among them like a demented skier. They heard a squawk from Troll and looked up from their bickering just in time to see him dive for the ground as something glittery swooped over his head and dove straight for them. Haakon broke to the right and Rama to the left. They both hit the ground rolling and came up behind trees. Rama was holding the beamer, her slit pupils darting from side to side, in search of enemies.

Haakon had the powerblade in his fist and was feeling a bit underarmed. ''What the hell was *that?*'' There was no sign of the thing in any direction.

Then three of them came whizzing in among the trees; the only sound they made was the whoosh of displaced air. These were moving slower than the first and Haakon could get a better look at them. The craft resembled a conventional ship's scout sled, but they were not made of any conventional metals, plastics or other synthetics. From every part of the craft glittered gold, platinum, gems, precious substances of every description. The riders were harder to make out. There were three to a craft and they were dressed in armor as bizarre as their sleds. From time to time they popped away with long weapons that sounded and behaved like old-fashioned rifles, complete with smoke.

Rama squalled and hissed, firing the beamer every chance

she got, but the bewildering movement of the sleds made accurate marksmanship difficult. The hunters were doing much better. Their missiles were whacking into the soft bark of the tree Haakon was trying to shield himself with, and some of the shots were landing distressingly near him. All he could do was try to keep the trunk between himself and the sleds.

Rama darted away from her tree, trying desperately for a straight shot. Two of the sleds peeled off and the third darted away from her, turned, and headed straight for her in a relatively slow charge at low altitude. Haakon watched, gaping. It looked for all the world like two knights squaring off for a joust. Rama went down on one knee and held the beamer straight out before her in both hands, forefinger on the firing stud. Several shots came from the sled but she didn't flinch. When the sled was no more than ten meters away, she fired. The helmet of the apparent driver fused and exploded, and at the same instant Rama dove to one side. Her dive took her straight into the path of a bullet. It struck her high on the right shoulder, tumbling her into an awkward spin, the beamer flying from her hand to land many meters away.

The sleds began to close in again. Haakon broke cover and ran to Rama. He had almost run for the beamer instead and knew that he might soon regret his ordering of priorities. She was sprawled, cursing, on the dense leaf-mold, half-stunned, one hand clutching her shoulder. Haakon got an arm under her and tried to get her to her feet. There was no way he could carry her; she would have to hoof it herself or stay.

"Come on!" he shouted. "Running's our only chance!"

The sleds were settling around them at a range of about twenty meters. Rama tried to lurch to her feet, but her unfocused eyes betrayed her dizziness. She ripped something free from her shoulder and stared at it lying in her palm. It was a small pellet of solid gold, once spherical and now slightly flattened from striking the armorcloth. It bore no rifling marks.

"*Muskets!*" Haakon exclaimed. "They're firing muskets at us!"

Rama muttered incoherently. It was plain that she wouldn't be running anywhere for some time to come. He couldn't do her any good. He was about to drop her and run when he saw the circle of hunters. More of the silent rafts were settling in around them. He'd had his chance to run and had made the wrong choice. He'd just have to live with it.

They were as weird-looking as anything he had encountered so far. They were human-shaped and human-sized, but not a square centimeter of skin was visible. All was covered by metallic armor so baroque in design that it was difficult to tell whether it was functional or purely decorative. It was not flexible like his armorcloth, but made up of intricately jointed plates that were etched, engraved, repousséd, inlaid, chased, acid-washed and otherwise decorated in fantastic designs. The helmets had face plates that lacked any holes for sight, hearing or breathing. If the contents were human, the suits had to be more sophisticated than they looked on the outside.

"All right," Haakon said, to break the silence. "Are you going to kill us, or what?"

Some stubborn if somewhat self-destructive streak in his makeup kept him from dropping Rama and running for it or else attacking. After all, they only had muskets, notoriously slow weapons to get into action. He didn't though. And the sleds and armored suits indicated that they might have more sophisticated weapons available to them. And furthermore, since there was a little cover in these open woods, they would undoubtedly find it relatively easy to run him down in the swift sleds.

But mostly, he finally admitted to himself, he did not want to drop Rama in an undignified sprawl in front of these sadistic sportsmen. He owed her better than that, although for the life of him he couldn't imagine why. One of the hunters pointed at him and several others came forward. They grabbed Rama from him and she tried, weakly, to claw at them, but her claws slid from the metal without even scratching the decorations. Haakon's hands were jerked behind him and fastened somehow. He stood it resignedly. It was not as though being a prisoner was a new experience. He saw another armored hunter come up with Troll under an arm. The little man was bundled into his own net and was grumbling.

Haakon was led and Rama half-carried to a sled. They were fastened by their wrist bonds to crystal rings set into the craft's decking. Somehow it was not surprising to find that Rama's wrists were confined by golden chains. Troll was dumped in unceremoniously next to them. Apparently he was not enough of a threat to bother tying up.

As the sled lifted, Haakon examined it. It was luxurious almost beyond belief. The decking was of a beautiful, hand-rubbed wood he'd never seen before that glowed with streaks of yellow-brown in a darker red-brown matrix. The rails were of gold, although he saw a sled next to his with silver or platinum rails, and one beyond that with what might have been carved ruby. The steering rod looked like amber. He took a closer squint. Sure enough, he could see tiny preserved insects in it. The other controls were carved from coral or jade or jet. There were some archaic needle dials, and the indicator needles were of sapphire mounted on silver disks. The numerals were in a system Haakon was unfamiliar with, but they were inlaid with emerald. He was sorry that Rama was so groggy. She'd love this.

The oddest thing, though, was that the craft was just an ordinary ship's scout sled except for the fancy materials and trappings. It was as though somebody had mistakenly sent the design to a jeweler instead of to a shipwright.

There were three of the armored hunters in the sled with them. So far he had not heard a single word pass among them, but that was not necessarily significant. They probably used sensors in order to see and hear through the helmets, so communication devices were in order. And it was always possible that these were robots of some kind. He looked around to see if he could catch sight of the one Rama had blasted. It would be informative to see what was coming out of the stump where the helmet had been. It was not in sight though. Pity.

He played the events of the last hour through his mind, while they were still fresh. He had nothing better to do, and he had been taught in intelligence school to do just this, to fix things in his mind immediately after they happened. Even a wait of a few hours could rearrange things, make the sharp edges fuzzy, make changes in events on a basis of wishful thinking. One thing was certain: He thought of his captors as "hunters" for a reason. Their actions had not been those of soldiers or police. Almost everything they had done had been stylish but inefficient. They were the actions of people enacting a ritual, or a sport. Things had been done that had no purpose except to give the prey a slight chance, to make the game more exciting. If it was warfare, it was of the primitive, coup-counting kind that valued risk more than kills.

Above all, though, one sight stood out, burned into his memory as brightly as anything he had ever seen: It was that of Rama leaving the cover of her tree to kneel in a wide-open spot, bracing herself with perfect calm for one perfect shot at a machine bearing down remorselessly with her almost certain death. Gods, what guts the woman had! It was tactically ridiculous, but you didn't run across a sense of style like that very often.

"Hey, Troll," Haakon said. "Who are these people?"

"Dunno," Troll answered from inside his net bag. "Never seen 'em before. Mountain folk, most likely."

"Did you ever see machines like these where you live?"

"Nope. What's keeping 'em up?" The little man sounded puzzled but not frightened.

"It would take too long to tell you. Doesn't it scare you, flying around like this for the first time?"

"Seems like what these things should do. *They* wouldn't be in 'em if it weren't safe, now would they?"

It made sense, after a fashion. The sleds were progressing toward higher ground, climbing through the titanic trees to an area of snow above the timberline. It struck Haakon that since nothing else obeyed the rules, the tree line and snowcap were probably there for purely artistic purposes. Atmospheric considerations had no business here. Xeus or whoever could have put a desert or a tropical rain forest on top of this mountain if so inclined.

The sled rose over a saddle between two peaks and descended the opposite side, but not before Haakon caught a glimpse of a mountain range beyond that was higher than the one they had just crossed, a range much higher, and beyond that a single mountain that towered over them all just as the mountain trees had towered over those of the lowlands. Its sides were covered halfway up with vegetation; the rest was rock and snowfield. Above the snow was a vicious crag of rock, angled and canted grotesquely, its sheer sides slanting in twisted attitudes as though designed to defeat any effort to climb it. No question about it; that had to be the Fang.

Then they were descending rapidly into a valley that was filled with structures almost as elaborate as the sleds. Buildings were packed tier on tier up the steep sides of the mountain cleft, colorful with polished marbles, abrupt with oddly cantilevered balconies and ajangle with eye-boggling decorations. Fragrant smokes arose from braziers on the balconies and strange music came from inside the buildings. In the midst of the interlocked community there was a broad esplanade surrounded by sculptures, and it was on this plaza that the sleds set down. In the surrounding sculptures Haakon thought he could recognize the style of the frog idol of the day before, but he was no judge of art.

"How are you feeling?" he muttered to Rama.

"Better. Still a little sick. Shoulder feels like something's broken."

"Well, act helpless. It can't hurt and it might give us a slight advantage if they think you're no threat."

"That won't take much of an act. I don't think I could use my claws for anything more strenuous than scratching my—" She was interrupted by two of the hunters who jumped into the sled and set about unhooking their bonds from the deck rings. More hunters arrived and they were hauled to their feet and hustled off the sled. Troll was picked up, sack and all, and dangled from an armored hand.

People appeared on the balconies overlooking the esplanade, clapping and calling out to the hunters. Haakon tried to get a good look at them, but they were too far away. He could see that they were colorfully garbed, although they did not glitter quite as brightly as did the armored hunters. The random clapping gradually became synchronized and rhythmic, and a chant began that became a song. The music was weird and unearthly, a multipart

counterpoint of incredible complexity. For a few moments
Haakon thought they were playing musical instruments;
then he realized that what he was hearing was made up
solely of human voices.

The hunters accepted the praise solemnly, raising their
weapons above their heads, turning this way and that to
acknowledge the applause. It figured, Haakon thought.
Ritual.

"Where have they brought us?" Rama asked.

"Your guess is as good as mine," Haakon answered.
"This must be their city. Whether they're for real or just
make-believe is problematical."

She looked about the esplanade. "At least they're
civilized. That's a first for this place. Maybe it'll be better
than another night in the wilds."

"Don't count on it. They were hunting us for some
reason. They might be planning to eat us."

"You would have to say that. I might feel better if I
could just see what they look like. If I could focus, that
is."

As though in answer to her wish, one of the hunters
came to stand before them. From the decoration of his
armor, Haakon thought that this was the one who had
acted the part of leader earlier. He had disposed of his
musket and, ceremoniously, he reached up with both gaunt-
leted hands and removed his helmet. Haakon blinked and
heard Rama's hiss of indrawn breath.

He was as beautiful as an angel. His skin was alabaster,
his hair of spun gold, his eyes emerald. His features were
of such perfection that in repose they would have lacked
character, but he was smiling so engagingly that there was
nothing sculpturesque about him. He made Haakon feel
brutish and shabby, and he had a suspicion that he recognized the scent that Rama began to emit. The man spoke to

them. Neither understood the tongue, but it was full of aqueous vowel sounds and consonants so fluidly enunciated that they might as well have been vowels too. No wonder these people could sing so beautifully.

Haakon almost shook his head, then decided that would look stupid and he didn't want to appear even more inferior than he already felt. "Why have you hunted us?" he demanded. "We never intended you any harm, yet you attacked us without provocation. We demand to be freed to go about our business."

The other just continued to smile radiantly. Well, at least they had established something, if only mutual incomprehension.

Other hunters gathered around. Apparently the ritual was over. They unhelmed, and children came running to help them out of their ornate gear. Hunters and children were of both sexes, all of the same unearthly beauty. They spoke among themselves in low, musical voices. There was no homogeneity in their coloration. Hair, skin and eyes were in all the usual human colors and several others besides. Haakon saw one with scarlet hair, blue skin and yellow eyes. Despite the garish colors, it was as beautiful as the rest.

"Makes you feel drab, doesn't it?" Haakon commented.

"Speak for yourself, bald one," Rama said. "I still say I'm more beautiful and that all their agreeable smells are artificial." Haakon smiled inwardly. If Rama was getting her old spirit back, things couldn't be all bad.

An honor guard of hunters flanked them and they were marched across the esplanade to a gigantic arch of yellow marble. Under the arch the light was dim and the walls were full of shrinelike niches with small statues, all beautiful, most of them emitting fragrant smoke. Haakon held his breath as he passed them, remembering the last time they had encountered smoky sculpture. Many of the statues were of nude men and women, some of animals, but a few were of the frog thing, the only jarring note of the grotesque among the beautiful.

A corridor opened off the archway and they were marched up it until they reached a door of massive wood. It swung open to reveal a chamber of carved marble and onyx. They went inside. The light came in from overhead, through skylights set into the ceiling, which was at least seven meters above. The walls were beautiful but smooth and had no windows. It was a pretty room, but it was also a prison. No question about it.

Haakon and Rama were casually but firmly divested of their armorcloth coveralls. Although Rama hissed a little, she was still in no shape to put up much of a fight. Several baskets of bright cloth were brought in by small drab people who looked and behaved like slaves. The gaggle of captors who now crowded the room went over the strips of cloth and argued for a while, then tied the chosen pieces intricately about the loins of both captives.

Another basket was carried in, this one full of chains. Two incredibly beautiful women sorted through them and came up with two, one of carved amber, the other of ruby. They held the two chains stretched across Rama's cheekbones, studied the effect with tilted heads and discussed it between themselves.

"I swear to all the gods, Rama, they're trying to color-match your chains with your eyes!"

"Chains?" Rama said, emerging from her groggy state, her eyes going wide and panicky. She hissed and struggled and fanned her hair, but to no avail. The ruby chains were clamped about her wrists and ankles and then the captors turned their attention to Haakon. He gave them no trouble, having been through this kind of thing many times before.

Apparently despairing of achieving any real artistic effect with him, they chose plain steel.

Haakon examined the chains after the captors left, shutting the door behind them. Not so plain after all. The chains were forged with a Damascus pattern-welding process, using different varieties of steel and color-treating them chemically to create streaks and swirls of varying shades of blue, all quite subtle and pleasing. He reflected that if you had to be chained up, it might as well be with pretty chains.

While he was admiring his shackles, Rama was going through some kind of psychosis. She was writhing on the floor, jerking madly at her chains, biting them, futilely slamming them on the floor. She shrieked and squalled and unleashed a battery of scents. Haakon decided to let her get over it in her own time. She was still too weakened to do herself any real harm. Finally, and most shockingly, she sat up and burst into tears. It was one of the few genuinely human things he had ever seen her do. He fought down an urge to put an arm around her shoulder and try to comfort her. Weakened though she might be, she'd probably disembowel him.

After a while she looked up at him with a tear-streaked face. "I can't stand this. I'll go mad."

"You'll get used to it. When you've been in the pokey as many times as I have, you learn to adjust. You'll never really gain a taste for it, but you learn to live with it."

"I'll go mad!" she reiterated.

"Hell, your sane state's nothing to brag about."

She snarled and lurched to her feet and tried to rip his face off with her claws, but the chains tripped her and shortened her reach.

Haakon grinned. "There, feeling better already, aren't you? Doesn't it feel good to hate me again?"

"Again? I've always hated you, you pasty-skinned grub. As soon as I've regained my strength, I'll tear your tripes out and eat them."

"Now that you two are back to normal, may I come in?" They whirled to face a doorway in one wall of the room. The light was dim in the room beyond, but Haakon recognized the voice.

"Soong?"

"The same." The assassin came in, dressed in a plain white loincloth and dark chains. "It grieves me to renew our acquaintance under such circumstances, but I rejoice to find you both still alive."

"Same here. How did they get you?" Haakon asked.

"In good time. We shall have much leisure to catch up on each other's stories, but I think Lady Rama needs attention. Is that a bruise I see on your shoulder?"

"I need nothing from you two!" she spat, but she allowed Soong to take her by the hand and lead her to a luxurious bed beneath one of the skylights. Haakon felt a twinge of conscience that he had forgotten the woman's injury. She sat on the bed and slumped over, exhausted. With great gentleness Soong probed and manipulated her shoulder. Troublesome as she was, and even in this condition, she was an astoundingly beautiful sight. The loincloth they had given her was brilliantly striped in silver and black to match her hair. Someone had hung a necklace of huge white pearls alternating with black ones around her neck, apparently to complement her white skin and black nipples.

"No serious damage," Soong reported. "But you will be sore for several days. The best medicine is rest."

Unprotesting, she let him press her back against the soft bolsters of the bed, prattling to her in his quiet voice. Gradually her eyelids drooped and her breathing deepened.

Soong removed his hands and signaled Haakon to join him in the other room.

"That was a neat trick," Haakon said. "I wish I could put her out like that."

"It is a skill I have. It wouldn't work for you. The emotions you arouse in her are too powerful."

"I'll go along with you there. Now, tell me what happened."

For the next hour Soong told him of events since their parting on the river—of his capture by the dinosaur people, of Alexander's peculiar visitor, their trek at the visitor's behest to find and climb the Fang. Like Haakon and Rama, they had been attacked by the ornate hunters. Soong and Rand had been captured. He was not certain about the others. They had been separated early in the combat.

"So," Haakon mused, "as of a couple of days ago, we were all still alive. Amazing, under the circumstances. Why did they put the three of us together, but not Rand?"

Soong shrugged. "What became of your little companion?"

"I don't know that either. Last I saw of him was when they unloaded us from the sleds. They didn't seem to take him very seriously. Maybe they just turned him loose. I hope so. I liked the little guy, even if he was kind of spooky and I couldn't really trust him. What do you make of this bunch that nabbed us?"

"Do you remember," Soong said, "when we first checked out *Eurynome* and I pointed out that only one culture remained that had the secret of giving bronze the true *shakudo* finish?"

"Yes. What of it?"

Soong held up his shackles. In the light from the ceiling Haakon could see the green-black finish of *shakudo*. "So," he said, "another link, however tenuous, with the real world. Not much help though."

"No help in remedying our predicament, no," Soong agreed. "But I think we have learned much about the nature of our adversary."

"How so?" Haakon asked. He sat down on a bed and leaned back against a massive perfumed bolster.

"Consider what we have encountered since arriving here: a gigantic river full of outsized creatures, including the incredible Leviathan; forests and jungles of outsized, exotic trees; creatures beautiful and frightening; and nothing at all that is dull. We have encountered savages, but not one bureaucrat. There are giant dragonflies, but no petty, annoying, biting insects. Everything is either beautiful or hideous. Have you not felt your senses overloading from the sheer intensity of sensation they have encountered?"

Haakon nodded. "What conclusion do you draw from all this?"

"I can draw none as yet. We have much data, but we are still lacking the vital element that will draw it all together; the key to unlock the puzzle, if you will. But I have formed an impression. This place is a playground. Nothing natural evolves in this way. It is artificial, but whoever created it has all the forces of nature at his disposal. It is a frightening thought, is it not: some pleasure-loving, jaded creature building a planet as easily as a rich man creating a resort, and then populating it with reasoning creatures to play out his games."

"And what's our part in all this?" Haakon wondered.

"Perhaps we're a random factor. Even the most passionate gamester grows bored with the same old rules and likes to introduce a random, unpredictable factor. What was the old expression—'a wild card'?" He chuckled. "Yes, perhaps that is what we are. Wild cards."

THIRTEEN

Alexander shivered. It was cold up here, and he hated cold. He hadn't encountered cold many times in his life, and when he had, he'd never liked it, not even once. He cursed quietly and slapped his palms against his sides. Why did this have to happen? Just when things seemed to be getting better, they were hit and lost Rand and Soong. At least he was still with Jemal and Mirabelle. That was a relief. Especially Mirabelle. He'd have *really* despaired without her.

And why hadn't he grabbed one of those insulated suits from the ship? It would have been uncomfortable—none of them were his size and none were altered to fit a tail—but his tail was likely to get frostbit as it was. Then what would happen? He had a mental image of his poor tail, gradually growing stiff and crystalline, then breaking off and tinkling along the hard-crusted snow, sliding downhill until it was out of sight. It was a terrible picture and Alexander sniffled a little at it. Poor tail.

"Alex?" it was Mirabelle.

"Over here," Alexander shouted, a little embarrassed at being caught in the midst of his self-pitying reverie. Mirabelle came to join him, comfortable and warm in her insulated armorcloth suit. He couldn't find it in him to resent or envy her though. She was just too nice and cuddly.

"Come on down," she called. "We're going to get a fire going. You need to thaw out, and to hell with the people on the fancy sleds."

"I'll be down in a minute," he said.

A fire. That sounded good just now. He had gone on ahead on his own reconnaissance, not expecting to accomplish much but not wanting to feel useless either. He'd found nothing so far, and he hated to go back without any useful information. He was feeling pretty wasted up here, not like down in the lowlands. Then he spotted the footprints.

His heart did a flip-flop. They were the prints of big, bare, human feet, but whoever they belonged to had a short stride. He wondered whether he hadn't ought to find his friends and tell them. Some wayward element of pride stopped him though. He'd just go get a look at this person before he went back. He proceeded cautiously since the footprints indicated somebody in the two-meter-plus range. He followed them for about five minutes until they ended at a mossy rock. He stood by the rock, scratching his head and shivering, wondering what had happened. Then the rock turned around.

"Whothehellre you?" Alexander squawked, powerblade out.

"I'm Troll. Who're you?"

Jemal watched Troll as the little man gnawed a bone clean. Troll had led Alexander to a cache where he had hidden the carcass of a goatlike animal, and the two had brought it back to camp. Mirabelle had been beside herself with worry over the monkey-boy, but her scolding had stopped in her larynx when she saw Troll. They had heard the first part of his story while the meat was cooking; then conversation had slowed for a while as they all ate ravenously. It was the first solid food they'd had in two days.

"Please try to describe the city as well as you can, Troll," Mirabelle said patiently. The dwarf's oddly limited vocabulary had already been a stumbling block to communication.

"Big," he said, picking his teeth. "Pretty. All made of shiny stone, only smooth, not like natural stone."

"And the people?" she prodded.

"Pretty too." He looked up at her from where he squatted and took out his pipe, lighting it with a twig from the fire. The pine trees surrounding them were, mercifully, of no more than ordinary size. "Prettier than you, even," he went on, "or that woman with the stripy hair."

"Why did they let you go?" Jemal asked.

"Can't say. Just looked at me and laughed some, then walked off. I tried to get in, maybe find your friends, but they wouldn't let me. Wasn't doing no good there, so I headed back for Troll's Wood. You looking for Xeus too?"

"Not right now," Jemal said. "First we have to get our friends out of there."

"They didn't tell me nothing about you."

"They didn't know we were still alive," Mirabelle said. "Thank you for trying to help them."

"Wanted to," he said.

"How come?" Alexander asked. Troll just shrugged.

"Tomorrow, as soon as it's light," Jemal said, "we're

going to go look for that city. Will you guide us, Troll?
We won't ask you to take us any farther, but it would save
us a lot of time and suffering if we could go straight to the
place.''

"I'll take you," Troll said, puffing his pipe and wreath-
ing himself in his own private cloud. Mirabelle leaned
over and kissed the top of his mossy head. He chuckled
and dug his toes into the ground.

Jemal and Mirabelle trudged along behind Troll and
Alexander. The sunlight was dazzling on the snow, and
the sky overhead was a glorious blue.

"Convenient for us that he came along when he did,"
Jemal said.

"Mm-mm," Mirabelle replied affirmatively.

"Damned convenient."

"Mm-mm."

"This is a big mountain range. What are the chances
that one small humanoid, just ambling on home and mind-
ing his own business, would stumble across our camp?"

"He didn't," she said. "Alexander found him."

"Same thing. It's too pat. I don't like it."

"Maybe you're too quick to look for conspiracy," she
said. "There might be another factor at work that we
haven't considered.

"Say on."

"A lot of natural laws don't apply here. Maybe coincidence works differently as well."

"Hmm. That's getting pretty rarified."

"It's something that's never been quantified, you know.
We had to study it as part of metaphysical physics at
technothief school." She warmed to the subject, her breath
fogging in the cold air, her cheeks turning red. "Chance,
fate, odds and coincidence are the primary theories con-

cerning the proper juxtaposition of two events or more. Conventional physics favors chance and odds; religion and supernatural-power theory favor fate."

"And coincidence?" Jemal asked. It was a tail-chasing conversation as far as he was concerned, but it helped pass the time. Hell, just watching this woman *breathe* was a pleasure.

"Coincidence is pretty much the province of individual experience and drama. When an individual experiences a remarkable juxtaposition of events—say, running across the name of a person one has not thought of in years, then later that same day receiving a communication from that person—the individual generally puts it down to coincidence. The philosopher looks for deeper meanings but usually comes up empty-handed. There was a philosopher of the nineteenth or twentieth century—I don't recall his name—who tried to formulate a systematic interpretation of the nature of coincidence. He called it 'synchronicity,' but it never caught on. The other great field of coincidence is drama, or literature. In the earlier centuries of literature, coincidence was a legitimate plot device, used to advance the action and bring about a resolution."

"Do tell," Jemal encouraged.

She looked at him and smiled. "Don't get so bored that you miss the vital point when I come to it."

"I await it eagerly."

"Good. Here it comes. Since about the middle of the nineteenth century it has been considered very poor, lazy and sloppy style to use coincidence as a plot device, and ever since that time it has been the province of the second-rate artist *or* the writer who is deliberately employing an archaism."

He caught the emphasis she had put on the last type, but

he was still mystified. What the hell was the woman getting at? "I followed you, but you lost me anyway."

"Look, there's somebody fairly close by here who plays around with planets and laws of nature like an artist with his medium. Suppose this person, or persons, can handle laws that we don't fully comprehend, like chance, fate, odds, et cetera, with equal facility? What's to stop that person, or persons, from decreeing a certain coincidence factor in his game?"

"I don't like it," Jemal said. The whole idea made him feel helpless, at the mercy of forces that were incomprehensible and implacable. "Conspiracy and treachery are a whole lot easier to accept."

"Sure. Back in the real world. But we're not in the real world anymore. We're stuck on a god's chessboard, and we've got to get off that board."

"Mirabelle," Jemal said.

"Yes?"

"Next time you get one of these deep, depressing, philosophical thoughts, would you please keep it to yourself?"

She smiled again. "Not a chance, love. It's my duty to educate you."

Despite his misgivings, her speech made him feel a little better. It was screwy, but it would go to explain a lot. Not everything, but a lot. Maybe the little guy was all right, after all. Maybe.

They bellied down in the snow and looked down on the city. It was dazzling in the light of the setting sun. It was also in an absurd place for a city. There were no fields this high up, therefore no agriculture. No meadows, so no domesticated animals.

"Maybe they eat freeze-drys," Jemal hazarded.

"Maybe they eat people they catch wandering around on their mountain," Alexander postulated.

"Quiet, Alex," Mirabelle said.

"Just one more thing, and then I'll shut up."

"Go ahead," Jemal said resignedly.

"Just what do we do now?"

"You had to ask that one, didn't you? Well, I've got a confession to make: I'm plumb out of ideas. Suggestions, anyone?" Jemal looked around and encountered three blank looks. "I thought so. I'm the one who's going to have to come up with the plan. I knew it would come down to this."

"Stop bitching and come up with a plan," Mirabelle said helpfully.

Rama sprawled back on the luxurious coverlets and furs of her couch and took a deep sniff of the perfumes impregnating them. She had a platter of delicacies balanced on her belly and a goblet of perfect wine in one hand. She was royally soused.

Haakon was eating too, but from a table. He and Soong sat on the floor, where they ate and drank with far more circumspection than Rama. They did not resent her boisterous state. Each of them was coping with the situation in the way that seemed best: Haakon and Soong trying to be ready to escape as soon as the opportunity presented itself, Rama trying to maintain her sanity.

They had been here for five days now. At least once each day Rama had gone into one of her stupendous rages. She was just not cut out for a life of captivity. The rages were becoming increasingly dangerous as she regained her strength. Haakon was sure that she would be more stable without the chains, which seemed to be especially galling to her. They looked like carved gemstone, but they would not shatter.

Several times in the last few days inhabitants of the city had come to visit them. The purpose of the visits was not clear. The people had the appearance and attitude of visitors to a zoo or museum or art gallery. Haakon had tried to communicate to them with signs that the chains were not necessary, that the room was escape-proof without them, but the captors seemed to find them indispensable, perhaps for aesthetic reasons. Kinky bastards, he thought.

Haakon picked up a meat-filled pastry with his fingers and popped it into his mouth; they had been allowed no eating utensils. The food was delicious. It always was, and there was always a great deal of it. It was an agreeable change from the conditions of prisoner status Haakon was used to, but it made him suspicious.

"Why are they fattening us up?" he asked Soong. It was not the first time he had asked.

"It's not the first time you've asked me that," Soong pointed out.

"You never can tell. You might have had some fresh thoughts. Have you?"

"Alas, no. Just the usual ones. They might be fattening us for cannibalistic purposes, I suppose, but with food such as this," he gestured gracefully to the heaps of delicacies on the table before them, "why eat the stringy likes of us?"

"Maybe they're just hospitable and like to treat their guests right," Haakon conjectured.

"Mindless optimism has its place," Soong said. "It confers comfort in distressing situations. It would be unwise to confuse this kind of fantasy with reality."

"I really wasn't putting forth the theory seriously," Haakon assured him.

"These people have a fine appreciation of how to live well," Rama said in a slightly slurred voice. "They could almost be Felids." She had five different canapes speared on the spread claws of her right hand. Her left hand held her goblet. One after another she ate the canapes, washing down each with the exquisite wine. When the canapes were gone, she refilled her glass.

"You'd better go easy on that," Haakon said. "When we get our chance to make a break, we won't be able to carry a paralytic Felid."

Rama glowered at him. "Find us a way to escape, dear one, and forget about carrying me. I'll never be so drunk that I won't be able to run from a prison. Just keep out of my way. In my haste I've put footprints on the back of more than one person who stood between me and freedom."

"I'll keep it in mind. Meanwhile, consider that you'll run much faster if you don't get fat. The way you've been gorging on these goodies, it won't be long before you're seriously cutting into the cargo capacity of your ship."

"Felids don't put on fat, hairless one. Our metabolisms are superior to yours. I could eat like this every day for ten years and still look as perfect as I do now."

Haakon looked her over critically. She was probably telling the truth. She had the rangiest musculature he had ever seen on a female of any species. Her curves were unmistakably feminine, but her level of subcutaneous fat was so low that the slightest movement made purposeful ripples beneath the skin. Even in her harem-slavegirl outfit, Haakon concluded, she was one damned deadly looking female.

The door opened and the hunter who had captured them came in. It was one of the disconcerting inconsistencies of their captivity that their captors showed equal parts of polite deference and arrogant presumption. They were fed and kept comfortable with great care, yet they clearly had no right to privacy. Visitors came and went at any hour without announcement or so much as a knock on the door.

The beautiful captor (they had been unable to come up with a name for these people) smiled and said something that sounded like a pleasantry. Haakon and Soong stood, but Rama lay at her ease, watching the man over the rim of her goblet. Still chattering volubly, he walked up to Haakon and felt his muscles, going over his body like someone buying livestock. He poked, prodded and felt, obviously with not the slightest regard for his captive's dignity.

"I'm in fine shape, friend," Haakon said. "Just take these chains off and I'll show you how fine." Paying no attention, the man grabbed a handful of Haakon and hefted. "Yes, that's right," Haakon said, "no ruptures, but if you squeeze, I'll break your goddamned neck, chains or no chains."

The man paid him no heed and repeated the performance with Soong, who bore the treatment with the same stoicism Haakon had shown. When he was satisfied with Soong, he went to Rama.

"Just sit there and take it," Haakon warned. "It won't do you any harm and you can amuse yourself fantasizing ways to kill him."

Rama lay back on the couch, not cooperating with her captor but gritting her teeth as he ran his hands over her and tested her muscle tone. He seemed especially impressed with her abdomen, poking repeatedly with a stiffened forefinger and watching the muscle leap into washboard prominence at each poke. Then he dipped his hand inside her loincloth. She growled dangerously and shed an acrid scent.

"Easy, Rama," Haakon ordered. "I know you can kill

him, but don't do it until we're out of these chains!'' His voice was low but urgent.

Satisfied with his examination, the man went to the door and turned to briefly address them in an affable fashion. They had, of course, no inkling of his meaning. Then he left and shut the door.

''I don't know if my pride can take much more of this,'' Rama said. Her voice was steady and her face composed, but tears streaked her cheeks, and Haakon found this heart-rending in a way her rage never was. ''Why did he have to be so beautiful?'' she wailed. ''I love beauty. It will tear my heart to kill him, but that is what I will do. I swear it!'' She flung the goblet across the room with all her force. Fragile as it looked, the goblet only rebounded from the wall with a musical ring.

FOURTEEN

They were taken from the room the next morning. In spite of their chains, they were escorted by a heavy force of hunters in rococo armor. They were marched through endless corridors, each adorned in the customary over-decorated style.

"This place makes *Eurynome* look shabby," Rama said.

"It lacks elegance," Soong affirmed. "There is a certain vulgarity in the lavishness of its adornment, unlike the understated good taste of *Eurynome*. Our ship might have been designed by a Zen master. This place was built by a drunken sybarite."

While his companions passed the time discussing aesthetics, Haakon studied the mechanism of the musket carried by the guard next to him. Like so much about this culture, it was a peculiar combination of the primitive and the sophisticated. Its materials and fittings were predictably lavish, but it was a muzzle-loader. A golden powder flask and a chain-mesh shot pouch hung at the guard's belt. The lock mechanism was fully exposed, a bewildering jumble of wheels, gears, levers and springs, many of the moving parts on jeweled bearings. It appeared to be some sort of wheel lock, but it was so complex that even that was not certain. Despite the elaborate lock, the sights were crude: just a silver blade in front and a notched plate at the rear. It had no shoulder stock, only a rudimentary pistol grip, a bit like some of the archaic Japanese muskets he had seen pictures of. The guard also had a long sword-like knife and a shorter dagger. He clinked slightly as he walked.

They passed nobody as they negotiated the endless corridors of the mountain city. The walls were riotous with tapestries, windowed and skylighted with stained glass; the floors were inlaid with mosaic and otherwise decorated to an extent undreamed of in any human culture of which Haakon was aware. Sculptures lined the walls, fountains tinkled, mobiles dangled from the ceilings, which in turn were covered with frescoes. Even the air was filled with perfumes and colored smokes. They came to one room in which multicolored fumes swirled in complex but regular patterns, apparently through the use of artistically arranged air currents. Another room was walled in glass, behind which a similar swirling effect was achieved with colored liquids.

"If it weren't for these chains," Rama said, "I could get to like this place." She purred as her bare feet crossed a floor covered in fur. She was in her element.

The guards halted abruptly at an enormous circular door. Writing ran around the circumference of the doorframe, the language and script known to none of them. The door itself was severely plain but covered in yellow lacquer.

"Looks portentous, doesn't it?" Haakon said.

"Is this one of those 'abandon hope' gateways?" Rama asked.

"It has that look," Soong commented. "If it were not for the futility of running while in chains, I would suggest we make a break right now. Somehow I don't think that we will find anything agreeable on the far side of that portal."

The door opened. The far side was disappointing. Five paces from the door was a blank wall. With muskets trained on their backs, the trio went through the door. It slammed behind them. To the right and left stretched a corridor, each end of which stopped at a right-angled turn. Walls, floor and ceiling were of plain rough stone.

"It's kind of dull after all that decoration," Haakon commented. "What next?" What happened next was that, with a click, their manacles and anklets popped open and the chains fell to the floor. "That was a neat trick," Haakon said. "Now that we have freedom of movement, I suppose we're going to pick a direction and see what we find."

"I am sure that that is what we are intended to do," Soong concurred.

"Then let's not," Haakon said. He turned and pounded at the door. "Let us out of here, you bent-brained perverts! We've had enough of your games and we have business elsewhere." The door didn't budge.

"Well, so much for that," Haakon said. "Which direction?"

"Any way we go, we're unarmed," Rama pointed out. She prowled a few steps in one direction, then whirled and prowled in the other.

"Not entirely," Haakon said. He picked up the chains he had been wearing. They consisted of wristlets connected by a half-meter chain, anklets almost identical except for size, and a meter-long piece of chain connecting the two. He grasped the mass and doubled the length of the central chain, whirling the result around his head. He had an efficient four-lashed chain flail. Soong and Rama did the same with their bonds.

"It's no beamer," Rama said, "but it beats being bare-handed. Let's go."

The Felid set off to her left. It seemed as good a direction as any, and Haakon and Soong followed. While the walls, floor and ceiling appeared to be featureless, and there were no signs of sensors or peepholes, they had the unmistakable sense of being watched. They came to the first corner and took the turn. Another corridor stretched ahead, dimming in the distance to complete obscurity.

"Do you think they are watching us?" Soong asked.

"I can't see them doing anything else," Haakon replied. He held the chain easily in one hand, always poised on the balls of his bare feet so as to dodge in any direction. "These people are spectators, voyeurs. I think we're about to put on a show for them."

"Well, let's give them something worth watching!" Rama hissed. "I want out of this place!" She bent low and darted down the corridor. Haakon and Soong followed at a more deliberate pace.

"I do wish you would be less impetuous," Soong told her. "Whatever we're in for, we'll encounter it soon enough." He thought for a second, then amended: "Maybe too soon."

"Let her have her head," Haakon said. "I pity anything that gets in front of her." But when the first danger came, it was from behind.

Rama was well ahead, Soong second and Haakon a few paces after him. The only warning Haakon had was a faint clink behind him; then he was whirling, ducking and lashing out all in one movement. Closing on him was a single hunter in armor, armed only with a long sword-knife. Haakon's chain weapon whistled out with all his years of pick-and-sledge work behind it, and the flail crunched into the armored shape with such force that blood sprang from the joints. Haakon struck again as the shape hit the floor; then he wrested the sword-knife from its grasp. Soong snatched the dagger from its belt; it seemed to bear no other arms.

"Dead?" Rama asked. She had silently returned.

"Who knows?" Haakon shrugged. "Out of the fight anyway."

"You should make sure," she said. "Kill him."

"It might not be a him," Haakon said. "We're wasting time here. Let's go."

Now a little better armed, they left the armored form inert upon the stone floor and proceeded cautiously. Oddly, Haakon felt a little comforted by the bare walls. All the overdone decoration had made him nervous, and more of it would be distracting. This he could handle.

They came to a fork. Rama, still in the lead, stopped and turned to him. "Which way?"

"It seems that we're in a maze," Haakon said. "Go left. We'll keep going left until something stops us. That way we might be able to keep track of our route."

"A labyrinth," Soong said. "Our host continues to exercise a classical bent."

"What can we expect next then?" Haakon queried.

"A Minotaur," Soong answered.

"What's that?" Rama asked. She was keeping closer to them now.

"Half-man, half—" He was cut off short as three of the armored hunters sprang from gateways that appeared without warning in the walls. The fight was brief and brutal. Haakon smashed his attacker against the wall with his chain flail and stabbed at the joints until the form stopped struggling. Soong took his out with the blade of his dagger placed neatly in the joint where the helmet met the shoulder plates. Rama's adversary made a thrust with his short sword, which she sidestepped easily; as he went past, she wrapped her ruby chain around his neck and jerked him back, after which she lifted him from the floor to dangle by his neck. He kicked violently for a few moments; then there was a faint pop and he hung limp. She dropped him and freed her chain.

"Anybody hurt?" Haakon asked. There seemed to be no injuries.

"They are not very efficient at hand-to-hand combat, are they?" Soong said.

"Be grateful," Haakon pointed out. "They outnumber us."

"They'd do much better without that silly armor," Rama said. "It's almost insulting. There's so little challenge to this."

"Ritual," Haakon said. "It's all some kind of ritual. I suspect that this is just a preliminary. The real challenge must be up ahead."

"Then I suggest we conserve our strength and sharpen our lookout," Soong cautioned. They proceeded, coming to several corners and forks, always taking the left turn.

"Fighting bulls," Rama said once.

"What's that?" Haakon asked.

"I was on Espagna Nueva once. They have a sport there, supposed to be very ancient. They pit a lone man with nothing but a cape and a little sword against a huge bull. There's only one quick way to kill the bull with the sword, and the bull has to be tired before the vital spot is exposed. It's very graceful and exciting. If the man makes a wrong move, the bull can whip his guts out in a second." As she spoke, she did not relax her alertness in the slightest. "The whole sport was surrounded with a lot of ritual, just drenched with it. Prior to the fighting the bull was treated almost like a god. It was given the best quarters and the finest food. But before it met the matador—that's what they called the man who actually killed the bull—it was harassed by a lot of second-string fighters. Some of them stuck barbed sticks into it and others rode up on horses and struck it with lances, not fatally but enough to bleed and weaken it. When the matador came into the arena, the bull was in a killing rage.''

"A ritual killing," Soong said. "A foregone conclusion, not a real contest at all."

"Almost foregone," Rama said. "But not quite. I saw a matador killed once. He was grandstanding. It's a point of pride with matadors to work closer to the horns than any of the other fighters do. This one leaned just a little too close to make the kill. The bull hooked a horn into his gut and tossed him ten meters away."

"I'll bet you loved it," Haakon said.

"It was a beautiful event," she agreed. "I'd been getting a little bored because it had begun to look like a sham—just the form of danger with no substance."

"I'm glad to hear you weren't disappointed," Haakon said. No question of it, he thought; she was right back in form. "Let's keep in mind that there's real danger here too. And we haven't been weakened yet."

They came to an open area where six intersecting paths made a six-pointed star. The space was perhaps ten meters across. They stopped cautiously before proceeding.

"How do we take the left here?" Rama asked.

"We don't," Haakon said. "We go straight across, but not all at once. Five'll get you ten that something is set to happen here. Rama, you go first. If nothing happens, Soong follows you, then me. All right?"

She nodded, giving him no back talk. He liked that about

her. She was as ornery as a rattlesnake with piles most of
the time, but in action she was all business. Even though
she might resent not being in charge, she knew the value
of discipline and subordination in times of danger. She had
passed up one of the long knives and carried a dagger in
her left hand. The chains were held bunched in her right.
Avoiding the wide-open center space, she skirted to the
left until she reached the corridor on the opposite side.
She crept down it for a few paces and encountered nothing.
Returning to the juncture, she signaled for Soong to come
across.

The assassin imitated Rama, skirting the open area but
taking the direction opposite the one she had taken. Haakon
kept his attention on the way they had just come from.
When trouble arrived though, it was from none of the
corridors. This time it dropped from the ceiling.

In ridiculously melodramatic fashion a massive trapdoor
dropped open in the center of the groined vault formed by
the junction of the six corridors. Through the trap dropped
a monster. The thing was reptilian, bigger than a man, and
obviously mad and mean as hell. It was in form a bit like
the Tyrannosaurs they had seen, but smaller and more
slender in build. Its feet were equipped with a pair of
outsized, forward-pointing claws shaped like sickles. Its
forelegs were bigger in proportion than a Tyrannosaur's,
and had powerful-looking hands. Its neck was long and
serpentine, terminating in a wedge-shaped head with a
gaping, toothy mouth. It stood for a moment, hissing and
surveying its surroundings. It looked ready to eat them,
merely indecisive about which one to begin with.

It seemed to decide on Soong, stretching its hands
toward the assassin. Haakon darted in and kicked the reptile
in the tail. It whirled and headed for him and he backed down
the corridor; then Rama slid in, stabbed it in the tail and

was away. It twisted again, apparently able to keep its attention on only the source of the most recent stimulus.

As it strode toward Rama, Soong ran in and whipped his chain around its nearest leg. He hauled back and the beast stumbled and lashed out with a foreleg, opening a slash on Soong's arm, but the little assassin held on while Haakon jumped on its back, where he wrapped his chain around its throat and pulled back on its head, striving to break its neck. The small dinosaur wasn't cooperating, however. It twisted its head and managed to latch a couple of teeth into Haakon's shoulder. Rama picked up the sword-knife Haakon had dropped and tried to hamstring the thing. It lashed out with one of the sickle claws and just missed disemboweling her. Only by sucking her abdomen in at the last possible instant did she limit the injury to a shallow but bloody slit from one hipbone to the other. Clearly this wasn't going to be easy.

"Goddamnit!" Haakon shouted. "Its neck won't break and the damned thing won't choke! Somebody do something!"

Risking dismemberment, Soong took a dive under the beast, hanging on to his chain and wrapping another turn of it around the opposite leg. Even though the lizard began to wobble, it was still biting and slashing out with its forelegs. Rama tried to stab at its flank, but even her strength was insufficient to pierce the tough hide and all she got was a backhanded slash for her trouble.

"Somebody kill this thing!" Haakon yelled. "I can't hold on much longer!"

"You kill it," Rama said, slumped against a wall and trying to regain her breath. "I'm tired."

"Pry its mouth open," Soong said calmly. "Just grab the upper jaw with one hand and the lower jaw with the other and pry them apart."

"Are you crazy!" Haakon shouted. "Stick my hands in there? Hell, I'm trying to keep out of its goddamn mouth!"

Nevertheless, he gave it a chance. Wrapping his legs tightly around the thing's serpentine neck—while it stumbled about on half-shackled feet, beating him bloody against the walls—he inched his fingers between its stiff lips, trying to get a good hold without getting his fingers caught in its buzz-saw teeth.

Finally, groggy from all the bashes he was taking, he felt that he had sufficient purchase and pulled with all his strength. Centimeter by centimeter the toothy mandibles separated, and the animal hissed like a broken steam valve. Risking the flailing forelegs, Soong stepped in with a fencer's lunge and drove the tip of his sword-knife through the roof of the reptile's mouth and into its brain.

Dead but not down, it thrashed wildly for several seconds. Its spastic convulsions threw Haakon clear and he staggered to his feet, only to be slammed against a wall by its flailing tail. It took several minutes for the beast to die properly, an interval the three accepted gratefully, getting their breath back and examining their wounds. Eventually it lay still.

"Damn!" Haakon said, shaking his hairless head to clear its store of stars and cobwebs. "I don't think I can take another one like that. Do you suppose that was the grand finale?"

"I doubt it," Rama said. "We're still alive."

"Is anybody too crippled to go on?" Soong asked. They checked themselves and each other out. Rama had the worst cuts, Haakon the worst battering. Soong was hurt the least but was still in poor shape. All in all though, it might have been worse.

"Anybody remember which way we were going?" Haakon asked. They looked about. They had been spun around so many times during the fight that they had lost their orientation. All the corridors looked alike.

"Well, hell," Haakon said. "Let's just pick one and go."

"Not quite yet," Rama said.

"Why not?"

"I'm hungry." She walked over to the dead dinosaur and thumbed the edge of her dagger, looking for a meaty spot.

"You're not serious," Haakon said. "You're really going to eat that thing?"

"Why not? It wanted to eat us." She probed it in several places and found that the skin of the underside of the tail was a little thinner than the rest. She worked away at it until she had made a small cut. "I wish we had a powerblade. This would be much easier."

While the other two watched bemusedly, she laid back a flap of skin and cut out a hunk of almost bloodless white meat. The amorphous lump of flesh quivered and pulsed in her hand, the dinosaur's life force not quite departed. She bit off a piece with her small sharp teeth, jerking her head from side to side to worry it loose. After chewing for a while, she swallowed. The others awaited her judgment eagerly. "Not bad," she pronounced finally. "Could use a little seasoning though." She took another bite.

"At least it's fresh," Haakon pointed out.

"True. You should try some." Haakon and Soong declined, but they waited until she had satisfied her appetite. From the armpits down she was covered with her own blood. When she had had enough, she licked her fingers clean and picked up her knife. "All right, let's go."

Haakon picked a corridor at random and led the way. He had a store of adrenaline because he was just about out of conventional energy. At least they wouldn't have any trouble in finding their way back if they had to make a retreat; they'd just follow all the blood. There was a good aspect to almost everything if you looked at it in the right way. He thought about telling this to his friends, but he realized they would take it the wrong way. They would think he was going batty. They would be right, of course, but yet he didn't want them to think he was losing his touch as a fearless and competent leader.

They wandered for quite a while without event. At least it seemed like a long time. Time was always long when you were suffering. Haakon hoped that whatever was going to happen would happen soon. He'd seen lots of combat and suffered plenty of wounds, and he knew this was the kind of situation in which the last thing you needed was a little rest. Anything short of a week's convalescence would be useless and counterproductive. Their injuries were already beginning to stiffen, and he knew that if he lay down for an hour, he would be unable to get up again.

The corridor ended at a room full of smiling people. They were the radiant, beautiful people of the city, the people they had learned to admire and loathe so much. A woman with rainbow-striped hair came up to them with a tray of goblets. She smiled and Haakon knew that teeth so perfect could only grace the gums of the gods. The stunning people stood around a pool in the center of the room from which arose bubbles.

Haakon looked at the goblets. They were of clear crystal and beaded with droplets of condensation. They contained a pale rose wine; he suspected it was the rose wine he had been drinking for the last few days, the most delicious wine his palate had ever experienced. He was so thirsty and so tired. Never, even after his longest, hardest day busting rocks in the pits, had he been so in need of a cool drink.

"No, thanks," he said. "I think I've accepted quite enough from you people." He turned to his companions. "They couldn't kill us. Their pet couldn't kill us. Let's not let the bastards poison us."

Rama brushed past him and picked up a goblet. "Don't be an idiot, beloved Captain. The real test is still ahead of us and I don't intend to meet it thirsty." She drank the goblet down, tossed it empty into the pool and grabbed another.

"Yeah, what the hell," Haakon said, taking one himself. "If they're poisoning us, it can't be worse than what's probably in store for us next."

"The lady has a fine grasp of the practicalities of this situation," Soong said. He took a goblet also.

Haakon took a long, cool drink. He felt relief seeping into every muscle, every tissue, every cell of his body. God, there was nothing like a good drink after a hard day of monster-slaying. But the day wasn't over yet. Like Rama, he finished his first drink, tossed the empty goblet into the pond and grabbed another. The spectators looked on with evident approval.

Rama was on her third glass, already beginning to get tipsy, when she spotted the man in the crowd. He stood at the edge of the pool, dressed in a short flowing tunic of a fabric finer than silk. She growled and loosed a scent that made the whole crowd draw back toward the walls. It was their captor, the man so beautiful that in his radiance she had momentarily forgotten her indignities. The man who had put her in chains and taken liberties with her body that would shame her to her dying day—a shame that could be obliterated only with his blood.

The goblet clattered to the floor and she loosed the longest, loudest hiss Haakon had ever heard. All her claws came out at once and her hair fanned out so wide that the stripes were almost invisible. Her whiskers quivered and her muscles tensed and trembled. Haakon watched with fascination. Standing like that, streaked with blood and radiating bloodlust on every visual, aural, olfactory and psychic spectrum, she was a jungle beast so deadly that she transcended all human standards of morality, decorum, beauty or decency.

In her presence the glamorous crowd faded into drabness. In a tingling, gestalten instant the gap between ape-human and cat-human was bridged, and Haakon wanted nothing more than to see Rama kill this man who had wronged her. Hell, he wanted her to kill him and eat him, just as she'd eaten the big lizard. He'd help her. She was about to spring when the bubbles arising from the pool suddenly became thicker and the water began to roil as though something down there were disturbed and about to surface.

For an insane moment Haakon had a vision of Leviathan coming up through the surface of the pool. Of course the pool would not have admitted a fraction of Leviathan's nose; even so, that didn't stop the image from forming. Leviathan was a super-whale, awe-inspiring and majestic, but far beyond ordinary good or evil. What came up through the surface of the pool, though, was infinitely worse.

The water seemed to hump in the middle, cascading in waves from a pair of bulky shoulders, the skin green and warty, slick and slimy in texture, making the hard dry scales of the reptile seem wholesome by comparison. The body kept on emerging as though there were no end to it. Dangling down the back were a pair of absurd vestigial wings, translucent-skinned and bat-ribbed. Worst of all was the head. It was flattened and triangular, with a V-shaped mouth surrounded by ropy, writhing tentacles lined with a double row of sucking pads. The eyes were pure

transparent gold. They would have been beautiful anywhere else except in the head of the abomination in the
pool. In that batrachian head the golden globes were a
fearsome, blank, depthless pit of ancient evil. Before their
blind gaze even Rama in her rage wilted.

"Now," Soong whispered, "what do we do with this?"

"Let's run," Haakon suggested.

"No," Rama said, rallying a little. "There's no style in
that. We'd be chased down like rats. Let's end it here, one
way or the other."

"It looks hungry," Haakon said. The creature, beast,
demon, god or whatever it was, watched them in turn. It
was difficult to read anything in the alien countenance with
its pupilless eyes, but hunger was there, and also a deep
and disturbing *amusement*.

"Then let's give it something to eat!" Rama cried. She
ran straight for the creature.

"No!" Haakon shouted, beginning to dart after her.
Soong put an unexpectedly strong restraining hand on his
shoulder and he halted.

Rama spun abruptly and grabbed the man who had
insulted her. For the first and only time, his expression
changed from its habitual mask of affability. His eyes
widened as he struggled and felt her inexorable strength.
The frog-thing was leaning forward now, looming above
the striving couple. With a surge of power that reopened
her wounds and made blood spurt in all directions, Rama
heaved the man above her head and cast him straight into
the nest of tentacles around the thing's mouth.

The victim shrieked as the tentacles wrapped about him
and the mouth opened to engulf him. The creature's clawed
hands came up to help force its reluctant dinner into its
mouth. There were horrible crunching and slobbering sounds,
mixed with the victim's hideous screams. Rama watched

the show with an intense satisfaction that even Haakon found shocking. Eventually the cries ceased and the man was gone. Haakon half-expected the monster to emit an obscene belch, but he was spared that.

Rama whirled to face the crowd. "Next!" she yelled. Then she keeled to the door in a dead faint. Haakon expected the frog-thing to gobble her up right then and there, but it just looked at her with that same maddening air of amusement. The hunger seemed to be gone and it slowly slid beneath the surface of the pool.

Haakon and Soong went forward to pick up Rama. The city people were backing away silently, seeming to fade a little, but Haakon had no attention to spare them. Gently he and the assassin picked up the big Felid, trying not to aggravate any of her already serious injuries.

"Damn good woman to have around in a tight spot," Haakon said.

"I fully concur. But where are we going to go now?"

They looked about. The people had disappeared. There were two small doorways leading from the room in addition to the corridor they had come in by. They picked one and followed it.

FIFTEEN

"All clear, boss," Alexander said.

As the best climber, the monkey-boy had been picked to clamber over the wall and precede the others into the city. He was crouched on a broad terrace and gaping at the fabulous ornamentation they had been examining from a distance for three days. There was nobody about. Jemal came up over the wall, then Mirabelle and Troll, followed by Rand.

"Where is everybody?" Jemal asked.

"Inside, where else?" Alexander replied, shivering. "That's where we should be too."

"Then let's go," Jemal said.

He led the way into the vast complex of buildings. It was warmer inside, although the source of the heat was nowhere apparent. They admired the decorations, but seen up close, the adornments seemed a little shabby and crumbling, as though the place had been abandoned for many years. Some of the tapestries were falling apart from their own weight.

In one corridor they found a suit of the ornate hunter's armor. Alexander picked up the helmet, only to jump back as a skull dropped out of it, smashing to tiny chips on the pavement as the helmet itself crumpled in his hands like foil.

"This place ain't quite what I expected," he said.

"It's a big palace," Mirabelle hazarded. "This wing may have been abandoned years ago."

"Let's find someplace that's still occupied," Jemal said. "I want to find one of the inhabitants and get some answers."

They continued, wandering from corridor to banquet hall to courtyard, meeting everywhere with the same air of decadence, age and decay. It went on for hours. From time to time they abandoned all caution and called their friends' names, but there was no answer. Finally they came to a sizable room buried in the depths of the palace. Inside they found two men leaning over a third person who rested on a pile of disintegrating cushions. Jemal saw that it was Haakon and Soong and that Rama lay inert between them. Haakon looked up, his eyes deep-sunken and dark-ringed from lack of sleep.

"What have we here?"

"The U.S. Cavalry," Jemal answered, a little miffed at his friend's lack of enthusiasm.

"The what?"

"They're the people who always arrive just in the nick of time," Jemal said. "What the hell happened?"

"The nick of time was a couple of days ago." Haakon returned his attention to Rama. "I think she's dying."

"Let me see." Mirabelle shoved the two men aside and pulled the coverlet away from the Felid's body. She sucked in a shocked breath. The ragged slashes were infected, the body itself appearing shrunken and bloodless. Rama's eyes were glassy, feverish. For a change, she seemed to have no smell at all.

"The food gave out almost as soon as all the people disappeared," Haakon said.

"Disappeared?" Jemal echoed. "You mean they just vanished?"

"That is what happened," Soong said. "And this place began to crumble. We would have headed for the lowland, but we were too weakened, and we could not risk moving her too far. Now it seems we made the wrong decision. We should have attempted it."

Troll waddled up to Rama and bent over her, prodding and sniffing her wounds. Finally he straightened up. "I'll go find us some food. Find something to fix her up with too." He turned and shuffled off. The rest watched him go.

"What do you make of him?" Haakon asked.

Jemal shrugged. "Spooky little bastard. We'd be lost without him though. He's kept us fed and on course for days." He sat down. "While we're waiting for him to come back, let's hear your story."

Hours later Troll returned, carrying a dead animal twice his own size and a bagful of herbs, bark and unidentifiable substances that he brewed into poultices for Rama's wounds, and medicines the others had to force her to swallow. They had scant faith in Troll's primitive medicine, but it could do little harm. Rama had only a few hours to live in any case. Alexander found enough wood for a fire and they cooked and ate the beast Troll had brought in, boiling up some broth and forcing Rama to choke it down. Now there was nothing to do but wait, and they brought each other up to date on their doings since splitting up.

"That frog-thing—" Jemal mused "—it sounds familiar."
He turned one of the statuettes of the thing in his hands. It
was now pitted and crumbling. "It reminds me of something I must have read years ago, when I was a boy. I used
to read lots of old weird literature in those days. I can't
quite call it to mind though." He put the ugly thing down.
"But I don't think it was historical or mythological. I
think it was purely fictional."

Haakon leaned back against a wall, tossing aside a
well-gnawed rib. He had several of Troll's evil-smelling
poultices tied here and there about his ravaged anatomy.
They really did seem to be drawing some of the pain
from his hurts. The places where the lizard had bitten
him had been especially virulent, and now they seemed
almost comfortable. "So what's our next move?" he
mused.

"That's for you to decide," Jemal replied. "You're
captain, after all."

"I'd almost forgotten," Haakon said, his face sagging
into lines of exhaustion. "It's been hard to keep my mind
on anything. The Cingulum, *Eurynome,* Timur Khan—they
all seem like something from somebody else's life, kind of
unimportant."

Jemal leaned forward and gripped Haakon's shoulder
painfully. "You better snap out of that, buddy. This place
is beginning to suck you in. Sure it's like a dream, but it's
somebody else's dream, not ours. We have to get out of
here, back to the real universe, or we're lost for good.
What do you think happened to this city, to the people
who lived here? They were part of the game. They played
their part and when Xeus was finished with them, they just
vanished." He squeezed Haakon's shoulder more urgently.
"What if the son of a bitch loses interest in *us?* We have
to find and confront him before that happens."

Haakon looked at him groggily for a moment. "You're right of course. But I'm not going to be worth anything until I've had some rest. Same for Soong. A full belly helps a lot though." He stretched out on a layered mat of rapidly crumbling silk. Then he propped himself up on an elbow and looked over at Rama. She was asleep, apparently comfortable, and her color was a little better, but she might have been in a coma. He turned to Jemal. "Wake me if she dies."

He felt something prodding him in the ribs. He was so dead tired he wanted nothing to disturb him. He rolled over and went back to sleep but the prodding came again. "Wake up," a voice said. Who would want to wake him? Then he remembered his last instruction to Jemal and sat up suddenly. He looked over to where Rama lay, and even in the dim light he could see that she was breathing regularly. He flopped back down with a sigh of relief; then his mood turned to one of annoyance. He rolled over to face Jemal.

"Why the hell—" He cut off short. He was looking at a pair of shoes with big silver buckles on their fronts. Nobody in his crew wore shoes like that.

Above the shoes were a pair of calves clad in silk stockings, and above those a pair of fawn-colored knee breeches with a buttoned flap in front. The wearer had on a long vest and a brocaded coat, and although his face was in obscurity, Haakon could see that he wore a powdered wig atop which sat a tricorne hat. There were a few other details Haakon could make out. The man had a lace fall at his throat and similar lace at his wrists. He wore a delicate smallsword at his waist. He was leaning on a cane, which had probably been the source of the prodding.

"Let me guess," Haakon said. "You're the archetypal messenger, right?"

The man laughed musically and made an elaborate, formal bow. "The same."

"Well, you're an archetypal son of a bitch for waking me at this hour. Can't you come back and deliver your message after I've had a little more sleep?"

"No style," the man said. "No style whatever."

He reached into a pocket of his vest and drew out a silver snuff box. Parking his walking stick adroitly beneath an arm, he took a pinch of snuff between thumb and forefinger, then returned the box to his vest. He sprinkled the snuff on the back of the opposite hand and raised it to his nose, simultaneously pulling a handkerchief from his cuff. He snorted the snuff up his nostrils, sneezed, returned the handkerchief to its place, retrieved his walking stick from beneath his arm and resumed leaning on it.

"You see," he said, "the final watches of the night form the proper time for dastardly deeds, ghostly apparitions and mysterious messages delivered by persons of doubtful nature."

"That so? Would you mind coming to the point?"

The messenger went on as though Haakon had not spoken. "Now that one"—he pointed with his cane at the sleeping form of Rama—"she has a real sense of style. Absolutely magnificent. Of the lot of you, only she has not been a disappointment."

"I'm just sorry as hell we haven't been sufficiently entertaining," Haakon said. "I've kind of developed a fondness for her myself, even though she's a real pain in the ass sometimes." He decided that the messenger would get around to having his say in his own good time and that he wouldn't be rushed.

"You have one more task to accomplish to prove yourselves."

"I know. The Fang, right?"

"Exactly. Climb the Fang and you will meet with Xeus and he will consider your petitions."

"Well, I've seen the Fang, and if you expect us to climb the goddamn thing, you're crazy. We don't have any special climbing equipment and we haven't a way of making any. We're weakened and half-dead from exhaustion."

"If it wasn't difficult," the messenger said, "then it wouldn't be much of a test, now would it?" His teeth shone white in the dimness of his face. "You may of course rest, but I must warn you that Xeus is distractable. He may lose interest in you. That would be sad indeed."

"Look, you tell Xeus—" but Haakon was talking to an empty space. There had not even been a pop of inrushing air. He flopped back down on his pallet. "Shit!" he said, and went back to sleep.

"Hey, look what I found!" Alexander said. He was carrying an armful of garments as he entered and he dropped them in the middle of the room. It was the first cloth they had seen in days that was not disintegrating. Haakon picked up one of the pieces. It was an armorcloth coverall—the very ones taken from him, Rama and Soong when they had been captured.

"Hot damn!" Haakon exulted, finding his own and scrambling into it. His powerblade was still at its belt, and Alexander had found his boots too. Something from the bundle clunked to the floor and Haakon found his two steel bracelets. Zipped up, armed and braceleted, he felt almost himself again. The insulation took away the chill; the palace had been growing cooler by the day. He separated Rama's from the pile and went into the next room.

"Nice going, kid," Jemal said.

"Yes," Mirabelle agreed. "Where did you find them?"

"In a trash bin, I guess it was," Alexander said. "I been looking all over this place for anything useful and not finding anything. I seen this big pile of junk off one of the courtyards and was gonna walk right by it; then I seen the handle of that powerblade sticking out. Once I found it, I dug out the rest. Funny, ain't it? This place is so big I coulda looked for years and never found that stuff—then I practically tripped over it."

"Just a coincidence, I suppose," Mirabelle murmured.

"This is splendid!" Soong said, scrambling into his own and sighing with satisfaction as his body heat warmed it. "Now we can think about attempting that mountain. It was unthinkable as long as half of us were nearly naked."

Then they heard a voice from the next room: "Get your paws off me, you slick-skinned simian! I can dress myself!"

Jemal smiled ruefully. "Well, I guess we can go now. Her ladyship is herself again."

"What about Alex?" Rand asked. "He's got no all-climate suit like everybody else. He'll freeze his tail off up on that mountain."

"You're right," Jemal acknowledged. "Alex, you may have to stay at the foot of the Fang and wait for us."

"Not a chance!" Alexander protested. "I'm going with you even if I do freeze my butt. We been separated once and I didn't like it a bit. Uh-uh, I go with you."

"Look, we may need somebody to stay with Rand," Jemal said reasonably. "His power-pack's running low and he may not be able to make the climb. We can't just leave him there alone, can we?"

"Well," Alexander said grudgingly, "if he really needs somebody to stay with him. But let's wait and see."

Haakon entered the room. "She's getting ready. She's mean as ever too, so I guess she's all right. Anybody seen Troll?"

"I'm here." The little man was standing in the corner of the room unnoticed, puffing his pipe.

"Then let's pack up and get going," Haakon ordered.

"Pack up what?" Alexander asked. "We've already lost just about everything we had."

"Just a manner of speaking," Haakon said patiently.

Rama came out of the next room, fastening her coverall, her step as springy and confident as ever. Her eyes were clear and her striped hair glossy and her steel-tipped claws freshly shined. She smelled tangily rank. She was one point nine meters of vicious Felid, and she was ready to go.

"Let's go get this Xeus," she said, adjusting the fit of her cuffs. "There are a few answers I want from him."

They followed the valley below the city, which was fast collapsing behind them. The natural declivity of the ground formed a path, and runoff from the melting snow made a pleasantly tinkling brook flanking their line of march. It grew warmer by the hour as they descended, a distinct relief to Alexander. He jumped onto a rock in the middle of the stream and scampered from one rock to another while the others tramped more sedately alongside.

They left the evergreen forest behind; then they were below the snowline and into deciduous forest again. It seemed that the worst of their troubles were behind them, and it took a conscious effort of will to remember that they were still in deadly peril, that a long trek lay ahead of

them, that there was no guarantee they would find any
satisfaction at the end of it.

Once they stopped, seeing something ahead. They had
an impression of an enormous and catlike shape, with a
pair of fangs half a meter long and lambent yellow eyes.
Then the thing disappeared into the underbrush.

"What was that?" Rama breathed.

"I thought you might be able to tell us," Jemal said.
"It looked like a relative of yours." She didn't even
bother to hiss at him.

"Stick close," Haakon cautioned. "We're not out of
the woods yet." He looked around at the dense forest.
"Quite the contrary, in fact. Alexander!" The boy came at
his call. "Don't be getting so far ahead of us. The beasties
grow big around here."

They proceeded cautiously. Once the sun was momentarily blocked by the wings of an immense flier. They strained
to see it, but only a silhouette was visible against the
bright sunlight.

"The Rukh?" Mirabelle hazarded.

"Maybe," Haakon said. "Maybe it was a dragon. Hell,
it might've been an angel with a harp for all I could see. It
was big though."

That evening they huddled around a small fire. Rama
had done the hunting this time, and she had brought
in some plump fowl. There were bloody feathers everywhere, but it was a welcome supplement to their diet.
They had given up all pretense of stealth. It was easier to
let trouble come to them than to go blundering into it in
the dark.

They traveled for days, and the mountain called the
Fang seemed to get little closer. Their way wound through
the valley of a river smaller than the first they had been
on, but still big. Once, from a distance, they caught sight

of an ape so huge that they made a circle of miles through
rough, swampy country just to avoid it.

"Big birds and reptiles on the other side of the mountains," Jemal puffed as they pulled themselves along through
the mud, "and big mammals on this side. The place is laid
out like a damned zoo. What next? Giant amoebas?"

"Don't borrow trouble," Haakon cautioned. "That may
be exactly what's next."

The ground began to rise and they left the valley behind.
They had become adept at avoiding anything that seemed
to be dangerous. Many times they hid as large, toothy,
hungry or just plain strange things went by. At one point
they tiptoed past half a kilometer of inert snake at least ten
meters thick. They never saw its head or tail, for which
they were duly grateful.

"Jeez," Alexander wondered later, "what does a thing
like that *eat*?"

"Better we shouldn't know," Jemal said.

They came to a plateau covered with mushrooms that
ranged in size from a few centimeters in height to ten
meters or more, with caps even greater in diameter—
all in a riot of color and shapes. Alexander bumped into
a purple puffball half his own height and the fungus
ruptured, shooting a cloud of spores many meters into
the air.

"Get back!" Haakon warned. "That stuff may be dangerous to breathe."

As they climbed, the mushrooms took on more bizarre
forms: ram's horns, clusters of veils, convoluted masses
like gigantic brains, spikes, trumpets; there was even one
variety that looked like a bird's nest full of blue eggs.
Once Haakon saw Mirabelle and Rama chuckling together
and wondered what prodigy could cause the two women to
put aside their antipathy for even a moment. Then he saw

that they were studying a mushroom shaped like a five-meter phallus. It was shockingly lifelike.

"Where's that damned mountain?" Jemal growled when they took a break in an area that was clear of vegetation and fungus. The grotesque peak of the Fang, which had dominated the skyline for days, was nowhere to be seen. "Don't tell me we're lost again!"

"Nope," Haakon said. "I know exactly where we are, and exactly where the mountain is."

"Then enlighten me."

"We're on the Fang right now. We've been on its lower slopes since morning."

Jemal looked around. All he could see was gently sloping ground. "Are you serious?"

"Umpf," Troll nodded, mouthing his pipe. "Been on the Fang since morning, we have. Can't see no mountain that big when you're on it, no you can't."

"Well, the climb's starting out easy enough then," Jemal said. He turned to Rand. "How are you feeling?"

The engineer was spreading lubricant on his knee joints. Some puffball spores had made their way into a number of his joints and had to be constantly cleaned out. "I feel fine. But my little box here," he patted a metering device at his waist, "says that I'm running low. Another day, maybe two, then I'll have to shut down functions to maintenance level until we can get back to the ship, and that had better not take too long."

The next stage of their trek took them above the mushroom forest. They followed the course of a stream since they needed a source of water in any case. The mushrooms dwindled in size until they were no more than ankle-high and then they ended at a near-vertical cliff that stretched to right and left as far as they could see. The stream was gushing from a cleft in the cliff face.

"Anybody bring along any ropes or pitons?" Haakon asked. "No? I thought not. It's a cinch we're not going to climb this rock. We'll have to go to one side or the other until we find a way up. Any preferences as to which direction?"

"Just a minute," Alexander said. "Let me take a look at something." He went up the stream to where the low waterfall emerged from the face of the cliff. There he found a cave just high enough that he could enter upright if he stayed in the center of the stream. After a few minutes he emerged. "Come on in," he said. "There's a door in here."

"My hearing must be getting bad," Jemal said. "I could've sworn I heard you say there was a door in there."

"Quit clowning," Alexander said. "It's a door all right. Come on in and see."

They filed in, all but Troll having to stoop low to get beneath the rock ceiling as they waded knee-deep through the water. The ceiling rose inside, and there was a sandy bank beside the stream. They walked up onto the bank and waited for their eyes to adjust to the dimness. As the blackness faded to grayness, they could, sure enough, make out a door at the far end of the cavern. It was rectangular, to all appearances an ordinary human-sized door made of wood.

"Think we should knock?" Alexander asked.

"Not today," Haakon said. "It's late, we've been climbing all day, and there's going to be nothing but trouble on the other side of that door. Let's go back outside and make camp, see if we can scare up something to eat. In the morning, when we've rested, we'll try the door."

They filed back out and shook the water from their feet. Rama and Troll took off in different directions to hunt, while Alexander and Mirabelle went to gather dried mushroom stems to make a fire with. Haakon, Soong, Rand and Jemal sat in the dimming light, watching the impossible planets rise above the horizon.

"There's a new one," Rand said. He pointed to a yellow-green globe they had not seen before.

"Looks poisonous," Haakon observed. "I wish we had a ship. I'd like to see if those planets are real or just illusions. They're probably as fake as that eighteenth-century dandy I talked to a few days ago."

"I think they're real," Jemal said. "There's somebody around here who can build a planet any way he wants. Be honest, Hack. If you could play God like that, wouldn't you make a few planets just for fun and hang them right out there where you could admire them?"

"I don't know," Haakon said. "Maybe. I don't think I'd torment people like rats in a maze though. Xeus has a lot to answer for."

Eventually the fire was built and the hunters returned with their game. Troll also brought in some mushrooms he insisted were edible, but nobody would risk eating them.

"This is the last leg of it, isn't it?" Mirabelle asked as the fire burned low.

"If you want comforting words, I'm out of them," Haakon said. "I have no idea of what's on the other side of that door, and unless there's been a sudden change of policy around here, we're not going to like it. Whatever Xeus is, we know he's a sadist. We know that he enjoys thinking up colorful ways for us to suffer and die. And he's doing it for reasons we can't understand. At least with Timur Khan we knew where we stood. That miserable bastard's a thoroughly human tyrant, loathsome as he is."

"He still has his finger on the button controlling our little head bombs, don't forget," Jemal interjected. "Any time you find yourself getting nostalgic for the good old days in the real universe, you might remember what we're in for when we return. If we return.''

"I'll take it anyway," Haakon said grimly. "I want to live in a real world, not a fantasy." Gradually the others nodded agreement.

Except for Troll, who puffed his pipe contentedly.

SIXTEEN

"No sense in waiting around," Haakon said. He pointed at the door and turned to Jemal. "Open it."

"You open it," Jemal said. "You're captain." He folded his arms and returned Haakon's glare. Haakon turned to Rama.

"Not me, ape-man. I'm just your follower, remember?" She smiled maliciously.

"Hell, I'll open the damn door," Alexander said. "I'm getting cold waiting here." He reached for the metal ring that hung from the door.

"Wait, kid," Haakon said, but the door was already swinging open and he jumped for it, shoving Alexander behind him as he leaped through, landing in a crouch with his powerblade humming. The others came crowding after, weapons ready. There was nothing but an identical cavern on the opposite side, except that this one had no stream. They looked at one another sheepishly, feeling a little foolish.

"Well," Jemal said, "there *might* have been something really awful on this side."

"Sure," Alexander commiserated. "I mean, who would've thought it was just a door to another room, like any other door?"

"Alexander," Haakon said.

"Yeah, boss?"

"Will you just shut up please?"

"Sure."

"Thank you. Let's find a way out of this place and go look for Xeus."

They split up to search the area, which was a big one, with rough rock walls and floor. They couldn't make out any ceiling. There was no light source, but a faint ambient glow kept them from being in total obscurity.

"I found something over here," Alexander reported. They joined him at a portal in a wall. It had no door.

"A stairway," Mirabelle murmured. "It looks dark up there."

"We should've thought to bring along torches," Haakon said. "Alex, go back outside and get some of those mushroom stalks we didn't burn last night."

"Right, boss." He disappeared.

"Where did the kid get this 'boss' stuff?" Haakon queried. The others just shrugged, if they took any notice at all. A few minutes later Alexander came back with an armload of stalks. He dropped them to the floor and shook drops of water from his feet.

"I'm getting tired of getting my feet wet," he reported, but nobody seemed to sympathize.

They twisted some of the thinner stalks into bundles and set them ablaze with a beamer. With Haakon in the lead, they ascended the stair. It turned gradually to the right, the spiral getting steeper and tighter until it resembled the turnpike stairway of an ancient castle. They began to cough as the smoke built up in the narrow confine. They also began to grow claustrophobic as they thought of how impossible defense would be were they attacked in the cramped space.

"How far does this go?" Jemal demanded testily.

"Now wouldn't I just go and leave my guidebook back on the ship?" Haakon said. "Run back and fetch it, will you, Jem?"

"Heavy sarcasm ill becomes you," Jemal retorted. "Kindly respond to rhetorical questions in the spirit in which they are asked."

"This stairway runs forever or until I say otherwise." Then, "Well, otherwise is now."

"Good," Mirabelle sighed. "My legs were about to give out. I counted five hundred and forty-two steps."

"Trust a technothief to record the data," Jemal said. "What do you see up there?"

"You'll just have to come and see for yourself," Haakon reported. "This is too good to miss."

They filed into the room behind him, massaging sore and cramping legs. Then they saw what kind of room they were in. "Well, I'll be damned," Jemal exclaimed.

It was a parlor, with a fireplace. There was a cozy coal fire burning on the grate. Overstuffed furniture dominated the room, the backs of the chairs and sofas neatly set with antimacassars. On a small table in the center of the room stood a decanter surrounded by cut-crystal glasses. Every available space was cluttered with knickknack shelves and potted plants, and the walls were hung with velvet drapes. Above the mantle there was a hunting print of pink-coated sportsmen with horses and dogs.

Haakon tossed his torch into the fireplace and sat on one of the overstuffed armchairs, which turned out to be a platform rocker. He released a sigh of relief. "I wonder why they don't make furniture this comfortable anymore."

Jemal sniffed at the decanter and poured the glasses full. "Port," he reported. "Not bad." Beside the decanter and tray of glasses was a humidor. He took out a cigar and ran it under his nose. "Havana, I'd guess."

"How would you know?" Mirabelle asked.

"That's what people are always saying in books," he explained. "They sniff these things and say, 'A-h-h, Havana!' I'm not sure what it means." He looked into the humidor. There was a small compartment full of pipe tobacco. "Troll, stuff your pipe with this. I'll bet it's better than that weed you smoke."

The little man did as instructed. He packed his stubby pipe and took a mushroom stalk from the fireplace to light it. He puffed for a while, considering it. After his mossy eyebrows rose and fell for a few minutes, he said: "Good."

"What now?" Rama asked, sprawled on the sofa. "I, for one, am content to wait here for our host's arrival."

"I don't think the port's going to hold out for very long," Haakon said. "This is a breather. My guess is that Xeus provided it to let us recover from negotiating that stair. I also suspect that he has ways of making this place unpleasant for us if we hang around here too long."

"Let's make the best of it then," Soong said, leaning back in a plush chair. "Wake me when the unpleasantness starts." The unpleasantness started all too soon.

"The ceiling's getting lower," Mirabelle said. They looked up. Silently the molded-plaster ceiling was lowering at a rate of no more than an inch per minute. Jemal went to the door through which they had entered. Three steps down the stairs he encountered a stone wall.

"You know," he reported, "it's a good thing the Victorians went in for high ceilings."

They tore at the drapes lining the walls and encountered only paisley-pattern wallpaper.

"Start tearing up the rug," Haakon ordered as he pounded on the walls. "There may be a trapdoor."

Rama drew her beamer. "I'll burn us a way out of here." She pointed the weapon toward a wall.

"No!" Haakon shouted. "We try that only as a last resort. If we set this place on fire, we could suffocate before we get squashed."

"Anything you say," Rama said, holstering the beamer. "But let's come up with something quick."

Beneath the rugs the parquet flooring did not look promising. "Gods, this guy's a demon for detail," Jemal said, studying the bewildering complexity of the wood-mosaic floor. "How are we doing for head space?"

"It's just about to the top of my head," Rama reported. She was the tallest of the group, topping Haakon by several centimeters. "Find us a way out of here quick or I'm going to burn us a way out!" She was beginning to radiate her scent of distress, which was oddly flowery and pleasing.

Troll was trying to hide in the fireplace, pushing the andirons aside to make room for himself but having to step back every few seconds, his beard smoking.

"Forget that," Alexander said, frantically pounding at a wall to see if he could find a hollow sound. "You'll just cook in there."

"Looky here," Troll said. With a grating noise, the fireplace—and a goodly part of the wall into which it was set—was swinging back, disclosing a dark passage beyond.

"Is there no end to the melodrama around here?" Jemal asked as he dashed through. The others followed, crowding against each other in their eagerness to escape the collapsing room. The wall closed behind them and they stood in absolute darkness. There was silence except for their breathing and the faint sound of furniture being crunched behind them.

"Did anybody think to grab a torch as we came in?" Mirabelle's disembodied voice asked. There was no reply.

"Welcome," said another voice. It was not one of theirs.

"Xeus?" Haakon asked.

"The very same. You are doing quite well."

"I'm pleased to hear it," Haakon replied. "Now that we have your attention, we have a few favors to ask. Primary among them is that we'd like to get back to our ship and return to the Cingulum."

"But this is the Cingulum."

"Ah, maybe you don't quite understand. The Cingulum is a chain of worldlets orbiting—"

"I know quite well what the Cingulum is. I created it, you know."

"Good for you," Haakon said. "But it didn't look like this place when we arrived. We went into a worldlet the Cingulans called Meridian to see what had become of several former expeditions, and we ended up in never-never land."

"It is still the Cingulum, all of it. It always has been."

"Look, we're not interested in whatever mathematical principles are involved here. We're only interested in returning to what is, for us, normal space. We've done nothing to earn your animosity. We've played this game by your rules; now we'd like to go home."

"But the game is not over yet."

"Dear, beloved Xeus," purred Rama in a voice that could have caused an erection in a bronze statue, "between whose toes I would love to lick, please grant us this boon. Just grant us a way out of here and we will raise temples in your name wherever we travel. We will establish shrines and endow a priesthood. We will—''

"Cat-woman," interrupted the voice of Xeus, "if you had the sincerity to match your courage, you would be a truly superior being."

"What do you mean, you game-playing psychopath?" she hissed. "I *am* a truly superior being!"

"I really must be going now," Xeus said. "Rest assured that I shall be giving your requests close attention and following your progress with interest."

"Xeus," Jemal said, "before you go, just one more little request?"

"I am listening."

"How about a light?"

"Assuredly."

They waited for a few minutes and then saw, faintly, a point of light in the obscurity. It came closer, resolving into a disk and then becoming a globe of orange radiance. It hovered overhead, a ball about the size of a typical human head, bathing them all in a welcome, if somewhat unflattering, light.

"I've never liked direct overhead lighting," Rama said. "It makes one look older." She looked at Mirabelle. "Especially you, dear one."

"Does anyone see a promising direction to take?" Jemal asked. "I don't know about the rest of you, but I'm getting hungry."

They were in yet another featureless cavern. No ceiling was visible, and they could just barely make out walls to the sides. It was cold and the air was still and damp. The light began to move.

"That relieves us of any choice in the matter," Haakon said. "Either we follow it or we get left in the dark. Let's go."

The globe set a leisurely pace, and it bobbed slightly as it moved, making their shadows shift disconcertingly. Alexander jumped a little every time the shadows twitched. He didn't like the dimness of the cavern. He felt exposed to invisible dangers, and so did the others to judge by the way they were huddling together.

The hike went on for some time. In the featurelessness of the cavern, time was easily distorted. They stopped when they reached the shore of an underground lake. At least it seemed to be a lake. They could see no farther shore and could detect no current; the only sound was the lapping of gentle waves on the rocky beach.

"Are we supposed to cross it or go around?" Rand asked.

"I don't see a boat," Haakon said. "And we haven't passed anything we could build a raft with."

"We could try swimming, I suppose," Mirabelle hazarded.

"You try it," Haakon said. "I'll bet anything there's something big and hungry out there."

"You take things too literally," Mirabelle grumbled.

"Let's go around it," Jemal said. "After all, we're inside this mountain. Granted it's a big mountain, but the lake can't be all that big."

"Why not?" Soong asked. "As you'll recall, we discovered a whole cosmos contained within the tiny worldlet of Meridian."

"Yeah, I'm still trying to figure that one out," Jemal admitted.

"Well, it's a cinch we ain't going anyplace without that light." Alexander pointed up at the globe. "It led us here, so let's see where it goes next."

"Good idea," Haakon said. "Only, it's just hanging right there. Let's go that way." He pointed to the left and they started off. After a brief hesitation, the globe followed. "Now we try the other way," Haakon said. They did as they were told—and again the globe followed them.

"This isn't much help," Jemal said.

"What happens if we split up?" Alexander asked, and they took up the suggestion; half went one way, half the other. The globe stayed right where it was.

"So we have to pick a direction," Haakon said, "but we also have to stick together. Which way do we choose?"

Suddenly there was the sound of something large breaking water out beyond their range of vision.

"Whichever way we go," Jemal suggested, "what say we don't stay quite so close to the lake?"

Haakon spat into his palm and smacked it with the base of his fist. The spittle flew to the right. "That's the way we go," he announced.

"By God," Jemal said admiringly, "I just knew there was a logical way out of this dilemma. Hack, you've done it again!" He clapped Haakon on the shoulder.

"I'll kill you when we get out of this," Haakon promised.

It was rough going at first. The beach was composed of small rocks that continually turned under their feet and made for sore ankles. From time to time disturbing sounds came from the water: slappings, as of broad tails or flippers; the hissing of breath through large mouths, or nostrils; splashings and displacements of water attributable only to a large animal, or animals. Their attention was so preoccupied with the water that they almost forgot about possible perils right there on the shore.

"I wish that thing—gaah!" Mirabelle jumped back convulsively, colliding with Jemal, who was following close behind.

"What is it?" Haakon demanded. Then: "Gods!" It was an exclamation compounded of fear and disgust. They had walked into a nest of enormous crabs, the biggest a meter across. With spindly legs the crustaceans scuttled all over one another. There were hundreds of them, with beady eyes on stalks and mouths that were nests of writhing, jointed palpi. They hissed and chittered and squeaked.

"Ugh, what disgusting creatures!" Mirabelle exclaimed.

"I wonder if they're any good to eat," said Soong somewhat more pragmatically.

"We can soon find out," Rama said, drawing her beamer.

One of the hideous things was moving closer and she swept the beam across it. The crab stopped in mid-scuttle, steam pouring from its joints. Within seconds other crabs were on it, chittering ecstatically. With big powerful claws they ripped it to pieces and devoured it. Almost before the steam had cleared, there was nothing left of the cooked crab except a few scraps of chitin.

"Actually it smelled kind of good there for a few seconds," Alexander said. "But if we're gonna eat one, I think we got problems."

"Let's just get away from them," Mirabelle urged. The crabs were closing in, and their intent was plainly not friendly.

"Rama, cook a few and we'll make a dash for it," Haakon ordered.

Nothing loath, she swept her weapon in a wide beam, killing dozens of the despicable creatures. The rest of them erupted in a cannibalistic frenzy, and the air was full of the sounds of ripping shells, of jointed legs torn off and crunched up. The little band took advantage of this gourmandizing preoccupation and ran through the nest of crustaceans, trampling the smaller crabs underfoot and kicking the bigger ones out of the way. The crawling horrors reached for them with slow, clumsy claws but never managed to get a good grip on the armorcloth. Alexander scampered across on all fours in record time, his tail high. Troll made creditable speed on his stumpy legs, punching a few of the bolder crabs with his knotty fists.

Then they were well beyond the nest of crabs, panting and gasping. When they were assured that no crabs lurked nearby, they sat and stared at each other in the light of the globe, which had kept up with them.

"I'll get even with Xeus for that," Jemal said when he had breath. "I'd take the dinosaur any day. It's bad enough to get killed, but why be so disgusting about it?"

"Hey, where's Troll?" Alexander asked. The little man was not among them.

"You don't think those crabs—" Mirabelle began. "Oh, gods, no, not that!" She lurched to her feet and started back the way they had come.

"Hold it," Haakon said. "I hear him coming."

The shuffling sound of Troll's big feet came closer, and then he entered the circle of globe light. He was carrying something almost as large as himself that writhed mindlessly. It was a crab a half-meter across. Troll held it by the back of the shell, where its horrible claws couldn't reach him.

"What the hell's that for?" Jemal asked.

Troll plunked the ugly thing down on its back in the midst of them. Its legs, claws, eyestalks and palpi waved mechanically in the air. "Lunch," he announced.

"Oh, no," Mirabelle said, sitting down and looking sick. "I don't think I could. Not after the last five minutes."

"I could," Rama announced. She beamed it. Dead and still, bright red in color and steaming fragrantly, the thing was not nearly as unattractive as it had been when alive. Eventually even Mirabelle overcame her repulsion and scooped the delicate meat from a claw.

"Not bad," Jemal pronounced. "Not bad at all."

"I believe," Soong said, "that classical gourmets insist

upon butter sauce with this particular delicacy, but hunger makes palatable many things one might otherwise eschew.''

"What's butter?'' Alexander asked.

"It's something they get from cows on terraformed worlds,'' Mirabelle explained.

"Never heard of it,'' Alexander said. "Do we keep on going that way?'' he asked Haakon, pointing along the shore they had been following.

"I suppose we have to, that is unless somebody wants to go back through the crabs?'' He raised his hairless eyebrows in query but got no takers.

"Why does it have to be so dark?'' Mirabelle asked. "If Xeus wants heroic doings, they're much more impressive in good light.''

"As well as being easier to carry out,'' Jemal agreed.

"Very true,'' Soong said. "This kind of obscurity is oppressive and conducive to malaise, the very antithesis of what one really needs for the proper inspiration, for the kind of atmosphere that urges one to the performance of great and impressive deeds.'' Each was hoping that Xeus was lurking about someplace near and would take the hint.

"No sense hanging around here,'' Haakon said. "Let's be going. Rand, how's your power supply?''

The engineer checked his meter. "Another twelve hours or so. Then you carry me or leave me.''

"No time to waste in that case. Rama, you take point. Your night vision is the best. Keep your beamer ready. I'm through fooling around. If it looks hostile, shoot it.''

"Captain, darling,'' she purred, "how long I've waited to hear such sensible words. And from such an unexpected source too.''

He let that one ride. "Soong, you go next. I'll follow. Rand, you go after me. I don't want you to fall behind under any circumstances; if you drop, nobody will see you. Alex, you and Troll take flank. Go out there a few meters and warn us of anything you see or hear.''

"Right, boss. Come on, Troll,'' The two went outside the little circle of light.

Haakon shook his bald head in exasperation. "Boss. Where the hell did he get that? Mirabelle, you go next. Jemel, you take drag. We're tactical from here on in. Try to keep a five-meter interval, but don't, under any circumstances, let the light out of your range of vision. Everybody understand?''

Jemal gave a low whistle and whispered in a voice everybody could hear: "Hey, isn't he getting as organized as all hell? I'm sure glad I signed on with a captain who knows the value of discipline.''

"I'll settle with you later, Jem. Now let's move out.''

"Forward, ho!'' Jemal called after them.

"Gods,'' Haakon said, "the things I put up with.''

They marched parallel to the lake for at least three hours, making slow time over the rough, rocky shore. Haakon was about to call a halt when there was an outburst of shouting and a scuffling from the flank.

"Assemble, everybody,'' he called. The column gathered under the globe and there was a quick nose count.

"Where are Alex and Troll?'' Haakon demanded. Then Alexander came scampering in, breathing hard.

"They got Troll!'' the monkey-boy gasped.

"Who got Troll?''

"How the hell should I know? It was dark. We was barely keeping you in sight. Next thing I knew, there was a whole bunch of them all around us, trying to grab us. I think I cut a few with my powerblade, but I heard them hauling poor old Troll off.''

"Any idea of what they looked like?'' Jemal asked.

"Not much bigger than me, that's about all I could make

out. They had hands, and I saw some eyes glowing a little—reflecting the light from the ball up there, I guess. Are we gonna go get him back?''

"We don't know what we're getting into," Haakon said.

"We owe him nothing," Rama declared. "He elected to tag along with us on his own. Leave him."

Alexander looked up at her with outrage and indignation. "Why, you ungrateful bitch! You would've died back there in that fancy city if it hadn't been for him. It was his doctoring that brought you around, even if you won't admit it."

She hissed. "Watch your tongue, apeling." But her voice lacked its usual conviction.

"There's Rand to consider too," Haakon pointed out. "We have to get him to a power source soon, and he *is* part of the crew."

"Well, I'm not part of your damn crew. I'm a stowaway, and I'm gonna go find Troll!" Alexander began to stalk off in a huff, tail aquiver with rage.

"Oh, come back here," Haakon ordered.

"I vote we go get the little man," Rand said. "I don't trust Xeus worth a damn anyway. Not to help us. The dwarf's been a friend, even if he is a little weird." They were all surprised to hear such a lengthy speech from the engineer.

"Yes, let's go find him," Jemal said.

"I agree," Mirabelle put in.

"So say I," from Soong.

"What's this?" Haakon said. "Democracy rearing its ugly head again? Ah, what the hell? Rama, you're overruled. We go find him."

Alexander in the lead, they made their way away from the lake. The glowing globe followed obediently.

"It was right around here," Alexander said. He was

down on all fours, straining his eyes in the dim light and sniffing the ground.

"Can you really track by smell?" Mirabelle asked.

"Sometimes, if there ain't too many other scents around. Ol' Troll don't have much scent, but these other buggers smell wors'n Rama in a bad mood." There was a hiss from behind him.

"Look!" he said. "There's a footprint." He pointed to an odd track in the sandy ground. It was roughly human, rather small and peculiarly curved, almost into a crescent. Closer examination of the ground disclosed a number of the prints, along with Troll's much larger ones. They followed the confused mass of prints—until Troll's disappeared.

"Must've just hoisted him up and carried him," Alexander pointed out.

Haakon bent low and picked up something from the ground. It was several strands of long hair. In the orange light it was difficult to judge, but it seemed to be dirty white and rankly greasy; it smelled awful.

Haakon passed the evidence around. Mirabelle wrinkled her nose at it. "I once had to ride on a ship that was ferrying farm animals. It smelled something like that. Only that's worse."

"So what do we know about them?" Jemal asked as they proceeded cautiously. "There's a lot of them and they smell bad. Not much to go on."

"Having second thoughts?" Rama asked sweetly. "I said this was a fool's mission."

"No second thoughts," Jemal replied. "I just like to keep our information in order." His voice betrayed his uneasiness though.

"There's light ahead," Alexander reported.

The monkey-boy was a little in front of them, on all

fours and following their quarry with his nose to the ground. They had been in the dark for so long, with only the mysterious globe for illumination, that the light ahead seemed somehow unnatural.

"Do you think it's a way outside?" Mirabelle asked hopefully.

"Don't count on it," Alexander cautioned. "These tracks head straight for it, and I'll bet those buggers avoid the light of day."

The light was coming from a rough, arched entrance to what looked like another cavern. "Rama, Jem," Haakon called, "come with me. The rest of you follow ten meters behind. Be ready to run."

The three crept forward silently. Haakon and Jemal took one side of the arch, Rama the other. They kept out of line of sight from the entrance, going well to the sides and closing in on the opening after reaching the cavern wall.

Haakon crept the last few inches and peered cautiously inside. He was looking into a wonderland of crystals that grew from the floor and walls and ceiling; crystals of all sizes, either creating or reflecting light, breaking it into all the component colors of the visible spectrum. Nothing moved in the glittering space. He whistled the others in.

"Hey, that's more like it," Alexander said. "We got light again. This sure beats where we been."

"I certainly hope that this environment proves superior," Soong said, "because we can't retreat."

"Why not?" Alexander asked.

"Because our light's gone," Jemal told him. There was a general craning of necks and turning of heads. The glowing globe was nowhere to be seen.

"Ever feel like a piece on a game board?" Haakon asked.

"Only since we met Timur Khan," Jemal answered.

They proceeded slowly into the crystal forest. Their relief at being out of the dark was quickly superseded by confusion in the dazzling refraction of light all around. The quick changes in color were at first pleasant but soon became disconcerting, even a little nauseating. To make matters worse, many of the crystals had mirror properties, disconcerting to the sense of direction, and to identity as well. Several times one of them would find himself talking to someone else, only to realize that he was addressing a reflection.

"This would be a bad place to be attacked in," Jemal said. "I'd hate to throw a punch at somebody and smash my knuckles on a crystal."

"Do you recognize any historical or literary precedent for this wilderness of crystal?" Soong asked him.

Jemal thought hard for a while. "No," he said finally. "I must have missed this one, but that's nothing unusual. I'm no scholar. I just did a lot of reading when I was younger. I liked the myths and epics and the imaginative writers from the eighteenth to the twenty-first centuries. I was never systematic though. I just picked up whatever looked interesting and read it."

"You mean you used to read real books?" Alexander asked wonderingly. "On paper? How'd you learn to do that?"

"Jem went to a weird school back on Delius," Haakon explained, not taking his attention from the possible dangers surrounding them. "They made kids learn to read and write without screens and symbols, just with letters and numerals."

"That's right," Jemal agreed. He jumped away from an intruder, only to realize that it was Mirabelle's reflection. "Believe it or not, I learned basic arithmetic by totting up columns of numerals. The art almost died out several generations ago, you know, during the First Communications Revolution. Letter and numeral literacy came back in only when a bunch of artists started the Graffiti Revival a generation or so back.''

Haakon didn't try to discourage the pointless conversation. Everybody was too keyed up to relax vigilance, and it served to dispel excess nervousness. ''Where'd you learn to read, kid?'' he asked. ''I know you can.''

''Oh, I mostly picked it up from the screens back home,'' he answered. He kicked a few loose crystals out of his way and they tinkled off, each ringing in a slightly differing tone. ''They didn't try to teach us exactly, but there was screens everywhere. They was set into the tree trunks most places, and they used the old-fashioned phonetic letters sometimes, as well as the modern symbols. I figured I ought to learn them since they were used at the port to announce the schedules of the incoming and outgoing shuttles.''

''Contemplating stowing away even back then, eh?'' Haakon said.

''Among the Han,'' Soong contributed, ''classical Chinese characters were revived almost as soon as our worlds were settled. The ancient writing, like the modern symbols, were cross-lingual. No matter what dialect of Chinese one speaks, the characters mean the same thing. Of course we use symbols as well. These days, though, only a few artists can form the old characters with brush and ink. Keying them has made it too easy.''

''I never learned letters,'' Mirabelle admitted. ''My education was almost all in symbols, their meaning and their retention. It was believed that most other kinds of education would clutter a technothief's mind needlessly.''

''They started you that early?'' Haakon asked. The

forest of crystal seemed to be going on forever. How big
was this mountain?

"Almost from birth. After adolescence our training broad-
ened of course. There was charm school, naturally. A
technothief has to be able to move freely in all kinds of
society. Then, in the war, there was espionage and intelligence school."

"You're not old enough to have been involved in the
war!" Jemal protested.

"Don't I just wish. You'd be surprised to hear how old
I am, but I'm damned if I'm going to tell you."

"I'm losing them," Alexander said.

"What do you mean?" Haakon asked.

"I been tracking them by the stink those guys left
behind. Now it's so thick I can't figure a trail from it.
Their smell's all over."

"That means we're in an area they inhabit habitually,"
Haakon said. "Everybody stay alert."

"Do you think we've been sleeping?" Rama snorted.

"Don't be so touchy. You see that big, tall, green
crystal over there? That's our point of reference for
now. We head for it. By the time we reach it, I'll have
another one picked out. It's the only way to keep from
going in circles in this place. If we're separated, we rally
there."

"I'm getting a headache," Jemal said. "I'm almost
nostalgic for the dark, even if it was full of crabs."

"I'm feeling the same way," Haakon reported. "Rand,
can you see any better than the rest of us? If you can,
you'd better take point. I'm getting cross-eyed."

"I'm probably more confused than you," Rand said. "I
see farther into both ends of the spectrum, but that means
I'm getting more contradictory data than the rest of you."

"So much for that then."

"No headache though," Rand said. "And I don't get sick to my stomach anymore."

"Glad to hear it," Haakon told him.

"Of course I don't have a stomach anymore," Rand said.

"That might account for it," Haakon answered.

"What about the headaches then?" Rama asked maliciously.

"I guess I'm just healthy," Rand said.

"I kind of wish those smelly guys would attack us," Alexander said. "It'd be a relief." As though in answer to his wish, they were attacked almost immediately.

The creatures appeared from behind the crystals, their numbers difficult to guess because of the multitude of reflections they cast. They were humanoid, long-armed and bowlegged, pasty in color and having long white hair on head, arms and back. Their concentrated smell was worse than the danger represented by their crude weapons. They all carried clubs and knives of crystal.

Rama snapped a quick shot at one. It was a reflection in a crystal slab. The reflected backwash of her beamer scorched her face and hands, temporarily blinding her. She screeched and waved the weapon aimlessly. Then a blow from a crystal rod numbed her wrist and she dropped it.

Haakon lunged and slashed with his powerblade, cutting two of the assailants, but the short, hulking humanoids were swift and did not make things easy for him. He felt one land on his shoulders, and Jemal cut it away with his own powerblade. The two men stood back to back, surveying the action and carnage around them. After witnessing Rama's accident with the beamer, Haakon was grateful for their shortage of the weapon. In this place they were better off without beamers. Not that they were doing well in any case. The ugly creatures were all around, and some of them carried ropes and nets.

"They want to take us alive," Haakon said over his shoulder as he slashed the hand of an attacker. The wounded creature jerked back, sticking the bleeding, smoking hand into its mouth but making no sound.

"Well, if you're going to be taken, that's the best way," Jemal said. "Alive."

"Yes, but let's not," Haakon urged, holding off several of the attackers with the threat of the powerblade.

He looked about quickly. He could not see Rama. Blinded, she must have been taken and led off, kicking and clawing no doubt. Soong was fighting methodically, taking out an assailant with almost every motion. Mirabelle was gone. Rand lay inert upon the floor. Probably his power was exhausted at last. He saw a net descend over Alexander, and the boy yelled and fought to no avail. He managed to cut a hand free of the net with his powerblade, but one of the creatures simply snatched the weapon away as soon as it emerged.

"Let's get out of here," Haakon shouted. "Hey, Soong, we're going to run. Meet us at that big crystal!"

He and Jemal broke and ran, making for a gap in a crystal hedge. Haakon felt tears stinging his eyes. He had deserted his crew. Their attackers chased them, but their stumpy, bowed shanks were not equal to the adrenaline-powered leaps their quarry were making. Soon they were left behind, and Jemal and Haakon had lost themselves among the bewildering crystals. They stopped for a breather and a chance to get their bearings.

"Goddamnit!" Haakon swore as he tried to spot the big green crystal. "We ran! I swear it, Jem, when we find Xeus, I'm going to kill him!"

"How do you kill a god? Besides, we didn't run, we made a strategic withdrawal. They had all the advantage there. Why let the enemy pick the time and place?"

"Don't try to snow me. We ran, and we ran damned hard and fast."

"Yeah, I have to admit we were making pretty good time for a pair of old spacers."

"And they got our shipmates! They got Rama and the kid and Rand, probably Mirabelle too, and maybe they have Soong by now."

"They wanted us alive," Jemal pointed out. "That means we can go back and get them."

"Assuming they intend to keep them alive. We don't know anything except what we saw. No, we know one more thing. We told Soong we'd rally at the big green crystal, and there it is." He pointed, and Jemal could just make out the faceted green tip of the crystal. Distance was almost impossible to judge. It might have been a kilometer away; it might as easily have been five.

"Let's go then," Haakon said wearily. Toward the crystal they trudged, wary of attack but almost hoping for it. They had a lot of pent-up rage to dissipate.

An hour's trek brought them closer to the crystal. Unlike most, this one stood alone in a clear area, the floor around it resembling polished marble. They stopped at the edge of the clearing. This was a good spot to run into an ambush.

"You think he got here ahead of us?" Jemal asked.

"I don't know, but I'm sure as hell not walking over there to find out," Haakon answered.

"Allow me to compliment your caution," said Soong's voice behind them. They whirled to see the neat little assassin standing there. They had heard nothing.

"Are you trying to give me heart failure?" Haakon asked.

"I do apologize," Soong said. "I've been waiting here for half an hour. You made so much noise approaching that I thought it superfluous to contribute to it."

Haakon glared at him, looking for mockery in Soong's face but it merely wore its customary mask of blandness. Not that that meant anything. "Seen any of the others?" he asked at last.

"Not since breaking away from the ambush. I fear that they are all taken, although I saw none of them seriously injured. Did you see what happened to the Felid?"

"Yes," Haakon fumed. "Damn the woman! Blinding herself like that! Our best close-in fighter and she takes herself out of the fight on her first move." He spat, his outward disgust hiding inner anxiety.

"You are too hard on her, Captain," Soong said, "but that's neither here nor there. What we require now is a plan of action if we are to rescue our friends."

"We do nothing for now," Haakon said, "except sit, rest and get our breath back. It's possible that some of the others broke away or got loose somehow. If nobody shows up after an hour, then we try to track them."

"As you command, Captain," Soong said.

"Gotten respectful all of a sudden, haven't you?" Haakon said suspiciously.

"It is merely that in matters of such responsibility, I prefer to defer to higher authority."

Haakon grunted assent. It was probably true. An assassin, Soong had most likely worked as an independent agent, a loner. Such men were often uncomfortable in positions of authority and either yielded to the leadership of others or else ignored it entirely.

They rested for the required hour, keeping watch on the clearing around the big crystal. When the time was up, none of their friends had arrived.

Jemal looked at Haakon. "Well, you really didn't expect anybody to show, did you?"

"We can always hope," Haakon said. "So much for

that. I see a wall over that way." He pointed to a darkness beyond the crystals. "I'm sick of these crystals. Maybe we can find a way out. You can bet those white-haired bastards don't live here. Nothing will grow in this place, nothing will burn. It's too damned inhospitable."

"Lead on," Jemal said.

As they made their way, the crystals grew ever shorter until finally they were no more than ankle-length. This robbed the trackers of cover but it made progress easier. Their armament now consisted of three powerblades. Aside from that their only assets were their armorcloth suits . . . and desperation, the latter being their strongest point. They no longer worried about personal safety, and they had little hope of a favorable settlement from Xeus. They wanted their shipmates; they wanted some answers; and they wanted revenge.

By the time they reached the wall, they could already see a doorway. It was little more than a crack in the wall but large enough for Haakon, the broadest, to walk through without quite having to turn sideways. The stench that hit them upon entering made their former assailants seem fragrant by comparison.

"I think we've found their latrine," Jemal said, gagging. There was light in the room they had entered; it came from a source on the low ceiling, probably a glowing fungus of some sort.

"Not their latrine," Soong corrected. "Their pantry, or possibly their midden heap." He gestured to the piles of indistinct objects strewn around, and they went closer to examine them.

They saw heaps of bones, some of them showing marks of having been gnawed, some cracked open to extract the marrow. There were many skulls in evidence, most of them with their craniums broken open to get at the brains.

The skulls were human. At least they were close enough to human to pass a cursory examination. Scraps of rotting flesh clung to many of the bones, and there were clumps of greasy, foul-smelling and blood-matted hair everywhere.

"Cannibals," Jemal said after a few minutes of dry heaves. "That's all we need. Now we know why they wanted us alive. They like fresh food. We'd better find our people quick. That fight must've sharpened those loonies' appetites."

With a new urgency they stepped gingerly among the ghastly remains. There was a path of sorts, relatively free of bones, but bloody clumps of hair kept sticking to their feet. Although they tried to breathe through their mouths, the stench was so dense they imagined they could smell it orally too. The light held and it was not too difficult to see their way. They were trying to make all possible speed but they had a horror of tripping and falling into the piles of putrescence on all sides. Then they became aware of a rhythmic, pounding sound, primitive and compelling. Haakon held up his hand and they stopped for a moment to listen.

"My god!" Jemal gasped. "Native drums!"

"What?" Haakon said.

"Native drums. It's one of the great adventure clichés. Now, if we were in one of those old books or vids, we'd have a native guide with us and we'd say something like: 'What do the drums say, Ngumbo?' "

Haakon looked at him. "Are you sane?"

"Sure. Drums were a pretechnological form of communication. Before radio even, I think. Anyway, these adventurers always come from a more technologically advanced culture, see, that doesn't use drums anymore, so they need their native guide to translate."

Haakon resumed the march, shaking his bald head. "It

had to happen sometime. I just hoped we'd be out of this before you cracked up. You're due for some hospitalization and counseling when we return, Jem."

"That so? Are you going to turn over my med file to Timur Khan so he can put his seal on it?"

Haakon ignored him. "Those drums are good for one thing—they let us know which way to go."

"Perhaps," Soong said, "that is what they are intended to do."

Haakon and Jemal stopped dead in their tracks. "I hadn't thought of that," Haakon admitted.

"It's good to have someone astute on the team," Jemal said. "Soong, your ancestors had a reputation for being subtle and wily. I'm glad you live up to their traditions."

"Your ancestors had a reputation for being barbarous savages," Soong said. "I shall forbear to comment on their descendants."

They proceeded with more caution now. The drums were louder, and to their unutterable relief, they were out of the charnel house. The smell was still awful, but anything was an improvement over the last five minutes. It seemed they had come to an area consisting of a chain of interlocking caverns, but with none of the evidence of erosion and deposit that ordinarily characterizes natural caverns. Yet these rooms looked to be of natural origin. Haakon commented on this.

"Volcanic action?" Soong hazarded.

"No," Haakon said. "It's fake, all of it. The lake, the crystals, everything. It's all stage dressing. Just like the trees and the animals. Dinosaurs, for God's sake! And Leviathan, and the Dragon people and the Eaglefolk. Great drama, bad nature."

"It may be fake," Jemal commented, "but it's come close to getting us killed on several occasions."

"I haven't forgotten that. Another room's coming up. Move careful now."

They walked slowly to the entrance of the next room. The drums were very loud. Light spilled from the archway, flickering as though the source might be flames. Cautiously they spied inside. It was an immense cavern, its roof and walls too far away to be illuminated even by the mass of flames dotting the floor. In the center, among the flames, hulked a shape, an immense combination of animal and human.

"What the hell's that?" Haakon wondered aloud, his attention half on the shape. The other half was on the humanoid forms capering about in the firelight. The flames came from cracks in the floor, and there was no smoke. Natural gas, was Haakon's guess, but who could tell around here?

The thing amid the flames had a catlike body and was crouching with forepaws extended and belly to the floor. The head was human—majestic and sinister in the light coming from below. It had a pair of immense wings, spread almost horizontally, and it was unmoving, made of stone.

"A sphinx," Jemal said. "There was something—"

"What?" Haakon said. "A sphinx? What's that?"

"Oh, a kind of chimera, a composite human-animal. Lots of cultures had them—but this one, it reminds me of something." He thought for a moment. "*The Time Machine!* That's it! It was a romance from about, oh, late nineteenth, early twentieth century, somewhere around there. It had a sphinx like that. That one looks a lot like the one in the illustration in the old book I read. And there were underground people called Warlocks. No, Morlocks. They looked just like these people, and they were cannibals too."

"So now we know where Xeus got the idea for this little horror. Does it help us any?"

Jemal pondered for a while. "No. The correspondence isn't complete. In the book the sphinx was above ground, for one thing. For another, the hero got away from the Morlocks by lighting things called lucifers, or matches. Those were primitive chemical fire-starting devices. The Morlocks lived in the dark and couldn't stand the light. The way these Morlocks are playing around those fires, it's obvious a little light doesn't bother them."

"It helps us in one way," Soong said.

"What's that?" Haakon asked.

"Now we know what to call them."

SEVENTEEN

Alexander dangled near a fire, trying not to go out of his mind with terror. His wrists and ankles were tied together and he had been hung by them from a horizontal pole, by which he had been carried from the scene of the ambush. The others were likewise trussed up, apparently for imminent cooking. They had passed through the boneyard and knew what was in store for them. Troll dangled there as well, a little askew since his arms were twice as long as his legs. He looked more like a wad of moss than ever. Somehow Alexander held on to the hope that Haakon and Soong and Jemal would arrive and get them out of this like—what was the expression Jemal had used—like the U.S. Cavalry, whatever the hell that was.

"Hey, Rama," Alexander called.

"What do you want, apescule?"

"You're pretty strong. Can't you break these ropes they got us tied with?"

"You think I haven't tried? I've pulled and twisted. I even used my teeth."

He could hear the shudder in her voice and winced a little himself. The nets and ropes they had been taken with were woven from the creatures' own rank hair and carried an odor so disgusting Alexander thought he would have it in his nostrils for as long as he lived. Which, he reflected, was a problem he might not have to concern himself with much longer. He craned his neck to see how Mirabelle was doing. Last time he'd looked, she'd been unconscious, or pretending to be. She still looked that way. He was worried about her, but if she were faking it for some plan of her own, he didn't want to interfere.

Rand was hanging like the rest and looked even more ridiculous. For a wild moment Alexander wondered how these cannibals planned to eat the engineer. Then he remembered how they had eaten the crab, and he almost threw up. Luckily, though, he had nothing left in his stomach. He wondered whether Xeus got a kick out of people upchucking. He was sure giving them plenty of opportunity for it. At least he himself had one advantage the others didn't: He could take some of the strain off his wrists and ankles by hanging on to the pole with his tail. He had already tried to use his unconventional manipulative appendage to some advantage, but to no avail. There were no nearby objects to grab, and since it had no fingers, he couldn't untie knots with it.

"Hey, Troll," he called.

"Humpf?" Troll said interrogatively.

"You been here longer than us. Got any ideas?"

"Nope. Guess they'll eat us." He pondered the prospect for a moment. "Cook us first though," he added at last.

"Hell, I coulda told you that," Alexander said.

"You miserable lump of ugliness," Rama hissed at

Troll. "It's because of you that we're here. If the others had listened to me, we'd have let these smelly things have you and you'd give them all indigestion."

"You come for *me*?" Troll asked.

"Sure," Alexander told him. "We wasn't gonna just let them haul you off." He looked around at their predicament. "Not that it did you—or us—much good."

"It was against my advice," Rama said. "Now the least you could do would be to come up with some plan to get us out of here. You've had plenty of time to hang there and relax while we were tracking you and fighting."

"Mebbe I'll think of something," Troll told her.

"Hah!" She radiated one of her more disagreeable scents at him.

The white-haired anthropoids were performing incomprehensible rituals around the fires that sprang from the floor. Their attention seemed to be on the big, winged, cat-human statue that stood in the center of the floor. There was a door in its chest between the forepaws, and they were doing a lot of bowing and capering in front of that door.

Then Alexander caught sight of something that wasn't white-haired moving stealthily at the periphery of his vision. He had to fight down the urge to stare in its direction. He had the distinct impression that not only was it not white-haired but that it had no hair at all. He thought that beneath the sound of all the barbaric drumming he could discern the hum of a powerblade. It might be his imagination though. Just wishful thinking.

He sweated and fretted. The figure was over by Mirabelle now, and there seemed to be another figure lurking near Rand. He and Rama were farthest from this new action. He began watching their captors, his heart in his throat, terrified lest the newcomers be noticed.

Not far from him squatted one of the humanoids, observing the dancing. It held a crystal club a half-meter in length. Whoever was messing around back there was making no sound, but some instinct seemed to tip off the creature because it was turning and straining its tiny eyes toward the direction of the others. Apparently eyesight was not its most reliable sense. It lurched to its full bowlegged height and began to head back to investigate, the hand gripping the crystal rod dangling just above its knee.

It stopped next to Alexander. The creature's shambling stance became more tense, more alert. It had seen, heard or otherwise sensed something. It began to turn. Desperately Alexander snatched the crystal club with his tail, and as the Morlock gazed at its empty hand, he whacked it across the back of the head. The thing crumpled in a limp, evil-smelling heap. Alexander looked around frantically to see if any of its cohorts had noticed the action, but there was no sign of alarm.

"Nice going, kid." It was Captain Haakon, and his powerblade was humming through the bonds that held Alexander to the pole.

"Jeez," the monkey-boy said, "where you guys been?" He dropped unceremoniously to the floor, where he lay rubbing his wrists to get his circulation going again. He jumped to his feet and promptly collapsed. It was as though his legs ended at his ankles. He felt, for a moment, as if there were pillowlike objects tied to his ankles, and he was slightly aware of a sort of feeling in them, kind of ticklish, but withal not sufficient to hold him up. He started to flop backward but got his tail behind him in time to keep from falling.

"Hey, boss, I think I'm all right, but you're gonna have to wait a minute or two before I'm like in top form, you know?"

"Make it quick. We don't have much time," Haakon said. "As we figured it, we've got about ten seconds of free time if we're lucky. If we're not lucky . . . well, we're out of luck. So get going!"

"Hey, that don't make much sense!" Alexander shouted, rubbing wrists and ankles.

"So what?" Haakon shouted back.

Jemal booted the boy just below the tail. "Get going, kid. We're all dead pretty quick anyway, so don't hang around. Move!"

Alexander moved. He rubbed his wrists and ankles, and he looked for shipmates in the same fix. He saw Rama being cut loose in similar fashion, hitting the ground, squalling and sputtering, flashing her claws and generally demanding an enemy to shred.

Then they were all heading in one direction. It seemed funny—until he saw that it was Troll who was leading them. The little man wasn't trying to get them out of the big room. Instead he was attempting to crowd them into the cramped space between the paws of the sphinx!

It would have been ridiculous, but Troll was no mean opponent when the quarters were close, and Rama was as formidable as any human adversary when her hair was up, as it was just at this time.

The Morlocks turned from their fires and their dancing, but it was too late for them to retrieve the situation. Their prey, contrary to any reasonable expectation, were heading straight toward the shrine tucked between the forepaws of the sphinx!

With one hand Haakon steadied the chattering, floppy angles of Rand over his shoulder; with the other he gripped a powerblade; and he followed Troll as though the little man were somehow the new brains of the unit.

Jemal was just behind him, with Mirabelle over his

shoulder, still to all purposes inert. But she was stirring. Her feet were kicking, causing Jemal some distress.

Behind them came Alexander, and Soong, but of all of them, Rama was the first to shake off the effects of their captivity, working her hands and feet, extruding her claws, wriggling her whiskers and generally acting like a Felid in need of a victim.

"Get up here!" Haakon yelled. With Rand over his shoulder, he had only one hand free for fighting, and he was having a hard time of it, with Morlocks beginning to pile on to him. The situation did not last long. Rama shook her hair into a sweeping mane, shot all twenty claws out to their full length, hissed and charged ahead, slashing right and left, sending Morlocks flying in all directions, bleeding and screeching.

Troll was determined to make their way between the forepaws of the sphinx, for whatever reason seemed sufficient to himself. The little man was not to be brushed aside lightly in his quest either. He met opposition to his goal with iron-knuckled fists that were nearly as discouraging as Rama's claws, but not quite.

"Why the hell're we going in there?" Jemal demanded. "Let's get out of here!" He waved an arm toward the far, dim archway through which they had entered the cavern. The others paid no attention. They followed Troll toward the narrow shrine between the forelegs of the sphinx, the focus of the Morlocks' frantic worship.

Then they were crammed between the paws. "Get in there!" Troll shouted, pointing toward the tiny shrine in the thing's chest. His voice was suddenly authoritative, as commanding and imperative as any thirty-year top sergeant's. Despite the apparent illogic of the order, they stepped lively, crowding into the interior of the sphinx. The Morlocks did not try to follow, but stood gaping as the door of the shrine closed.

"We're in the dark again," Jemal noted to nobody in particular.

"Not for long," said a voice.

"That you, Xeus?" Haakon asked. "How about it, is the game over? If it is, how about some light?"

The door of the shrine opened and light flooded in. They started and whirled, expecting an invasion of Morlocks, but it was not firelight coming through the door. It was daylight.

They walked out and found themselves standing beneath a clear blue sky. In the distance piles of cumulus clouds towered majestically, and they could make out tiny dots of flying creatures. They seemed to be standing on a mountaintop, probably the Fang, since all the other mountains they could see were much lower.

Automatically Alexander started shivering, even though it was not cold. They were in the midst of a snowfield and he *felt* like he ought to be cold. He looked back up at the sphinx. "You know, it don't look quite so big out in the open like this."

Haakon faced into the opening and said: "Come on out, Xeus. We want some answers from you. What's been going on and why have you done all this?"

"I get bored," Troll complained. They turned to face him, their mouths hanging open foolishly. He glared up at them from beneath his heavy brows, and suddenly he didn't look comical anymore.

"*You're* Xeus?" Mirabelle said, incredulous.

"Not much of a god, if you ask me," Rama snorted.

Troll began to change. Forehead and cheekbones widened and jawline spread and firmed. His mossy hair and beard became curly and chestnut-colored. He grew taller, his shoulders broadening, his knotty arms becoming muscular and graceful as his legs lengthened. Then he stood before them as a classical god-king, with the majestic head of a handsome, middle-aged man atop the body of a young athlete.

"Is this better?" Xeus inquired.

"You're still just a man," Rama said. "And one of the ape-breed at that."

"Then how about this?" He kept his form but grew to fifty meters in height. The sphinx metamorphosed into a throne, and he sat down on it. From somewhere a Rukh flapped in and perched on the back of the throne.

"Very impressive," Haakon said. "But cut the card tricks and give us some answers. You may be a god, but you're still a manipulating son of a bitch."

"Yeah," Alexander shouted up at him. "I liked you better when you was Troll. You're the one been playing around with us all along!" He walked over and kicked Xeus on the toenail.

Xeus leaned over them like a thundercloud, his face wearing a look of exasperation. "You are without question the most insolent species I have encountered in all my millions of years. I can call whole star systems into being, complete with their inhabitants. I can banish them to non-existence with a wave of my hand. I could destroy you and all your kind and it would be as though you had never been. Why should I not do that, you pernicious little beings?"

"Then what would you do for entertainment, you sadistic deity?" Jemal demanded.

Xeus leaned back in his throne and laughed, causing several avalanches down the face of the Fang. "What indeed? That's what I like about you. You are totally unpredictable, unlike the species I create myself."

"What are you?" Haakon asked. "I know damn well you're not a god, even if you can act like one."

Xeus leaned over him. "I might as well be a god, little man. I can do everything a god can do."

"Then how about shrinking again? I'm getting tired of looking up at you."

Immediately Xeus stood before them only slightly larger than human-sized. The throne was gone. "Enough," he said. "The game is over, as I said. I am not a single being, but millions. We are the population of the planets you have named the Cingulum. Once, many millions of years ago by your reckoning, we dismantled our system and rearranged it into that necklace of worldlets in order to make more efficient use of our energy and resources. Later that wasn't necessary. We became independent of conventional energy, independent even of conventional space and time. Then we faced a crisis.

"A wave of supernova energy was sweeping our arm of the galaxy. It would destroy all life in the Cingulum. We had plenty of time to work on the problem before the energy struck: millennia, in fact. We were far into the study of transtemporal geometry. I am sorry; I realize that is a new concept to you, but I have no proper words with which to express it in your vocabulary. We had progressed somewhat beyond language at that time, in any case. In essence, what we did was to turn reality inside out. We retreated into the worldlet you call Meridian, creating our own cosmos within. It is absolutely invulnerable to any force in the universe we left. Here we make our own reality, and we study and experiment in realms you could only call metaphysical."

"But you got bored," Haakon said.

"Yes. It seems the lot of all intelligent beings to fall prey to boredom. Also, we feel a nostalgia for our old universe; for the time when we, too, were mortal, short-lived creatures with a passion for survival and reproduction. We have lived here for so long, with our experiments and our work, that we have nearly exhausted the possibilities for diversion among ourselves. Even beings such as we require recreation.''

"Then we showed up," Haakon said.

"Exactly. You were not the first intelligent species to stumble into Meridian, but you were by far the most fascinating. A race of creatures relatively advanced in space travel, but barbarous beyond belief. Primitive in thought and ethic, but with a history of color and violence. Whole mythologies of such richness and complexity that it made up for your appalling deficiencies!''

"I think I should be insulted, but I'll let it pass," Haakon told him.

"Ethic?" Soong said. "You criticize our admittedly primitive morals when you play games with the lives of intelligent creatures?''

"You are all alive," Xeus reminded him. "Had any of you died, it would have been remedied.''

"What about the others, the ones who came here before us?" Mirabelle demanded. "What about the Ancestor?''

"When they first arrived, we believed your species to be totally without any redeeming virtues. The memories of the humans and the histories contained in their ships' memory apparatus were quite explicit on that point. For all your splendid mythologies, you really are an appalling species. We felt we should improve those who arrived earlier. Tell me truthfully: Is not the Ancestor a far more majestic being than any ordinary human?''

"It is not sufficient," Soong said. "If we are evil, it is for us to work out. You had no right to tamper with them.''

"Right? You creatures have the word, but not the concept. Still, as Troll I learned a certain grudging respect for you. You have a clumsy but sincere goodwill—when you are not blinded by passion or fear or hatred. You have loyalty to each other, even though that is rooted in a need for self-preservation. Best of all, when you thought Troll was in danger, you came after him to your own peril." Rama had the grace to look somewhat embarrassed.

"What is your true form?" Rand asked.

"I have none. We have become beings of pure energy. We went through many changes of form during our corporeal existence. Some of them would have been most displeasing to you. We can take on any form now, as you can see." He waved an arm in a broad sweep. "Except for yourselves and the Ancestor, every living creature you have seen is me, is one of us. We are a collective being, but we are individuals as well."

"A rather theological sort of concept," Soong observed.

"While taking these forms, we *are* those creatures, from flying insects to the likes of Leviathan. We have populated those other planets you saw with all the possibilities of your cultures and many others. We are the masters of reality; we make it what we want. I think you will keep us amused for a long time to come."

"In return for which?" Haakon ventured.

Xeus pointed. The G-102 was coming toward them. "Enter your ship. When you leave here, you shall enter the cave of Meridian from whence you came. Tell your friends of the Cingulum that that cave is now their refuge, by my wish. When they are within it, it will seem to them as though the Cingulum is uninhabited rock. No enemy will find or harm them. If there is any hope for your wretched species, it lies with people such as they. As for you, you are changed and better people for having come here. That you can take with you. Go now.''

The G-102 settled onto the snowfield, and suddenly the air was very cold; their ears popped with an instantaneous drop in atmospheric pressure. Xeus was gone.

"Jeez, let's get inside!" Alexander shouted, his voice tiny in the thin air. "My tail's gonna freeze off!"

The ramp descended and they scrambled in, Haakon and Jemal jumping into the pilots' seats and going over their instruments. Rand went to the engines and plugged himself into a power outlet.

Although the little ship was the same as ever, now it seemed alien to them, as though every angle and facet of its makeup had been subtly altered in their absence—but that was not true. The only change was in themselves.

"Everything checks out," Haakon reported, wondering why the data on the screens seemed to be in some language he had never seen before. "Let's get the hell out of here before that godlike bastard changes his mind."

EIGHTEEN

Lopal Singh jumped for his screen. "They're coming back out!" he shouted. The unmistakable shape of the G-102 was emerging from the tunnel. "Captain Haakon, report. What did you find?"

Haakon's features appeared in the screen, the same as always, yet somehow changed. "You still here?" he asked.

"Of course," Lopal Singh replied, mystified. "Where else would I be? Did you encounter anything in there after I lost contact?"

"Do you really expect me to tell you right now, over this screen? Let's get somewhere comfortable and you'll have a full report. It'll take quite some time."

"Do you have that much to report?" Lopal Singh asked suspiciously.

Haakon glared at him; then his expression changed. "How long have we been away?"

Lopal Singh checked his screen: "Eight minutes, forty-five seconds from the time we lost contact to your reemergence.''

The one called Jemal appeared on the screen now. He looked haggard and worn and somehow changed as well. ''Just get us to a hot bath and a cool drink, Singh. Have we ever got a story for you.''

''Your report seems to check out,'' Lopal Singh said, ''bizarre as it is.'' He studied the crew of the *Eurynome*, sprawled on the furniture of the guest suite he had made available to them. ''Of godlike beings and Leviathans and such our team was able to learn nothing, but it is true that some new phenomenon prevails within Meridian. There is more space within that cave now than is provided by all the worldlets of the Cingulum put together. That which goes in is utterly undetectable from the outside. It is the answer to a prayer.''

''What else are gods for?'' Jemal said. Lopal Singh ignored him.

''Now, about this business of Timur Khan.''

They stiffened. The interrogation they had undergone after their return from Meridian had not been gentle. The circumstances of their mission had come out.

Lopal Singh went on: ''Our scans confirm the presence of the explosive devices in your skulls. I am assured that we can do nothing about them without killing you. Because you completed your mission for us, we will do for you what we can. Our defense readouts you may have. By the time Timur Khan gets them, they will be of no use to him.''

''There was a matter of some heads,'' Soong murmured.

''I was just getting to that. While the investigation into your wild story was going on, I was cracking another case that had long been on my docket. I uncovered a nest of traitors within the Cingulum, persons who were about to sell us out to Bahadur—profiteers, even an undercover agent for Timur Khan. Certain arrests were made. Certain executions were carried out. Those heads should do nicely. One of them belonged to a man named Tagus, who sat on our Supreme Council. They should make convincing tokens. By the time Timur Khan makes his move against us, he will find nothing. He can hardly hold that against you, can he?

"You may go now. The heads, suitably preserved, shall be delivered to your ship. A shuttle shall take you to *Eurynome*. On behalf of the Cingulum, I thank you for what you have done for us; I extend my condolences for your plight; and I sincerely hope never to see you again." The huge NeoSikh went to the door, then turned. "Oh, yes, something occurred to me. This person Xeus. He truly had godlike power, you say?"

"That he had," Haakon agreed.

"Then why did you not request *him* to remove those devices from your skulls?"

Haakon and Jemal looked at one another for a long, pregnant moment. "Shit," Jemal said finally.

Timur Khan Bey shot his last arrow of the day. He unstrung his bow and hung it up. Then he turned his attention to the next order of business. He stepped into his broadcast room and said to the controller: "*Eurynome*." He continued to stand in that spot, but his surroundings became the luxurious appointments of the *Eurynome*. Captain Haakon and his crew were assembled as ordered. Although they did not prostrate themselves, Haakon gave him a proper military salute. There was also a curious little Singeur they had picked up from somewhere, a sort of pet apparently.

''I have examined your report and find it satisfactory. The readouts for the defenses of the Cingulum have proven to be authentic. The heads are acceptable. There was among them one who was an agent of mine, but he was expendable. Well done.''

''We are happy to have pleased you, Noyon,'' Haakon said.

Timur Khan studied him and the others. They were a tough-looking crew, no doubt of it. He had chosen them for their hardness; no other kind could have carried out the kind of mission he had assigned. But now there was something else about them: a sort of unity, a solidarity that had not been there before. It made them look different, and somehow a bit more dangerous. His hand hovered for a second over the control at his belt that would detonate their explosives. Then the hand fell away. If they were more dangerous now, that meant they would be more dangerous to the enemies of Bahadur. He could liquidate them at any moment anyway.

''You may go and play now, my children,'' Timur Khan said. ''I shall summon you when next I have use for you. Do not fail my summoning. Fear me and obey.'' He disappeared.

No one said anything for several minutes. They were all nursing their own bitter thoughts.

''So that's Timur Khan,'' Alexander said at last. ''No wonder you people are scared of him.''

''He was about to kill us,'' Haakon said. ''I know it. He was going to hit the switch and then he changed his mind. We came that close.''

''He saw that we are different,'' Soong said. ''We are no longer what we were.''

''What are we now?'' Mirabelle asked, her voice still slightly tremulous from the recent presence.

"Something new," Soong said. "Your old poets called it a 'sea change,' I believe. According to at least one of them, now every part of us is 'something rich and strange.' "

"Maybe it just means that we're a crew now, instead of a pack of convicts," Haakon said.

"Well, I haven't changed," Rama asserted. But she was wrong.

"Where to, Cap'n?" Jemal asked. "Do we go take on freight, turn smuggler or run up the Jolly Roger and become pirates?"

Haakon pondered. It had been so many years since he had had any independence of action that he was stymied. "What does it matter? We're still his slaves."

"But we can pretend for a while," Jemal said.

"All right," Haakon said. "Let's go to Tortuga. That place is wild and wicked and dangerous and fun. Rand, fire us up. Alex, you'll like it there. It's even better than Hold Six. Let's go and pretend we're free."

Haakon sat back in his chair. He felt good. Almost, but not quite, he felt like a captain again.